WASHED ASHORE

WASHED
ASHORE

KERR THOMSON

SCHOLASTIC INC. · NEW YORK

First published in the United Kingdom in 2015 as *The Sound of Whales* by Chicken House, 2 Palmer Street, Frome, Somerset BA11 1DS.

Library of Congress Cataloging-in-Publication Data available

ISBN 978-0-545-90420-9

10 9 8 7 6 5 4 3 2 1   17 18 19 20 21

Printed in the U.S.A   23

First edition, June 2017

Book design by Christopher Stengel

For Susan

Go gather by the humming sea

Some twisted, echo-harboring shell,

And to its lips thy story tell,

And they thy comforters will be.

—From "The Song of the Happy
Shepherd" by W. B. Yeats

ONE

Walls of black water rose on either side of the boat as it dropped through a crack in the sea. In the wheelhouse, Fraser Dunbar clung to an old wooden chart table and waited for those walls to collapse and send him to the bottom.

The windows rattled and the wind roared through the open doorway. The door banged hard on its hinges. He couldn't close it from where he stood, dared not move in case he slipped straight through the opening and out into the night.

Ben McCaig glanced at him from behind the wheel.

"How are you doing?" he shouted above the wind.

"Fine," Fraser lied. He had never been out at sea in a storm before. It was thrilling to begin with, but now it was just scary. No one in their right mind would go out in this kind of sea, in this kind of weather, yet Ben was whooping as if it was a fairground ride.

"Are you going to be sick again?" he yelled.

Fraser shook his head. "There's nothing left to puke."

Ben laughed and spun the wheel.

"My dad's going to kill me," Fraser shouted.

"Not if this storm kills you first!"

It was a definite possibility and only now did Fraser remember his father's fierce words that very afternoon: "You must not, under any circumstances, get on that boat again. McCaig is downright reckless and that boat should have been scrapped."

He'd ignored that advice, had told himself that he was fourteen and didn't take orders from anyone, not even his dad. Now it was both annoying and astonishing that perhaps his father knew best after all. As the boat plunged deeper into the dark sea, and his stomach turned to mush, he suddenly remembered the list his dad had taken great pleasure in sharing: the top five reasons why people drowned.

Number 5: *water sports accident*. That didn't apply.

Number 4: *alcohol consumption*. Good, he hadn't touched a drop.

Number 3: *inability to swim*. No problem, he could swim just fine.

Number 2: *failure to wear life preserver*. Fraser looked behind him at the ancient life jackets hanging on the wheelhouse wall. He could grab one if needed, but if Ben wasn't wearing a life jacket, then neither was he.

Number 1: *water conditions exceed swimming ability*. He swallowed hard as he looked out at the ferocious ocean. He wasn't *that* good a swimmer. Nobody was.

The walls of water were closing in; the little boat was about to be swallowed whole. Fraser let out a cry and hoped that Ben hadn't heard. Then at the last moment the boat rose, grabbing an edge of the swell and riding it slowly, casually almost, out of the watery canyon. Despite its peeling paint and shabby deck, an old island lobster boat like this was built for these wild seas off the northwest of Scotland.

Maybe they were not about to sink after all, Fraser thought. It had seemed certain for a moment there.

With one hand still on the wheel and his legs splayed for balance, Ben reached behind him and grabbed the banging door, pushing it shut and securing the catch. Fraser wiped a hand across his face, tasting salty water.

Ben patted the wheel. "This old piece of junk might just get us home." He peered through the window. "The harbor's around here somewhere."

The slow swish of a solitary wiper was fighting to keep the wheelhouse window clear. Fraser could see no sign of the lights of Skulavaig.

And then he remembered why they were here in the first place, sailing so late at night. "Where are the whales?"

Ben rubbed his stubbly chin. "They will have dived to deeper water . . . I hope. It'll be a bit daft if we miss the harbor and hit a whale." The grin was gone; there was no more whooping. Whales were Ben's life.

It was already a bit daft, Fraser thought, to go sailing into the night with clouds building and the wind picking up, but being with Dr. Ben McCaig, professor of marine biology at Aberdeen University, was beyond cool. He'd even given Fraser a job title for the summer: seasonal voluntary assistant researcher, which really meant "general grunt," but that was OK. It was enough that Ben let him come along and it was something to do over the summer holidays. The island of Nin was not the most exciting of places at the best of times, and these were not the best of times on his little island.

Ben pulled back on the throttle, and the throb of the engine died, the boat pitching hard. "I can't see a thing," he said. "I'll have to step outside to see where we are."

He lunged out of the door and Fraser staggered after him, with a glance at the unused life jackets. They stood with their backs against the wheelhouse and were pummeled by the wind and rain. The sea was a dark, heaving mass, broken only by the white flash of a breaking wave. It was impossible to tell where the water ended and the land began, but they could see the tops of the cliffs, black against the gray tumbling clouds.

With growing panic, Fraser scanned the coastline, working along from the cliffs to get his bearings. Twice he wiped eyes that stung from the spray. As his eyes refocused, he saw a dot of light farther up the coast. It was too far out to be on land.

"Another boat," Fraser said to Ben, but when he looked again, he couldn't find the light.

He turned his head and saw the faint glow of other lights emerging from the darkness. It was Skulavaig.

"Over there," he shouted, pointing.

"Aye, I see them," Ben said. "We're a half mile too far north. Five more minutes sailing on the same heading and we would have hit the cliffs." He turned for the wheelhouse. "Let's get home."

Fraser breathed a sigh of relief as deep as the ocean. The wind and the waves and the rocks would have to gang up some other night and try to sink their little boat. He looked again for the other vessel that was sailing for the open ocean. There was no sign of it.

He was stepping into the safety of the wheelhouse when he heard the cry. It was hard to hear anything above the roar of the wind and for a moment he thought he had imagined it. But it came again, and this time he recognized a word.

"Help!"

Fraser lurched across the deck, held on to the rail with both hands as he leaned out over the water. It came again, louder this time, clearer.

"Help me!"

There was someone in the water.

"Did you hear that?" he shouted at the wheelhouse.

"Hear what?"

"A cry for help."

Ben leaned out, cocked an ear for a few seconds, then

frowned and shook his head. "Just the wind playing tricks."

Fraser *had* heard something; he was certain of it. He focused his ears toward the ocean and listened. The wind roared and the sea boomed and the engine beneath his feet clunked back to life as Ben pushed forward on the throttle. He could hear nothing else.

He scanned the ocean, but the water was black and turbulent; it was impossible to fix his gaze on any one spot, but toward the cliffs there *was* . . . something. A hand, an arm maybe? And was that a head, or just a breaking whitecap? Fraser shouted back at the wheelhouse, but Ben couldn't hear. That other light, it had to be another boat. Had it lost one of its crew? Had it *sunk*?

He staggered back to the wheelhouse, pulled himself through the door.

"There's someone in the water," he said breathlessly, urgently.

"You're imagining it, Fraze," said Ben. He was concentrating now, making sure they got back to harbor.

"I saw something."

"Aye, the waves."

"I saw an arm."

Ben fixed him with a troubled look. "You're certain?"

Fraser hesitated. Was he certain? Was it not just a breaking wave? His confidence began to fade, the more he thought about it.

Ben saw the uncertainty. "In the dark your eyes play tricks."

But not your ears as well. "I heard a cry."

"The wind."

"No. A voice. We have to turn around."

"We're almost at the harbor. We're getting out of this storm before we go under."

"But the person in the water . . ."

"There's no one there, Fraser."

"There is."

"I'll chase whales in the dark, but I'm not chasing ghosts."

Fraser opened his mouth to argue, then saw Ben's narrow eyes and firm mouth and knew it was useless. He peered through the glass of the wheelhouse at the stormy night. Maybe he was wrong. Maybe he *had* imagined it. But he couldn't stop thinking there was someone out there among the waves, crying for help and disappearing under the black water.

TWO

Hayley Risso stood on the beach and faced the Atlantic Ocean, let the wind thrash her body and grains of sand sting her face. She was all alone, on a dark and stormy beach, thousands of miles from home. Her heart thumped in her chest; it was wild and frightening and thrilling too. Like nothing she had ever experienced. In Texas, at the first hint of a thundercloud, it was into the cellar in case a tornado should form.

It was crazy to be out so late and in such a storm, but she wasn't going back to the cottage, no way. Not until her mom had calmed down and, hopefully, gone to bed.

Hayley turned and looked back toward the harbor. At the far edge sat their tiny rented cottage; a light shone from the living room where she slept on a pull-down bed. Her mom was still up, still fuming probably. It had been another knockout of a fight.

The cottage had a painfully slow Wi-Fi connection, there was no cable, cell phone reception came and went. It was sleep or read a book. The jet lag still hadn't lifted, so she couldn't sleep, and reading a book was boring. She'd finally managed to get an Internet connection to chat with her friends back in the States, but her mom had discovered her on the laptop. They were the wrong friends. Her new ones. OK, most of the boys were jerks and some of the girls could be nasty, but she was fifteen now and could be friends with whoever she liked. It was fun picking ones her mom hated.

Hayley set off along the beach in the opposite direction to the cottage. It was hard to walk in a straight line with the battering wind and her eyes half-shut against the rain. At least she had dressed in her heavy boots and jacket before storming out into the storm. She'd tried to bang the door behind her, but it was an old house and the door was too stiff to slam. So annoying.

High cliffs loomed ahead. She could just make out a narrow path that climbed upward. The sensible move was to stay on the beach and avoid steep drops in gusting gales. Hayley paused, then bent into the wind and forced herself up, her expensive boots slipping on the muddy path.

"This could have been London," she shouted into the driving rain. "This could have been Paris. I get *Scotland*!"

If she had to go to Europe, she had pleaded to her mother, why not somewhere much more interesting? Her mother had simply told her there was research to be done for the book she was writing. Hayley knew there was more to it than that. Scotland was a long way from the United States, which meant a long way from Hayley's father. And her new friends.

A gust of wind grabbed her by the ankles, sending her to her knees with a squish. She scrambled a few feet on all fours before straightening up and flicking mud from her hands, pulling her shoulder-length, blond, bedraggled hair away from her face.

Stretching her long legs, arms pumping, she crested the slope and stood on the clifftop. The path was only a couple of feet from the edge, and the gale battered her body as if trying to push her over the drop. *Why am I up here?* she thought. Her legs ached from staying attached to the ground. *Where am I going?*

Up ahead was the outline of something big, a structure of some sort. As she drew closer, it took shape: a high tower, a curved archway . . . It was an old ruined castle, with high stone walls, dark doorways, and empty windows. Gray clouds scudded behind the outline of its crumbling turrets.

But there was something, a shadow, between her and those old stones. As the clouds briefly parted, in a glimmer of moonlight, the shadow became a silhouette. It was a figure teetering on the cliff edge. And from this figure came a sound, an eerie wailing, above the wind. The pitch rose and fell and it sounded almost like a melody.

Hayley moved forward, trying to breathe.

It was a boy, whose skin was even paler than most on an island where it seemed like everyone was pale white. He stood close to the edge, high above the surging waves spilling up the beach with a boom. He was young and thin and soaked to the skin. He stared out across the water, his arms outstretched as if he was trying to grasp the wind, head raised to the black clouds. Water dripped from hair that was white.

Hayley couldn't begin to imagine what he was doing up here alone in the dark. Was he stuck? Was he planning to jump? Did he realize how close he was to falling?

She took a few steps closer, heard him give another wail that was almost like a sob and a song together. She was desperate to grab him but scared to move any closer. Her stomach rolled like the breakers on the beach below.

She was about to shout, when he took a step away from the cliff edge, then another. He twisted his shoulder back, then flung his arm forward and launched something into the night sky. It spun in the air as it arced over the clifftop and was swallowed by the dark and the rain.

"Hello," she shouted, the word snatched away in the wind. Louder, "Hello!"

The boy slowly turned his head and she could see he was crying.

"Are you OK?"

He didn't reply.

"What's your name?"

She moved slowly toward him and remembered something her mom had told her their first night on the island. It was a warning really, about the son of the people who owned the cottage. *A little different* was her mom's description, *be nice*, her instruction . . . *He doesn't speak.*

The family was called Dunbar; there were two brothers; the younger one had a strange name. A blast of wind and it came to her as if blown in from across the sea.

"Are you Dunny?" she asked. He gave the slightest of nods. "I'm Hayley. I'm staying in your cottage."

The boy wiped rain from his face and slowly turned away from the sea, swaying slightly. Another blast of wind hit the clifftop and made him stumble, and suddenly he was falling. Hayley leapt forward and grabbed his arm; her foot touched the nothingness of air over the drop, then she lurched backward, clutching the boy, and they fell together onto the sodden grass. She lay there holding him with shaking hands, taking deep breaths of the wet wind.

"That was close," she said, picking herself up.

Dunny stood and backed away, kept watching her with the saddest, darkest eyes she had ever seen. Then he smiled, only for a moment, and his face changed and he looked grateful at least, if not happy.

"We should go home," Hayley said.

The boy reached into his pocket and pulled out something, stepped forward and handed it to her.

It was a scallop shell. It was pale cream in color with darker banding, its fan shape perfect, not a chip or crack across its surface.

"Thank you," she said, wondering what to do with it. Was this the award you received on the island when you saved a life? She put it in her pocket, realizing it was a shell he had thrown from the cliff. She didn't understand this place.

Dunny had already set off down the path. She hurried after him, no longer wanting to be alone in the dark and the storm. She took a last look out across the ocean and was surprised to see the faint lights of a small boat close to shore. It was battling the waves, bouncing around in the swell. She wished those on board a safe sail back to harbor. She smiled at the thought that there might actually be someone on the island crazy enough to be worth meeting.

THREE

The morning after the storm, Fraser sat on the stern of Ben McCaig's boat, his legs hanging over the edge. The glare of the sun made him squint and he rubbed his tired eyes and pulled a hand through his dark hair, which was needing a cut. The sky was clear blue and the air was warm; in the first week of July, it was the first hint that good weather had finally arrived. Fraser yawned; what little sleep he had had the night before was broken by dreams of drowning men crying for help. In the sunlight now, with the ocean calm, he was almost convinced that it had been his imagination and nothing more. Almost.

Ben pulled himself up from his position dangling over the hull and dipped a brush in the paint can Fraser was holding.

"That's *Moby* done," Ben said. "Now for *Dick*."

The boat that saved them from the storm was getting a new name in black letters that would stand out against the rusty white. *Moby Dick*, an appropriate name for the vessel of a whale scientist. Beneath the paint could be seen the faded port registration number, SK712, a Skulavaig vessel. The old lobster boat was almost forty feet long, the fishing gear removed but not the smell.

Fraser took a breath and asked his question. "So any reports of a body washed ashore?"

Ben sighed. "No bodies, no shipwrecks." He pulled himself upright. "There was no one in the water, Fraser, there was no one swimming. Let it go." He leaned back down and asked as he painted, "What did your dad say last night when you finally got home? You obviously escaped the killing."

"He didn't even notice I was gone."

"That was a bit of luck."

"Aye, I suppose."

It *was* luck; it would have been a grounding if not a killing. Fraser had hurried home to face his father's wrath and found the house empty. He'd thought with growing anxiety that they were all out looking for him and had slid beneath the bedcovers to await his fate. But when his parents arrived home, they had a wet Dunny in tow. This was a first for his brother: He was always wandering the beach or sitting up on the cliffs, but never at night.

Dunny had crept out of the house and quickly been missed.

Fraser had done the same thing and no one had noticed.

As always, it had been his mute brother who had somehow gained the last word.

Back in bed, in the dark, Fraser had thought, *I'm really starting to hate him.* And then he had heard a muffled

15

conversation between his parents, had learned it was the American girl staying in their cottage who had found his brother, high on the cliffs beside the castle. No one had explained what *she* was doing up there.

The sound of feet made him turn and he saw Willie McGregor walking toward them down the jetty. The tide was in and the boat sat high on the water, moored against the lowest section of the harbor wall. Willie hopped the gap between the jetty and the boat, landing unsteadily on the deck. In his sixties but fitter than most, he was one of the few fishermen left in town, and the old boat had once been his. He seemed to think he could still come and go whenever he pleased.

Willie pulled a face when he saw Ben painting a new name. "You survived, then?" he asked.

Ben hauled himself onto his feet and handed the paintbrush to Fraser. "Just about. She's a tough wee boat."

"Oh, aye. She's been in worse than last night."

Fraser said, "I can't imagine worse than last night."

Willie shook his head. "Laddie, you've not been in a storm until below deck is full of water up to your waist and St. Elmo's fire is dancing round the wheelhouse. Did I tell you about the time I caught the tail of a hurricane off St. Kilda?"

Ben laughed. "You told me that story when you were selling me this rust bucket."

"And did she not get you home last night in much the same kind of storm?"

"She did. And made a fine job of it."

"Aye." Willie McGregor moved across the deck and stood at the rail beside Ben and Fraser. "Next time you might not be so lucky." He looked sternly at the boy. "I dinnae suppose your father knew you were out on the water last night?"

Fraser shook his head. "Don't tell him, please."

Willie turned to Ben. "You, lad, you should know better."

Ben McCaig smiled and shrugged. "It was fine, there was nothing to worry about." He nodded toward Fraser. "Fraze brought up his dinner, that's all."

Fraser forced a smile, looked out across the harbor wall to a sea that was tranquil and sunlit. It was a completely different place from the previous night, but there was still the nagging memory of a shadow in the water and a cry for help.

Willie ran a hand across the stained wood of the wheelhouse. "Look," he said to Ben, "next time the sky's a bit gloomy, dinnae go anywhere, eh? She's strong but she's old."

"If there's so much as a breeze, I will stay in harbor."

"And you, laddie," he said to Fraser, "you stay in your bed."

Fraser nodded, having told himself that next time he would absolutely stay in his bed.

"One last thing," Willie said as he turned to go. "I hear there's a whale been washed up on the beach." He paused, then added, "But dinnae get excited. The beast is dead."

Five minutes later, Fraser was walking fast along the sand, trying to keep up with the purposeful stride of Ben McCaig, the straps of Ben's backpack cutting into his skin. He didn't mind; this was his job: seasonal voluntary assistant researcher.

The ocean sparkled in the morning sun, not a breath of wind to ruffle the water. The storm had cleared the sky of clouds, the pummeling waves had washed the beach clean; it felt like summer had finally arrived and everything was fresh and new. Almost everything.

The dead whale was high on the beach, pushed there by the storm, now out of reach of the tide. It lay partly on its side, a glassy eye staring at the sky as if wondering what in heavens it was doing there. Big gulls wheeled in the air above.

"Isn't that your brother?" Ben asked.

Dunny was standing by the whale, a hand stretched out, fingers gently touching its flank. His face was lifted to the sky, his pale hair shone in the sun.

"What's he doing?" Ben asked.

"Something weird, no doubt."

"Is he singing?"

There was a noise coming from the boy, a hum without a tune, a series of random notes, high and low.

"I wouldn't call that singing," said Fraser. As they arrived at the whale, he asked, "What are you doing, Dunny?"

The boy turned, his humming abruptly ending. He looked at Fraser for a moment, an intense sadness on his face, then walked away. He was barefoot and he moved so lightly along the beach that the sand barely rippled.

Fraser returned his attention to the whale.

It was smaller than he had imagined, its mouth slightly open, a line of jagged teeth glinting in the sun. It was also a little bit sad—the whale seemed out of place and abandoned. Ben walked slowly around the carcass.

On top of the whale, Fraser saw something else that caught the sunlight. He lifted it off and saw that it was a scallop shell. Dunny must have placed it there. In recent weeks his brother had started collecting shells and writing messages on them. Fraser had no idea why. He thought sometimes his brother faked the strangeness, that it was a bit of an act, but then again, maybe his brother *was* just weird. There was a message written on this shell in very small writing. Fraser refused to pander to Dunny's nonsense by reading it. He took the scallop shell in both hands, snapped it in half, then tossed both bits down the sand toward the breaking waves.

"So what kind of whale is it?" he asked.

"It's a pilot whale," Ben said. "You can tell from the dark skin, its round head, and this triangular dorsal fin. We need to measure it first."

Ben pulled a tape measure out of the backpack. With Fraser holding it at the head of the whale, he pulled the tape slowly to the tail.

"Ten and a half feet," he said, scribbling in his notebook. "It's a juvenile, only half the length it would have reached in maturity."

He dropped to his knees and placed both hands on the carcass. "Help me push it over."

The animal was cold to the touch and dry, covered in a sprinkling of sand. Together they pushed on the body and Ben examined the underside.

"It's almost impossible to tell the sex of a whale when they're swimming," he said, "but this close, there are some clues."

He pointed to a thin slit on the belly toward the tail. "This is the genital slit. If it was female, there would be two corresponding mammary slits. There are none, so it's a male."

They let the carcass fall back on to the sand, and Ben noted this information in the notebook. Fraser was on his knees, stroking the rough skin. It was an amazing thing to touch a whale. And such a shame it could be done only when it lay dead on the beach.

Ben said, "Your brother's back."

Fraser's heart sank at the sight of Dunny standing on the grass at the top of the beach, watching. And then something funny happened in Fraser's stomach as he noticed the pretty blond girl striding toward them from the same direction.

"Hi," she said as she arrived. "What you doing?"

Fraser had yet to meet the American visitors, but the girl's accent gave her away.

She stared curiously at the whale, then asked, "Is it dead?"

"I'm afraid so," Ben replied.

The girl looked into the eye of the animal. "What kind of whale is it?"

"It's a pilot whale. They're quite common in these waters. This is a young male."

She took two steps toward the tail. "How do you know all this?"

"I'm a scientist, I study whales. This part of the world has recently become a whale hot spot. I'm Ben."

The girl gave a quick smile but didn't offer her name.

"You're American?" Ben asked.

"That's right."

"Are you here on holiday?"

"Not really. Kind of. My mom is over here researching some book she's writing."

"Interesting. What's the book about?"

The girl shrugged. "No idea. Scotland, I guess."

"Then I suppose you've come to the right place."

The girl said, "This is never the right place."

"Have you met Fraser and Dunny?" Ben pointed to the brothers in turn.

Dunny's eyes were fixed on the whale. Fraser noticed that his fists were clenched and his back stiff, as if the whale was his and they were messing with it without permission.

"I've met Dunny, yes," the girl said. "Last night."

"This is Fraser, Dunny's older brother. Fraser's helping me with my whale research."

There was a twinkle in Ben's eye that Fraser didn't like, as if he was trying his hand at matchmaking.

Reluctantly, it seemed, the girl said, "Hello."

Both she and Ben looked at Fraser and he realized that it was his turn to say something. His mind went blank. His experience of making conversation with pretty girls was just about zero. In the silence that followed, Fraser heard the breaking of the waves and the pounding of his heart.

"And don't you speak either?" the girl asked after a pause.

Her rudeness broke the spell. "Not a word," Fraser said. "Mute as a brush." He gave her a withering look.

"What does that mean?" she said, rolling her eyes. She turned back to Ben. "So what will happen to the whale?"

"The town council will have to remove it or bury the thing before it starts to smell."

"That'll be a big hole." She surveyed the three of them as if deciding whether they were worth her company. "Well, I have to go. Nice meeting you, Ben," she said, pointedly leaving out Fraser. She turned and headed up the beach away from the town.

Dunny lingered at the top of the beach, watching, keeping guard, it seemed.

Fraser kicked the dead whale and dry sand fell from the carcass.

"Way to go, Fraze," Ben said with a smile. "That's how to impress the ladies."

"She wasn't worth impressing," Fraser said, peeved.

"No? A pretty American girl. How many of them do you see in Skulavaig?"

"One too many." He had been away at school the previous week when the American visitors arrived. His first encounter had not gone well.

"What's her name?" Ben asked.

"Hayley, I think."

"What's she doing with your brother?"

"Who knows. Who cares." Fraser did care, he cared a lot. He moved around the whale and looked at its back, which was more exposed now that they had turned it slightly. Three large grooves caught his eye.

"Look at these."

Ben joined him. He caught his breath and stared for a long moment, then exhaled slowly through pursed lips, shaking his head. "God," he said.

"What are they?"

"They might be marks made by the propeller of a boat."

"Is that what killed it?"

"Maybe." Ben looked out to sea and grimaced. A horrible notion struck Fraser.

"It wasn't us, was it?"

"No, it wasn't us. If you hit a whale, you would know it."

Fraser gave a sigh of relief. "I knew I saw the lights of another boat last night."

Ben's face had drained of color; he had anxious eyes. "Perhaps there *was* another boat out there somewhere." After a pause, he added, "It still doesn't mean there was someone in the water."

"But it's possible. And we did nothing to help."

Fraser was certain there was a connection between whale, boat, and swimmer.

Ben said grimly, "Let's get this finished up."

He retrieved a camera from the backpack, took a series of photographs, focusing on the propeller marks, then replaced the camera and pulled on a pair of rubber gloves. With Fraser's help, the whale was pushed all the way over so it lay on its back. From his bag, Ben extracted several plastic containers, which he laid carefully on the sand.

Ben unsheathed a large knife and rubbed both sides of the blade across his shirt. "This is the unpleasant bit."

Suddenly, Dunny was there beside the whale, his head shaking and his face full of anger. He grabbed Ben's arm, tugging it, and the knife fell onto the sand.

"Whoa, careful, wee man," Ben said.

"What's your problem, Dunny?" Fraser was shocked and a little frightened at such a display of rage and rudeness.

Dunny stood between Ben and the whale, breathing through his nose, his frown so deep you could hardly see his eyes.

"The whale is dead," Ben said gently. "I'm doing it no harm. I'm taking samples so we can find out what happened to it."

Dunny breathed, said nothing, didn't move.

"If we know what happened to this one, we can maybe prevent it happening to other whales."

For a moment more, Dunny held himself taut, then his whole body sagged. His eyes, which had been narrowed with anger, grew wide and watery, and he turned and moved away. Fraser watched him head along the beach in the same direction as the American girl.

"Sorry about that."

"Don't worry about it."

"He's getting weirder by the day."

"He was just concerned about the whale. He didn't understand."

Ben picked up the knife, grasped it firmly in the palm of his hand, and plunged it into the underside of the animal. He pulled the knife down the length of the stomach. A greasy solution of blood and fat seeped onto the sand. He prised open the incision with the flat of the blade and took a step back as the smell hit him.

"Well, that isn't nice," Fraser said, putting a hand to his nose.

Ben laughed. "This job's not all boat trips and dolphin rides." He delved a hand into the stomach and pulled out the animal's final meal. There were a few white fish bones and some squid beaks, black and sharp. He made some notes, then prodded around the guts with his knife until he found the liver. He cut off a piece, popped it into a plastic container, and labeled it. He took a few more samples, from the blubber, the kidneys, the skin, making notes as he went along. Finally, he took the fragments of viscera and pieces of tissue that lay on the beach and jammed them back inside the whale, kicking sand over patches of stain. He pushed closed the cut in the belly with his foot.

"Normally, we remove the head of the whale and send it to a collection housed in the National Museum of Scotland, but I haven't the heart for it today. I've samples enough. Now we need to go and see the harbormaster."

He stood and brushed the beach from his shorts. "One last task, though." He lifted the knife from the sand and moved to the mouth of the whale, the jaws slightly agape. He selected a blemish-free tooth and worked it from the gum. It popped loose and he caught it in his left hand.

"You can tell a whale's age from a tooth. It has annual growth layers that are visible under a microscope. But this one's for you." He handed the tooth to Fraser, then prised a second one loose for himself.

Fraser held the tooth between his fingers, marveled at its smoothness, the way it tapered to the finest of points.

"Thanks," he said.

"Keep that in your pocket and it will be your lucky talisman. When you spot a whale, it will circle back, thinking you're one of them."

Fraser didn't believe a word, but he placed the tooth carefully in his pocket just in case as they headed to see the Skulavaig harbormaster.

Mr. Wallace was responsible for the safe arrival and departure of the ferry twice a day. He also watched over the comings and goings of the town from his little office above the Fisherman's Mission. The mission, a social club for the town's fishermen, was deserted when Ben and Fraser arrived, a pool table standing idly among a clutter of chairs. Fishermen were rare now in Skulavaig; the mission served mainly as a meeting place for the old boys who gathered to talk about how things used to be.

Together, Fraser and Ben climbed the narrow wooden stairs that led to the harbormaster's office. The walls were lined with photographs of fishing vessels, some in color, some black and white.

Fraser had never been up these stairs before. He examined the pictures as he climbed and looked for Ben's boat.

"Where's the *Moby Dick*?" he asked.

Ben gave a gloomy smile. "The boats on this wall have all been lost at sea in the last eighty years. It's a stair of remembrance."

"Oh," Fraser said, wishing he hadn't asked. He had come close to being up on the wall himself.

They entered the harbormaster's office and found Mr. Wallace by a large window, scanning the sea with binoculars. He was a tall, thin man with neatly trimmed gray hair and beard. As well as harbormaster, he was also the unofficial coast guard and customs officer, but he rarely moved from his window. Nothing much happened on the island of Nin; there was never much to see through his binoculars.

"What can I do for you, Dr. McCaig?" he said rather coldly, without removing the eyeglasses.

Fraser knew that Ben and Mr. Wallace didn't like each other. Ben breezed in over the summer during the research season and ignored most of the harbor regulations. He didn't care much for figures of authority such as Mr. Wallace.

Ben addressed the back of his head. "There's a dead whale washed up on the beach south of the cliffs."

"Aye, I heard. Willie McGregor was up earlier."

"Can you arrange to get it removed before it rots?"

"It's already taken care of. Some men will be over later today. Are you finished with it?"

"I am, yes."

"What was it?" Mr. Wallace put down his binoculars.

"A pilot whale. A young male."

Mr. Wallace turned. "How did it die?"

"It was probably hit by a boat."

"In last night's storm?"

"Aye, the whale is not long dead."

"It wasnae your boat?"

Ben huffed and folded his arms. "No."

Fraser wanted to ask if there had been reports of struggling swimmers, but he thought better of it. The harbormaster would only wonder why they had done nothing to help.

"And you, Fraser Dunbar."

It took a moment before he realized he was being addressed.

"Aye, Mr. Wallace?"

"No more midnight sailings."

"No, Mr. Wallace." Willie McGregor had obviously blabbed.

The harbormaster turned back to his window, and Ben and Fraser stole silently from the room and descended the stairs. Fraser had the suspicion Mr. Wallace was disappointed not to be adding a new picture to his wall of wrecks.

He left Ben at the jetty and walked up the small hill to his house. His was the biggest house in the harbor, had belonged to the ferry master back in the days when ferries were powered by wind and sail. It had an old boathouse that his dad had converted into a holiday cottage to be rented out to tourists and visitors.

He was thinking about the American girl again. It was a small island and it was inevitable that they would meet again. The thought made him shudder—she was so annoying. But she was also very pretty and very American, like someone from a television show. Storms, sunshine, dead whales, American girls; the island of Nin suddenly seemed . . . seemed . . . he searched for a word, but only one seemed to fit. Nin suddenly seemed *interesting* and he couldn't remember when he last thought that about the place.

FOUR

Hayley stood at the base of the cliff she had climbed the previous night in the dark and the wind and rain. How different it seemed now, the red rock glowing in the sunlight. The path up seemed not nearly as steep, the cliff not so high. Hayley considered another climb but decided to walk farther along the beach instead.

In the opposite direction, there was just a dead whale and an irritating Scottish boy. In Texas she never walked anywhere, ever; it was the school bus or a car ride every time. A *combustion-engine culture*, her history teacher had called it. Here, it was either take a walk or sit in the cottage, and since the Internet connection was down again and she had listened to the songs on her iPod too many times and her mom was still in a mood, a walk seemed the only option. Her mom was waiting for an apology for her late-night wander, even though she had rescued a boy from certain death. The Dunbars had been eternally grateful when they had met at the harbor; she had brought their son safely home. That was how she had spun it anyway, although her mom was unconvinced.

Hayley wondered what would happen if she didn't apologize, if she just refused to say sorry. Would her mother punish her by dragging her away from her home, her friends, her life, and pack her off to some cold, desolate place on the other side of the world? No, wait, she had done that already.

Hayley stopped and glanced back again. Yes, he was still there, the weird boy, following at a distance but making no attempt to hide himself. At first it had been amusing, but now it was a little creepy. Whenever she stopped, he stopped.

The tide was out, so there was a large stretch of sand between her and the sea. The water glimmered in the sunshine, and the air felt surprisingly warm—she had expected only cold rain in this country. As her eyes moved from the ocean to the cliff, she saw a cave in the rock, a dark, menacing hole that gave her a jolt, along with an instant, overwhelming desire to know what was in there, despite not being much of an explorer. She would need to scramble up some boulders to get to the cave entrance. She was athletic and strong, on the school swim team, but she also had nice nails that were easily chipped . . .

Before she had the chance to choose between nails and curiosity, something touched her on the arm. She jumped in terror and let out a squeal. Dunny was beside her; he had closed the gap between them unnoticed and stood now biting his lip, frowning.

"Jesus, Dunny, you gave me a heart attack."

The boy pointed to the cave and shook his head.

"What is it?" Hayley asked.

Dunny just shook his head again.

"You really don't speak? At all?"

Dunny wrapped his thin fingers around her arm and gently pulled.

"Is there something in the cave? A wild animal? A monster?"

The boy smiled, as if she was being ridiculous. It transformed his face; he had a nice face when he smiled, with big soft eyes and cute dimples. Hayley wished he smiled more. He pulled again.

"OK, I get it, it's your cave. I'm not allowed in."

Dunny retraced his steps along the beach and Hayley followed, wondering to herself why, for the second day in a row, she was trailing after this mute Scottish boy. When his initial strangeness was overcome, there *was* something intriguing about him. His skin was so pale, but his eyes were so dark; he never spoke but sometimes wailed; he seemed to seek solitude but was always close by.

She turned to take a last look at the cave and saw a fleeting movement, a shadow, a shape. A man?

She gasped and it was gone.

Dunny kept to the top of the sand, away from the dead whale, and they reached the harbor in silence. Beside the Fisherman's Mission, Hayley saw her mother.

She sighed and walked up the road, leaving Dunny standing by the harbor. *No reason to say good-bye,* she thought. *He's not my friend and he won't reply anyway.*

Sarah Risso was slim and tanned from the Texas sun. Her blond hair was shorter than Hayley's but tied in a similar ponytail. "Hi, honey," she said with a smile.

This is promising, Hayley thought.

"Let's go for a coffee," her mom said.

"You can do that here?"

"They drink coffee in Scotland."

"It doesn't strike me as a Starbucks kind of town."

"There is a small café near the ferry."

Together they walked along a narrow street that led away from the old harbor. Around the bend, on the other side, was the slipway and jetty where the ferry embarked and disembarked. Unlike the wood and stone of the old harbor, this was functional concrete and steel. Beside it sat a small row of shops and a café. The town had no mall, so Hayley hadn't thought it worth exploring. The low stone houses had window boxes and some of the quaint chimneys were puffing smoke. There didn't seem to be very many cars or people. A little back from the ferry port stood a large sandstone church with a tower but no steeple.

A bell above the café door rang as they entered. The place was empty. They chose a table by the window that looked out on the ferry port. One small van sat in the boarding lane, but there was no one in it. The morning boat had come and gone; the afternoon ferry was not due for a couple of hours. The café smelled pleasantly of home baking, and a small, round woman appeared from a door by the counter. She offered a good-morning and menus. Sarah asked for a recommendation.

"We bake our own scones," the woman said.

"Two coffees and two scones, then," said Sarah.

"Fruit or plain?"

"One of each."

The woman bustled away and Hayley asked, "What's a scone?"

"It's like a biscuit."

"But Scottish biscuits are cookies."

"Our kind of biscuit."

Hayley stared out of the window and willed someone, anyone, to wander by and show that there were more than three people left in the world: her, her mom, and the scone lady.

"Was that you talking with Dunny Dunbar earlier?" her mom asked.

"Hardly," Hayley said with a scoff.

"You know what I mean. It's good to make friends."

Hayley physically recoiled. "Dunny Dunbar is not my friend."

"Have you met his older brother, Fraser? He seems like a nice boy."

"He's an extremely unpleasant boy."

Sarah sighed. "Hayley, honey, you have to make some kind of effort to get along with people. We might be here for a couple of months, remember. You will be going to school with these boys."

It was Hayley's turn to give a big sigh. "I can miss school for a few weeks, Mom. I'll catch up when I get back, I promise."

"You're behind as it is. Your grades have been terrible this semester."

"We know who's to blame for that."

"You can't blame your father for everything. You flunked those tests all by yourself."

"Yes, well, Dad didn't help."

Hayley stared out of the window again. She looked at the empty slipway and knew if she didn't get back in her mother's good graces, she would be catching ferries to school. The island of Nin had a primary school, but it was too small to have a high school of its own. Children from Nin went to the nearby, much larger Isle of Skye.

"Sorry for leaving the cottage last night," she muttered through gritted teeth.

"Just don't do it again," Sarah said. "I read somewhere that Scotland has more ax murderers than any other country in the world."

"Is that right?" Hayley asked disbelievingly. "More than Texas?"

"That's right. And I've heard they target moody, selfish girls."

"I'm not going to school here."

"It will only be for a few weeks."

"But the high school isn't even on this island. I have to stay in a hostel."

"Won't that be an adventure."

The distance between Skulavaig and Skye was too great to travel every day, especially in winter when seas were stormy and roads impassable. Children from small islands and remote locations stayed in a purpose-built hostel during the week, returning home on the weekends. Hayley had made it perfectly clear from the moment the idea was raised that she would not spend her weekdays with a bunch of hicks whose ways and accent she did not understand. Her mother had replied simply that it was not up for debate. Her mom thought her spoiled and self-absorbed; staying in the high school hostel would be a bit like summer fat camp. It would be summer *brat* camp.

Hayley had checked out the school website, half of which was written in Gaelic, the local language. Most of the words had consonants running together she couldn't even begin to pronounce. And the school seemed obsessed with a sport Hayley had never heard of: shinty. After searching every page of the website, the crushing realization slowly settled that her new high school did not, and would never, have a cheerleading squad.

There was a pause while Hayley seethed in silence before she finally asked, "Why are we here, Mom?"

"You know why we are here. I'm writing a book."

"A book about what?"

Sarah gave a laugh. "Now you ask. You've shown no interest in my writing up to now."

"I haven't been dragged from my home up to now."

"I've told you all this before. You don't listen. I am writing a book about displaced people."

"Like me, you mean."

"Not quite. These are people forced to move."

"Exactly. I can be Chapter One."

Sarah gave an incredulous smile. "Hayley, these are people forced to move because of poverty or persecution or war. It's hardly the same thing."

Hayley muttered, "It sure feels like it."

"That's why I was in Mexico in March. And London before that."

Hayley stated coldly, "I remember." Her mom's Mexico trip was the first time she had stayed with her father in his new apartment. The first time they had spent time together since he moved out. The first time she had met "Judy." It had not been a good few weeks.

"So why are we in Scotland?" she asked. "Why are we stuck on this little island in the middle of nowhere?"

"I have my reasons," her mom said. "But you don't need to know everything."

"I want to go home," Hayley said.

"You are home, honey, at least for a little while."

Hayley took in the view from the café window: the glittering ocean, the rocky headland, the sandy beach. It was picturesque for sure, beautiful even, but so was the Sahara Desert, so was Mount Everest, so was the *moon*. No one asked her to live there.

CHAPTER

FIVE

Fraser sat on the crumbling stones of Nin Castle and looked out over the ocean. The castle had been a ruin for a century and a half, abandoned when the last laird of Nin had died without an heir. Whoever had built it had chosen a good defensive position, but Fraser reckoned they had also loved the view. The air was warm, filled with the aroma of salt and seaweed. It was more than a scent; it was a memory, as if he had indeed crawled from the sea a billion years before. Not an idea he would bring up when the priest next visited the house.

He had been sent to find his brother and bring him home. Dunny was usually on the beach somewhere, but there was no sign of him. That meant he was up on the cliff or in the castle.

Fraser and Dunny had spent a lot of time in Nin Castle; it was their playground when they were younger. In the crumbling walls were nooks that led to small dark chambers and worn stone steps that took you down to dark passageways that led nowhere. The roof was gone and light spilled in from the top, but the castle floor was always dim.

It was perfect for hide-and-seek and Dunny was always better at the game; he could disappear behind a wall or up a chimney and it would take Fraser an age to find him. Whenever Fraser hid, Dunny always seemed to know exactly where he was.

Today, Fraser couldn't be bothered playing games. It seemed childish and Dunny was just annoying. Still, Dunny had to be found and shouting for him never worked. The best way to find his brother was by sneaking up on him.

Fraser scampered low along the ground toward the tower, crawled the last few feet until he came to a small wall. He edged around it and darted across to a doorway, ducked down and crept inside. He hugged the wall, staying in the shadows, paused and listened. From the corner of his eye he saw a flash of movement across the doorway. He scuttled to the entrance and peered out, enjoying the chase now that it was on. He crawled back to the low wall, could hear shallow breathing from the other side. Dunny was losing his touch. He threw himself over the ragged stones, crying, "Got you," and landed on top of the American girl.

"Get off me," Hayley cried.

Fraser rolled over and sat up. "You."

"Are you trying to kill me?"

If the first impression he had made earlier was lame, the second might be classed as criminal assault. Fraser held up his hands. "Sorry, I thought you were Dunny."

"Do I look like a small, weird Scottish boy?"

"Less of the weird; he *is* my brother."

"Well, I'm not him."

They sat on the grass, both frowning, Hayley looking at the castle and Fraser at the ocean.

"Have you seen him?" Fraser asked.

"I saw him earlier today but not recently."

"He's around here somewhere. Probably watching us and laughing."

"What is this place?"

"It's an old castle."

"Well, I get that, but is it real?"

"Of course it's real. This isn't Hogwarts."

"It's a bit of a ruin."

"That's because it's old."

"How old?"

"Auld, sae very auld," he said, putting on a Highland burr. "I dinnae ken exactly."

From her quizzical look, it was clear that she hadn't understood.

"I don't know exactly," he said by way of translation.

"It's your accent."

She was still proving difficult to like. "It's not my accent you can't understand, it's my dialect."

"OK, whatever."

Fraser thought to himself, *I've just been whatevered by an American girl.* A bit of him was outraged, a bit of him thought it was pretty cool.

"So why are you sneaking around an old ruined castle?" she asked. "I saw you."

"Why do you care?"

"It's very strange, that's all."

"And who made you the judge of all things strange?"

"I'm surrounded by it, it's hard to miss."

He snorted. She was implying that he was as strange as his brother.

"It's just a game Dunny and I play. A kind of hide-and-seek."

"Well, I found him last night, so it would seem I'm better at it than you." The girl looked behind her, along the path to the lip of the cliff. "He was standing over there, on the edge, in the storm."

"Aye, I heard. My mum and dad were out looking for him as well."

"At least one of us got to stay in bed."

Fraser didn't want the girl thinking he was safely tucked under the duvet while everyone else was out in the storm. "Everyone thinks I was in bed, but . . ." He shook his head.

"Where were you?"

He pointed toward the ocean. "Out there."

"Swimming?"

"No, I was on Ben McCaig's boat."

"Who is Ben McCaig?"

"You met him this morning on the beach. By the dead whale."

"Why were you on his boat?"

"We were trying to find a pod of pilot whales."

"In the middle of a storm?"

"Aye. It seems a bit daft now."

"And your mom and dad thought you were in bed?"

Fraser suddenly panicked. He had divulged information to a girl he didn't know and didn't like. "You can't tell anyone."

"Who would I tell?"

"My mum. Your mum."

"I don't know your mom and I've kept bigger secrets than that from mine. Much bigger than stupid sailing stories, believe me."

"Well, *my* mum doesn't need to know there were two of us out in the storm last night."

The girl gave a rueful laugh. "There were five of us out in the storm: your family and me. We all got wet."

"Six, actually."

"Ben the whale man."

Fraser had forgotten about Ben. "Seven."

"Who else?"

He looked in the direction of the sea, so different now from a day ago. He had a burden to share, a story to tell that none believed and it seemed important that someone else heard, even if it was an infuriating American girl. There was no one else to tell.

"I may have imagined it, but when I was out in the boat last night, I thought . . ." He paused, rubbed his chin.

"What?" she asked, suddenly interested in his stupid sailing stories.

"I thought I saw somebody in the water. I thought I heard a cry for help."

"What did you do?"

"Nothing. Ben wouldn't believe me. He thought I had imagined it. It *was* dark. It was some storm."

For the first time, there was something soft in the girl's voice. "But *you* don't think you imagined it."

"It doesn't matter now anyway. It's just a bit . . . strange, that's all."

"As I said already, this town is a bit strange. You're a bit strange."

"Thanks."

There was no venom in this insult; she laughed when she said it. Fraser looked at her, noted how pretty she was, tried not to be intimidated by it. There were a few pretty girls in his school, but he couldn't think of any with blond hair. Not that the dark-haired ones or the red-haired ones gave him much of their time. Girls were all a bit of a mystery to Fraser, intriguing, yes, a puzzle to be solved, but he wished there was some textbook that offered all the answers at the back.

"What are you doing up here anyway?" he asked.

"I was following you. There's nothing much else to do on this island except take a walk. I thought you might be going somewhere interesting. I was wrong."

"You don't think an old ruined castle is interesting?"

"Not really. Just kind of creepy."

"Well, Nin has other delights on offer," Fraser said. "We have a nine-hole golf course, there's the marina, a lighthouse on the north coast . . ."

"I left my golf clubs back in Texas," she said sarcastically.

They both laughed and for a moment it seemed that the ice, if not yet broken, had perhaps melted a sliver at the edge. Fraser thought he should venture another stab at friendly conversation. Deep down, she was probably a lovely girl. Deep, deep down. Way down deep.

"So how are you finding Scotland?" he asked. "It's a long way from Texas."

Hayley sighed. "It is a very long way, but my mom is writing a book about people far from home and seems to think *we* need to be far from home to do it. There are other reasons we're here as well."

Fraser waited for her to continue, but it became clear she wasn't going to say any more. He could tell from the way she chewed her bottom lip and stared into space that there *was* some other reason why this girl and her mother had traveled across an ocean to a different continent, then washed up on a small island on its far edge.

"Well, I better find Dunny, I suppose," he said after a moment.

He looked at the castle tower, lit by the afternoon sun, each weathered stone a different shade of gray. "He's in there somewhere."

"What's the deal with your brother? Why doesn't he speak?"

Fraser shrugged. "He has something called Selective Mutism. But I *think* he just chooses not to, never has.

"Which is just another way of saying *weird*."

Fraser shook his head and wondered if the girl realized just how rude she could be. Was it an American thing? Was it a girl thing? Was it just a Hayley Risso thing?

"He's on the autism spectrum, if that's what you mean. We don't call them weird anymore."

If he expected an apology, none came. Instead, Hayley said, "He gave me this last night." She reached into the pocket of her jeans and pulled out a scallop shell. "Right there on the edge of a cliff in the middle of a storm, he hands me a shell."

Fraser took the shell from her and examined it. "Another one. He's been doing this lately. Sometimes he writes on them."

"What's it for?"

He flipped the shell over, flipped it back. "My mother calls it a tell shell, some kind of island tradition. People used to send messages to one another."

"What kind of messages?"

"No idea. Load of nonsense."

He threw the scallop toward the castle wall. It hit the old stones and shattered.

"I might have wanted that," Hayley said.

"It's just a shell."

The girl stood and said, "Well, I'm going home." She paused. "God, I've just called that ridiculous little cottage 'home.'" She gave an anguished sigh and walked away. After a few steps she stopped and turned. "Oh, and FYI, there might be someone hiding in the big cave down there. Thought you should know in case he's kidnapped your brother or something."

"What do you mean?" Fraser asked, startled, but the girl strode off down the path and was gone.

He faced the castle again and his brother was there, standing under a shadowed archway like a phantom. Fraser sighed in relief that he was found, imagined some laird's son from centuries past plunging from the high cliff and only now returning, a pale ghost haunting the castle, moving through its dark, ruined rooms in silence.

"Time to go home, Dunny," he said, but he knew that this place, this cliff, beach, and ocean, was the only place Dunny seemed truly at home.

SIX

Hayley stood on the beach and stared at the endless ocean. She was stuck on this island, an Alcatraz of sorts, only wetter and with less chance of escape. And nobody ever escaped from Alcatraz.

She took out her phone, turned her back to the sea, and snapped a picture of herself. Later she would post the photograph on every one of her profiles, along with a challenge to her friends. She was alone on a beach, on an island where she knew no one, in a country far away from everything she understood. Could anyone she knew post a pic that was more of a *selfie* than that?

She climbed up from the beach onto the harbor wall and saw her mom. Sarah was talking to the whale man. He was good-looking in that older, stubble-on-chin, broad-shouldered way that boys her age couldn't muster. She moved up the jetty, and her mom saw her.

"Hi, Hayley," she said. "Ben was just telling me that you saw a dead whale this morning."

"It was gross."

The man laughed. "I prefer them alive myself."

"Do you see many?" Sarah asked.

Ben nodded enthusiastically. "This season has been amazing, actually. I've seen a bunch of minke whales, pilot whales, dolphins, harbor porpoises, a sei whale. And then . . ." He paused for a moment and looked at the ocean, smiled slightly. "I recorded a sperm whale. Can you believe it?"

"That *is* amazing," Sarah said.

Hayley blew a snort of disbelief. Her mom wouldn't know a sperm whale if it flopped onto the sea wall and introduced itself. What was she doing?

"Nin suddenly seems to be the center of the whale world," Ben said. "I'm thinking of packing in my research and starting a whale-watching business."

"You mustn't do that. Being a scientist is such a cool job."

What was that? Hayley wondered. That was dangerously close to flirting.

"I'm kidding. I love my job, although it can be a little lonely at times, just me and the whales."

Her mom laughed coyly.

Enough already.

"Here's something you might find interesting," Ben said. "You guys have a species of dolphin named after you. There's a Risso's dolphin."

"Oh, my goodness," said Sarah. "That's exciting." She turned to her daughter. "Isn't that exciting, Hayley?"

Hayley thought, *Not really.* "Sure," she said.

Ben looked at Hayley now. "There's also a Fraser's dolphin."

Why are you telling me? she thought.

"Is there a Ben's dolphin?" her mom asked.

"Not yet. Not until I discover a new species."

From around the headland, there appeared a large yacht, its white hull gleaming in the sunlight, its sail billowing in a gentle breeze.

"Whose boat is that?" Sarah asked.

"That's Willie McGregor's yacht," Ben said. "He's a big man in Skulavaig. One of the old fishermen. My boat used to be Willie's. As you can see, he's upgraded."

Hayley looked down at the old boat tied to the sea wall where they stood. Compared with the yacht, it was a rather sorry-looking thing.

"There must have been money to be made in lobster fishing," Sarah said.

"Aye, indeed."

Hayley saw a gleam in her mother's eye and she hoped it came from chasing a story, not from chasing Ben.

"I'm going for a sail round the island myself," Ben said. "Would you like to come?" After a pause, too long for Hayley's liking, he added, "Both of you."

"I can't today," Sarah said. "But definitely some other time. We would love that, wouldn't we, Hayley?"

"Sure," she said again, as unconvincing as the first time.

Ben said good-bye and climbed down a rusty metal ladder onto his boat. He moved to the wheelhouse and the engine spluttered and banged and came to life. He guided the boat gently away from the wall, spinning the wheel so the vessel turned to face the narrow harbor opening and the sea beyond. He eased forward on the throttle, the screw began to turn, the propeller churned water, and the boat sailed out.

Hayley and her mom watched the boat move away and then Hayley asked, "Why were you flirting with that man?"

"I wasn't flirting with Ben. I'm researching my book."

"*Ben*, is it now?"

"Well, that's his name."

"Do you like him?"

"Hayley."

"I think he liked you."

"Hayley!"

When she wanted to, Hayley could really twist the knife.

"What about Dad, what would he think?"

"Now, that's not fair."

"You're still married, after all."

Sarah took a large breath. "You know as well as I, honey, that your father couldn't care less who I flirted with."

"So you *were* flirting." Hayley gave a squeal of triumph.

Her mom gave her a look of both scorn and disappointment, turned on her heel and walked up the jetty toward the cottage. Hayley stood on the stone wall and realized she had just chased away the only person she knew on the whole island. In the whole country. On the whole continent. She reached into her pocket and pulled out her phone. It was time for another photograph. A completely, totally, utterly by-my-selfie.

SEVEN

Fraser thought again about Hayley's tale of someone hiding in the cave. First a man in the water and now perhaps a man in the cave. They must be connected, he thought as he watched the afternoon ferry come in. Two cars and two vans disembarked along with a crowd of foot passengers, most of whom were islanders. He gave a nod to a girl who was a year ahead of him at school. His one friend on the island, a boy called Malcolm, was away for five weeks in Lanzarote. Fraser stayed until the ferry departed; there were six cars on it plus some passengers on foot. That gave a net loss, more people leaving than arriving. Thus was the story of the island.

Fraser couldn't shake the notion there was something interesting lurking in the dark recesses of the distant cliff face. It was either nothing or it was adventure, and he'd had an afternoon of nothing. He could at least try for adventure.

A half mile north of Skulavaig were deep caves that must once have harbored pirates and smugglers and ship wreckers. He had explored them often, had even camped for the night in one with Dunny. It took ten minutes to reach the base of the cliff and he was sweating as he pressed a hand against the weathered sandstone of the first cave opening. His heart pounded as he peered into the dark entrance. This cave was not especially deep and the afternoon light made it to the back wall. The cave was empty except for sand and dried seaweed. The next cave along was a little deeper but equally empty. The entrance to the third cave could be reached only by a clamber up some fallen boulders. Fraser pulled himself up the loose rocks, sending a scatter of stone back down to the beach. At the top he peered cautiously into the hole. Sunlight reached only so far and the depths of the cave were inky black. There was a damp smell to the air and he could hear water dripping from the roof. He paused for a moment to let his eyes adjust to the gloom. The back of the cave remained in shadow.

"Hello," he said nervously, hearing the word echo back as if he had replied to himself. There was no other response. He needed a flashlight and some courage to venture deeper. He had neither, and there were other small caves to be examined farther along the cliff face. He turned his back on the entrance, searching the ground for a sure footing to clamber back down to the beach, and saw, in the thin layer of sand at the cave mouth, a set of footprints. They were not his own, for these prints were made by bare feet. Big feet. Fraser caught his breath, turned back to the dark opening.

"I know you're in there," he said, trying to sound confident. "Show yourself."

For a moment, there was nothing, just blackness, and then shadow became movement. The figure of a man emerged from against the back wall as if pulling himself from the stone. At first, all that could be seen were his eyes, white discs that shone as he moved into the light. The man was big. He wasn't young but he wasn't old; his head was shaven and he had the beginnings of a beard. He wore nothing except a pair of faded jeans. His skin was black.

Fraser gasped in fright, took a step back, then another, and found himself tumbling over the fallen rocks. He hit the beach with a thud and his lungs deflated. He knew he was only winded, but it felt like dying. After a long few seconds he caught his breath and slowly pushed himself up to a sitting position. The man was standing over him and Fraser couldn't breathe again; his heart hammered so hard it was painful, his whole body tensed at what was to come.

"Can you help me?" the man asked. He sounded tired and desperate, and his voice trembled.

Fraser picked himself up from the sand and, gasping for oxygen, he turned and ran, ran as fast as he had ever run in his life, his feet sinking in the soft sand, his arms pumping, fingers clawing at the air as if that might help. He heard the sound of whimpering and realized that it came from him. He dared to glance behind him and saw the beach was empty.

Fraser collapsed on the sand. When his breathing finally returned to normal, he sat up and felt embarrassed. True explorers didn't run away whimpering. And he remembered the man's words: *Can you help me?* That didn't sound like a murdering psychopath.

Then it hit him: He had heard those words before. In the middle of a storm-tossed ocean, someone had called for help. It was the same man, there *had* been someone in the water, and the man had made it to shore.

He got up and walked back toward the cave. When he reached it, he shouted, "Hello again." There was a sudden panic that he had frightened the man away and would never see him again. After a moment, however, the stranger stepped out of the shadowy entrance and slid down the boulders to the beach.

At first glance the man looked big and scary, but there was a nervousness in his eyes and his head twitched left and right as if he expected something bad to happen at any moment. "I did not mean to frighten you," he said.

"My fault. I overreacted."

"Still, I should not have jumped from the cave."

The man had a deep voice and a sharp accent, not Scottish, not English, not American, some kind of African, perhaps.

"You didn't jump. And it was me who told you to show yourself."

"Yes, you did."

"What are you doing here?"

"That would very much depend on where *here* is." He looked out to sea. "Where am I?"

"You're on the island of Nin."

The man frowned slightly, as if that was impossible. "An island? And in which country is Nin?"

Fraser hesitated, wondered if the man was joking with him. "Scotland. You're in Scotland."

The stranger leaned back against the fallen boulders and wrapped his arms around his bare chest. "Ah, Scotland. That would explain why I have been so cold."

"Where are your clothes?" Fraser asked.

The man gave a loud laugh that echoed off the cliffs. "It was easier to swim without them."

"Is that how you got here?"

"Yes, I am . . ." He scratched his stubbly chin as he searched for the word. "Shipwrecked."

This *was* the man who had been swimming in the storm.

"Well, you've landed not far from town. Come back with me. Or I'll go and fetch help."

"No!" There was a look of alarm on his face. He began again to glance up and down the beach. "You must not bring anyone here."

"Then let's go back to town."

"No, I cannot go to your town. I must stay here."

"But I want to help."

"You *can* help but only if I stay here."

"Why?" Fraser asked warily. "What have you done?"

"I have done nothing." The man's eyes narrowed and he pinched his lips together as if something hurt. "Except come here."

"Where are you from?"

"I will tell you all you want to know, but first . . . will you help me?"

"Yes." It was the least Fraser could do. In the storm he had lacked the courage of his convictions but not this time. The man looked cold and frightened and helpless. This time, Fraser would help.

The man stared for a few moments, breathing slowly, his hands clasped together as if in prayer. "Can I trust you?"

"Of course."

"You will tell no one of my presence here?"

"Not a soul." Fraser paused. "You must be hungry. And cold. I'll bring some food and clothes. I'll go right now and come back later with what you need."

The man sighed and said, "Thank you."

Fraser started back down the beach but was halted by a call.

"Boy, what is your name?" The man was at the entrance of the cave, almost hidden by the darkness.

"I'm Fraser. Fraser Dunbar."

"Thank you again, Fraser Dunbar."

"And what's your name?"

"My name is Jonah. Like the story in the Bible. Jonah and the whale."

Fraser sprinted all the way back to his house and arrived out of breath, heart pumping. It was not just the run along the beach; he had found a shipwrecked sailor in a cave. That was beyond astonishing! He slowed his breathing, wiped sweat from his forehead, and pushed open the back door into the kitchen, ready for the fight that would follow.

The kitchen was empty—no fuming parents, no dinner cold on its plate, only the smell of something cooking in the oven. His mum appeared from the downstairs toilet, wearing rubber gloves and holding a bottle of bathroom cleaner.

"Where have you been?" she asked.

"Just out."

"Down at that boat, no doubt."

Fraser said nothing.

"Your father's warned you, Fraser. He says it isn't a safe boat."

"It's a fine boat. Dinner's late tonight."

"Just as well for you. Our American visitors are eating here tonight." Jessie Dunbar ignored Fraser's sigh, and her voice softened. "Have you met Hayley yet?"

"Aye."

"She's a very pretty girl, don't you think?"

"I hadn't noticed."

"Well, take it from me she is. Now go and wash your hands; they'll be here soon."

Fraser hesitated. He had to get back to the cave. He had promised. "I'm not that hungry. I'll skip dinner."

"You'll do nothing of the kind." His mother pointed a finger encased in yellow rubber. "Go."

Fraser slunk from the hall and climbed the stairs to his bedroom. From the window he could see the *Moby Dick* sitting in the harbor, but there was no sign of Ben. He tried to work out a plan that would get him back to the caves that night, but nothing cunning or foolproof came to him. After a while he heard the doorbell and voices in the hall, and then his mother called to come and eat.

In the small dining room, his family was squashed around the table along with Hayley Risso and her mother. The table groaned under the weight of food. His mother had left him a seat beside the American girl. *Subtle*, he thought. She was certainly pretty but in that don't-I-know-it kind of way.

The main course was salmon, as Fraser knew it would be. His dad was production manager of the island's large fish farm, Nin's only industry apart from tourism. Fraser and Hayley said nothing to each other throughout the meal except for some polite passing of the plates. Dunny could offer no conversation, so it was the parents who did the talking. Small talk mostly, about the food and the weather and the scenery and life in Texas and life in Skulavaig. Talk also about how life on Nin was hard for young people, how most had to leave to find work if they didn't want a job on a ferry or a fish farm. Fraser chewed his food and thought only of the man in the cave who had nothing to eat. After a dessert of apple pie and ice cream, the never-ending meal came to an end.

"I'll clear the plates," said Fraser, seeing the surprised look on his mother's face. He never volunteered for chores.

"Put the kettle on," Jessie said as she ushered their guests into the living room.

Fraser carried the plates through to the kitchen and scraped the leftovers from the serving dishes into a plastic tub. He then put the remains of the apple pie into another tub. The man would have dessert.

He took orders for tea and coffee, to the admiration of his mother, then sneaked upstairs and stuffed the two plastic tubs into the bottom of his backpack, empty now of schoolbooks. He quickly searched and found two baggy sweatshirts, an old cagoule, and a couple of pairs of thick socks. These went into the backpack. Finally, he added a tatty blanket that had rested on top of his wardrobe for as long as he could remember.

He ran back down and made two cups of tea and one coffee. When he took them through to the living room, Dunny and Hayley were standing with their jackets on. The girl made a poor attempt at concealing a frown.

"There you are," said his mum. "Take Hayley and your brother and stretch your legs for twenty minutes."

"My legs are stretched," Fraser said.

"Don't be cheeky, and do as your mother asks," said his father.

"But I can't."

"Why not?"

Fraser could think of no convincing reason. "I've still to fill the dishwasher." It was not a convincing reason.

His father made a slight scoffing sound; his mother said, "The dishes can wait."

There was nothing for it, so Fraser moped from the room, followed by his brother and the girl. He would have to think on the move. He ran upstairs to fetch a jacket, grabbing his backpack at the same time. As he pushed Hayley and Dunny through the back door, he lifted a pair of his father's muddy boots from the step, waiting to be cleaned. He tied the laces together and strung them through the straps of his backpack. Hayley watched closely but he had little choice, it had to be done.

"What's with the boots?" she asked. "What's in the bag?"

"Some things I've to take to Ben."

This seemed to satisfy her and she let Fraser lead the way out through the garden and down the small path that led to the harbor. Dunny trailed a step behind. Fraser's mind was racing. He had to find a way to ditch them both.

The harbor was quiet, the only sound the slap of water against the stone walls and the cry of a distant gull. It had grown chilly and Fraser thought of Jonah, bare-chested and sockless. Wherever he came from, he would be feeling the cold.

At the *Moby Dick*, he could tell Ben wasn't home. A light usually glowed through the open hatch from the cabin below. He was probably having a drink with the old fishermen in the harbor pub.

"Ben's not here," Fraser said. "He probably walked along the beach. He won't be far."

"I've just got sand *out* of my shoes," Hayley said.

"Don't come, then. Just stay here."

"I will," Hayley replied.

Fraser moved quickly along the jetty and jumped down onto the sand. "I won't be long."

"Fraser," the girl shouted, "don't you dare leave me here with your brother."

Fraser put his head down and pretended not to hear. He ran along the beach, close to the waves where the sand was firmer. He knew Hayley would march Dunny straight back to his parents and he would be in deep trouble. But that was a worry for later.

When he reached the cliff, Jonah emerged warily from his cave, as if he expected a squad of policemen, the coast guard, or Fraser's father at the very least.

"You are alone," he said. His sigh of relief was followed by a gentle smile of gratitude.

He pulled on both sweatshirts and devoured the cold food, taking greedy mouthfuls as if he hadn't eaten in days. Fraser sat on a rock and watched him, wondered again who he was and where he was from.

A clatter of stones made Fraser spin around and there was Hayley Risso standing in the half-light, a dumb-struck look on her face.

"What are you doing here?" he said.

The girl didn't answer, asked instead, "Who is that?"

Jonah glanced around him, a fearful look back on his face, his body tensed to fight or run. "You promised you would come alone."

"I did. She followed me." Fraser turned to the girl. "Why do you keep following me?"

"Don't flatter yourself," she growled. "I refuse to be abandoned at the harbor with your little brother."

"Dunny, where is he?"

"He was right behind me."

"Great. You're here and Dunny's lost."

"What was I supposed to do?"

"You should have stayed where you were."

"And you shouldn't have run away." Hayley looked at the large man who was standing in a sweatshirt too small for him, holding a plastic dish in one hand and a fork in the other. "Who is this guy?"

"This is Jonah." He faced the man. "Jonah, this is Hayley. She followed me here. I'm sorry."

"Can she keep a secret?" Jonah asked.

"Yes, I can keep a secret," Hayley said.

"You are American."

"Yes, I am. And where are you from?"

The man's eyes darted from Fraser to Hayley and back again, seemingly weighing up the danger of telling them more. Finally, he sighed and said, "I am from Lesotho, a small country in Africa."

"I knew it!" said Fraser. He repeated the word. "Lesu-tu." He recognized the name, remembered it was pronounced differently from how it was spelled. He liked maps, liked looking at faraway places around the world that were a million miles from Skulavaig. Lesotho sounded like it might be even farther than that.

"Never heard of it," Hayley declared.

"So why have you come to Scotland?" Fraser asked.

Jonah gave a grim laugh. "I did not expect to come here. All I know of this land is that you have a monster in a lake."

"This is perfect," Hayley said. "My mom is writing a book about people like you. She could do an interview."

"You keep out of this," Fraser said.

"Oh, I don't think so. Either I'm part of this little game or your dad will no longer wonder what happened to his boots."

Fraser's outrage was instant and overwhelming. "You are the most . . . the most . . ." He fizzed as he searched for the words. "The most annoying, conniving, stuck-up . . ."

"Enough," said Jonah softly. He clasped his hands together, as if in thanksgiving. "What's done is done. The girl knows I am here." He turned to Hayley, a troubled dip to his eyebrows, his voice grave with a hint of pleading. "Will you promise not to tell anyone of my presence in this place? Especially your mother?"

"Only if you tell us what you're doing here. In Texas we have people called illegal aliens. Is that what you are, an illegal alien?"

"If you mean have I been invited by this country's government to come and stay, then the answer is obviously no. Otherwise I would not be hiding in a cave."

There was another term Fraser remembered. "Are you an asylum seeker?"

"Asylum seeker, illegal alien, these are just words." Jonah gave a deep sigh. "All I know is that I am very far from home."

"So why come to *this* island?"

"I did not come to this island. This island came to me."

There was no more talk for a moment and above the crash of waves they heard a sound like a chant, a single note that changed pitch from low to high and back again.

"Down there," Jonah said, pointing to the waves. "What is that?"

"That will be my brother."

"Your brother? Will he talk?"

"He really won't." Fraser gave a weary smile and said, "Dunny talks almost as well as he sings."

He trudged toward the breaking surf. Away from the cave it wasn't completely dark and he could see the figure of his brother standing at the ocean's edge. The moon had risen above the cliffs and cast a ghostly light on Dunny and the water. The boy stood motionless facing the sea, making a quiet humming sound now.

Jonah moved alongside Fraser and stretched out an arm. "Do you see there?"

Fraser followed Jonah's pointing, out beyond his brother, out beyond the breaking waves. Something moved in the water, something big and dark.

A fin.

"Is that a shark?" Hayley asked.

"It's not a shark," Fraser said. "It's a whale."

And he knew immediately that it was not just any kind of whale. It was the most wondrous kind. The kind you were not supposed to see off the coast of Nin.

"It's a killer whale. An orca."

The fin rose slightly from the water and he could see a white flank and a round head. The moonlight reflected on its sleek body as it cut through the water. Fraser took a step forward.

"That's amazing," he whispered.

"There's another one," Hayley said.

"And another," said Jonah.

Fraser looked and saw a pod of orcas swimming off-shore. In all his life, no one, not even Ben, had ever seen orcas off his little island. His heart pounded so fast he hoped the sound didn't scare them away.

He heard a splash and turned to see Dunny wading into the rolling waves.

"No, Dunny," he cried, and without thinking, he ran and plowed into the ocean after him. The water was icy cold and it snatched away his breath. He struggled to keep upright in the surf. Dunny was in up to his waist when Fraser reached him. He grabbed his arm and hauled him toward the shore.

"You can't swim with orcas," he shouted, panting. "They're carnivores, they could attack."

Dunny shook his head and tried to tug free. Fraser pulled again, but his brother resisted; he was stronger than he looked.

"Dunny!" he shouted again and he heard Hayley yell from the beach. A wave rolled over them and its crest slapped him on the face, giving him a mouthful of salty water. When he looked, the whales were closer; he could almost have reached out and touched a fin. He tightened his grip around Dunny's arm and heaved. The boy's legs gave out from under him, he floated for a moment, and Fraser pulled hard. Slowly, they splashed back toward the shore. Hayley and Jonah helped them onto the dry sand.

Fraser stood on the beach and dripped water and held on to his brother's arm. He could feel Dunny pull against him, as if he wasn't done yet with the whales. The orcas were farther out now, dark fins silhouetted against the dim horizon, cutting through the water with barely a ripple.

"We can't swim with them," Fraser said, taking deep breaths. They stood and gazed for a few moments. "A pod of orcas, can you believe it? I almost don't mind getting wet."

Dunny sat on the sand, and Fraser sat down beside him. He shivered in his wet clothes as they watched the whales and Fraser realized they were alone. He could see the figure of Hayley making her way toward town, and Jonah must have gone back to his cave.

"This isn't so bad."

He looked at his brother and saw him gently smile.

"We haven't done this kind of thing for ages." He laughed in amazement. "Well, we've never done this exactly. There's never been killer whales before."

And in turn each whale blew a deep whoosh that echoed across the waves, sending up a spray of water that glimmered in the moonbeams.

EIGHT

Hayley returned to the harbor alone, leaving the Dunbar boys captivated by the whales. It had been fascinating to start with, especially when Dunny had tried to get eaten, but there were only so many circling silhouettes she could enjoy. And it was time to head back—it had been two hours since dinner and her mom would be panicking.

As she climbed on to the end of the jetty, she heard laughter and voices, and one of them was her mom's. She didn't sound frantic with worry. Hayley listened some more and made out a man's voice with a Scottish accent. Ben McCaig! What was going on here?

Her first impulse was to march over, full of indignation, but then she thought she should listen for a bit. Get some evidence to back up her outrage. She dropped back down onto the beach and crept along until she was level with Ben's boat on the other side of the stone wall. Her mother was on top of the jetty, talking to Ben.

"Well, if you see her, you can tell her to get home."

Hayley thought again, *This is not my home.*

"They'll be by the harbor somewhere. Nowhere else to go."

"It *is* a lovely little harbor. Is yours the only boat that moors here?"

"There's a marina along the coast. Most of the boats berth there now."

"Are there many?"

"A few. There used to be a fishing fleet, before my time, but the fish have gone now, if not the old fishermen. A few still work, a few still have their boats."

So her mom was researching *and* flirting at the same time.

"You're all alone here, then?"

"Aye, the harbor's too wee for most of the boats. An occasional yacht will tie up in the summer and there's the ferry, although it doesn't always come, not if the seas are rough. That happens a lot. You need to be a lot more self-reliant if you live on an island."

"You seem to manage fine."

From the beach Hayley thought, *What was that?* She pictured her mom's coy smile, the gentlest of touches on Ben's bare arm. This was embarrassing.

"I'm only here for the summer, but it's a fine life. I have no money and my boat is falling apart, but I'm doing what I love."

"We should all strive for that."

Hayley's face crumpled in disgust.

"Well, you must love being a writer? What's your book about?"

"It's about displaced people—where they've come from, where they're going, how they get there."

"Why Scotland?" Before her mom could answer, Ben added, "Why Nin?"

"Your country has a long history of people on the move. Look at your Highland clearances. Even today, people are coming and going. There is a story here."

Hayley recognized the slightly evasive tone in her mother's voice. She had heard it often enough when her parents' marriage first hit the rocks and they were pretending everything was still all right. No, her mom wasn't telling Ben McCaig everything.

There was silence now. *Please God they're not kissing*, Hayley thought. She had to know, so she carefully grasped the top of the wall with her fingertips and slowly pulled herself up so her eyes peeked over the top. Her mom and Ben were gone. She turned and saw them wandering down the jetty toward the ocean. She dropped back onto the beach and moved down the sand until she could go no farther without paddling. The wall was higher here; if they kissed now, she would never know. Unless there were slobbering noises. Hayley shuddered at the thought and heard Ben say, "We've only one pub on Nin but three churches. It is a very religious island."

Sarah laughed. "At least you have one pub. I grew up in what was called a dry county. No liquor allowed. You can buy me a drink some night. It would be wrong to come to Scotland and not try a whisky."

Hayley expected her mom to say, *Pick one of three churches and let's get married.* She heard them laugh together.

"Come to the ceilidh tomorrow," Ben said.

"Is that a dance?"

"Aye, Highland dancing and the like. It's a good laugh and you won't be any worse at it than me."

"You'd be surprised."

OMG, Hayley said to herself, *now they've made a date.*

"OK," her mother said, "that's a date."

See, Hayley shouted in her head. *See, I told you: a date.*

"But for now," Sarah continued, "I need to find my daughter. Last seen heading that way."

"They'll be fine. Fraser is the reliable sort and Dunny knows every grain of sand on this beach. They're good boys; they've been out on the boat with me a few times. They will be exploring the caves, seeing if there are mermaids and monsters in them."

From her crouching position behind the wall, Hayley thought, *If only you knew what was in the cave.*

"Has Dunny never spoken?" Sarah asked.

"Not as far as I'm aware."

"That must be so sad for Jessie and Duncan."

"Aye, they're good people; it's a shame."

Sarah sighed. "I'd better go find my daughter. Sometimes she has too much to say."

"Well, don't worry, the view will still be here tomorrow."

"I do like this view. What will I see in the daylight?"

"Over there is the mainland, and over that side is the big island of Skye, which isn't really an island anymore since they built the bridge. In front of us, can you see that bit of land in the distance across the water?"

"Where there's a lighthouse flashing?"

"That's the tip of the island of Rona and beyond that there's Raasay and beyond that there's Scalpay. Nin is the most northerly island of the little archipelago."

"I have a map of Scotland," Sarah said, "but I couldn't find this island anywhere. It's as if it doesn't exist."

"That's because it doesn't," Ben said. "The island of Nin is a ghost isle."

"It does lack a little bit of life."

"Aye, it's not exactly buzzing, but a ghost isle is an island that doesn't appear on maps."

"Why not?"

"Because of bad geography and ancient history. The earliest maps were not always the most accurate maps. No Google Earth back then. Places were often wrongly mapped or not mapped at all. On the first map of Scotland, the island of Nin was missed out. Later maps just copied that first map and so the error kept going. Some maps today still have the mistake. Not every map, just some."

"I'll remember that. And what's the water called?"

"There's a deep channel that lies between the islands

and the mainland. Mapmakers named it the Inner Sound. The people of Nin know it by its older, Gaelic name, Caolas Mucmhara."

"What does that mean?" Sarah asked.

There was a pause before Ben said, "It means the Sound of Whales."

Sarah laughed. "I guess that's why you're here."

"It is. In the last couple of years, there have been a lot of whales in the sound. Way more than usual. I'm here to find out why."

"What's your theory?"

"It probably involves fluctuating ocean currents caused by climate change. But there's more research to be done."

"Sounds fascinating."

Ben laughed. "You're humoring the whale nerd."

"No, it's your work, and it's important to you."

"You best go find your daughter."

"No need. Come on, Hayley, let's go."

Hayley, crouching behind the wall, jumped in fright. How did her mom know she was there? She stood up and walked along to where the wall was low enough to climb up on top. Her mom and Ben were waiting for her.

"Good evening, Ben," she said nonchalantly.

"Hello again."

"Hi, Mom."

"Where have you been?" Sarah asked.

"The boys and I took a walk along the shore."

"And are they behind the wall as well?"

"No, just me."

Hayley gave them her most winning smile—her cheer-leader smile, her mom called it—and set off up the road toward the cottage. She heard her mom say good night to Ben, glanced back to see if there was a peck on the cheek, but her mother was right behind her, and Ben stood on the jetty in the dark, watching them go.

It had been quite a day, unlike any she had experienced back in Texas. For a ghost island on the edge of nowhere, Nin had a lot going on.

NINE

The morning sun streamed through the window and bathed Fraser's face as he lay in bed. It felt warm and inviting, calling him outside, seeking his company. But he was stuck indoors, grounded for the morning, having offered no reasonable explanation for his late return the previous evening. He couldn't talk of caves and strangers, dared not even mention the whales. He had considered faking a romance with the American girl but wasn't keen to even pretend. Dunny had escaped the grounding, had been judged an unwilling accomplice in some secretive shenanigan.

Typical.

Fraser was not to leave the confines of his house unless it was burning down. He thought about making toast for breakfast and leaving it under the grill.

Something else was calling him to the forbidden outdoors. He was desperate to find Ben McCaig and tell him of his late-night encounter with orcas. He had witnessed a pod of killer whales swimming just offshore and that seemed even more unbelievable than a shipwrecked man.

Fraser dragged himself from under his duvet and looked out the window, down toward the harbor. It made no difference that he was grounded; Ben was gone. The *Moby Dick* had sailed some time in the early morning. It had been gone when Fraser first looked, just after his mother had woken him to say that she and his brother were catching the early ferry to Skye to buy Dunny's school uniform. They would be away all morning, but Fraser was not to leave the house if he valued his life.

He turned from the window and noticed something lying on his pillow. It was a shell. Dunny! It was annoying enough that Dunny came into his room when he wasn't there. Now his brother was coming into his room when he *was*.

It was a razor shell, long and thin and shiny white, with speckles of blue. Inside, like a pearl, was a small lump of dull glass. As Fraser picked up the shell, the glass tried to sparkle in the sunlight. He took the shell to Dunny's room and tossed it through the door.

He returned to his room and lay back on his bed, in no rush for breakfast, or a wash, or clothes. He pictured the orcas again, the sleek black of their bodies hidden in the darkness of the ocean, the white parts shining in the moonlight, their high fins silhouetted against the horizon, circling slowly, his brother smiling at the water's edge, like lord of the whales . . .

A loud knock on the front door woke him from his doze. The sun still streamed through the window, but it had moved across the bed, no longer on his face, the world spinning on its axis. The knock came again and he hauled himself to his feet and pulled on a pair of jeans and the same T-shirt he had worn yesterday. As he was going downstairs, there was a third knock, an anxious, something-is-wrong knock. He hoped it was Ben, hoped the scientist had somehow heard about the orcas and wanted to know more.

Fraser pulled open the door and saw Hayley Risso. Her face was white and her bottom lip trembled.

"Come quickly," she said.

"I'm grounded."

"Put on your shoes and come quickly!"

"I'm not supposed to leave the house."

"You have to come."

"But what if I'm caught?"

"When this gets out, all that won't matter."

"When what gets out?"

"Just come."

Hayley moved back down the path, heading toward the harbor. She didn't look behind her, confident, it seemed, he would follow. Fraser had to walk fast to catch up.

"Where's your mum?" he asked breathlessly.

"Off to that big island, can't remember its name."

"Skye?"

"Yeah, that's it."

"Why she's gone there?"

"No idea. She said she would be back on the afternoon ferry."

Past the harbor, Hayley jumped down on to the beach and headed in the direction of the cliffs. Fraser wondered how many times he had walked this piece of sand in the last couple of days, wondered if he was walking in his own footprints.

The ocean was still and blue, the sand sparkled, but ahead lay a large, dark object.

"Oh, God," Fraser said, his heart sinking. "Another whale."

Not an orca, he prayed. Another pilot whale, a dolphin, a baby sperm whale, even. Just not one of the orcas from the night before. They had been too special, too magical to now be washed ashore, dead and decaying.

He moved toward it slowly, searching for a fin or a tail fluke. Then he heard Hayley behind him say, "No, Fraser."

He stood above it now, frowned slightly as his brain slowly made sense of what his eyes already knew.

That wasn't a fin. That was an arm. That was no tail fluke. That was a leg.

Fraser staggered back, fell onto the sand and tried to push himself backward, clawing hopelessly at the beach, which slid through his fingers.

It was a body, a human body. Just lying there on the beach of Skulavaig, on a warm July morning, with the ocean calm and not a soul to be seen.

"Is it . . . is it Jonah?" Hayley asked, as if the sand was clogging her throat.

Fraser stood and stared, didn't know what else to do when a corpse lay in front of him. Was this the man he was talking to only yesterday? It didn't seem real, it couldn't be real, but there he—*it*—lay, partially buried, facedown on the sand, twisted slightly, legs apart, arms by the sides. It had the frame and bulk of a man, and looked the same size as Jonah. The body was naked except for a pair of cotton underpants. The skin was wrinkled, as if newly emerged from a hot bath, grains of sand in the folds. And it was black.

"Is it Jonah?" Hayley asked again in a quiet voice.

Fraser stepped closer. "I don't know." He took a quick glance but couldn't see the face. Nothing else looked familiar, but there was nothing familiar about a dead man. He had never seen one before, had attended only one funeral, his grandfather's, and the coffin had been securely sealed.

"What happened?" he asked. "Did he try to swim for the mainland?"

He took another step closer, crouched down beside the body. Sand flies buzzed about Fraser's face and he was surprised there was no smell. That was the ocean's doing. Ben McCaig had told him once that the ocean washed everything clean. He pushed the revulsion back down and examined the corpse. It lay twisted with the stomach partly exposed. There was a dark stain on the sand beneath. The skin here was lighter and, peering closer, he saw that there was a wide tear across the abdomen. He was looking inside the man.

"Come here and look at this," he said. "There's a wound."

"No, thank you," Hayley said with a hint of panic. "We better go. We better tell someone."

She was right.

"Mr. Wallace."

"Who's that?"

"The harbormaster. He'll know what to do."

As Fraser straightened up, he saw something glint in the sun. It lay close to the body, mostly buried in the sand. He reached down and pulled out a knife.

He recognized it instantly: the wooden handle, the flat, sharp blade. He checked anyway and there on the handle were the carved letters *BM*. It was Ben McCaig's whale-gutting knife.

"What's this doing here?" he said.

Hayley moved a step closer. "What is it?"

"It's . . . Ben's knife."

"Where was it?"

"In the sand here."

On the blade of the knife, there was a dark glaze that could only be blood. On the dead man was a wound, a large gash across the abdomen. He had watched enough *CSI* to connect the two.

Hayley voiced a half-formed question. "Do you think he . . . ?"

"No. Absolutely not." But he was holding Ben's knife. "We can't tell anyone," he said.

"But we have to."

"We can't. They'll blame Ben. It's his knife."

"But if he's done something . . ."

"No. He wouldn't. He guts whales, not people."

"That knife could be a murder weapon."

Fraser knew as much. He held the knife gingerly where the blade met the handle, but he had to give Ben the opportunity to explain.

"Let me talk to Ben first. Then we'll hand over the knife."

"And what if he takes it from you and stabs you?"

"That won't happen."

They stared at each other for a few long seconds. Perhaps the tan was fading but suddenly she seemed pale—a girl far from home and unsure of herself.

"What's to stop me reporting everything?"

"Nothing. Except I'm asking you not to."

"And what about meeting Jonah last night?"

"I wouldn't mention anything about that. If last night we're with Jonah and the next morning he's lying dead on this beach, we'll spend the next week answering questions in a police station."

Fraser took a last look at the body, half-buried, face-down in the sand. It was unreal, not what happened in Skulavaig on quiet Saturday mornings. Not on this beach, his beach. Not in this life, his life. An event that had held the promise of adventure had suddenly become a trag-edy. There would be no more caves and castaways. A dead body brought all that to an end. As he moved back down the beach, he carefully slipped the knife inside his belt and pulled his shirt over the top.

TEN

Hayley followed Fraser back toward the harbor, not a word passing between them all the way. She wished she'd stayed in the cottage and not made her discovery, wished she'd told anyone but Fraser Dunbar, who made serious things even more serious. She wished she was back home in the heat of Austin, sitting on the bleachers, watching the senior boys at football practice, or strolling the mall with her friends, her old friends Kayla and Megan and Abbie, spending imaginary dollars on dates and dances and proms yet to come.

The wishes gushed out of her now, as if someone had shaken a soda and popped the top. She wished her dad had not left home to be with another woman, wished her mom was less concerned with the displaced people of the world and more concerned with a displaced daughter, wished she was trusted enough and smart enough and old enough to live her own life, do her own thing, on her own terms.

Her thoughts were interrupted by Fraser's whisper, as

if Mr. Wallace had listening devices hidden all over the harbor: "I'll stay here. You go on. Don't mention me."

"You're coming too."

"I can't."

"Why not?"

"I'm grounded, remember. I'm not supposed to be here."

"That doesn't matter now."

"It will to my father. Besides, I have this." Fraser tapped his waist where the knife was hidden.

"We should give that to the harbormaster."

"Not yet. You just go on; it will be fine."

Hayley scowled at the boy, but she wanted this particular episode in her Nin nightmare to be over, wanted to forget that there was a dead man close by. This was not her responsibility. "Where am I going?"

"Over there, in the Fisherman's Mission. The harbormaster's office is up the stairs."

"What will I tell him?"

"Just say you think there's a body on the beach. Point him in the right direction but don't linger."

Hayley had no intention of lingering. She was quite literally about to shake the sand from her shoes. She left Fraser crouched behind the wall and pulled herself on top of the jetty. She walked quickly to the building with the sign saying FISHERMAN'S MISSION, wondered what mission a fisherman might have except to catch a lot of fish.

She pushed open the door and crept inside. The room was full of empty chairs, with a pool table in the middle, a large-screen television and a dartboard fixed to opposite walls, and a smell of beer in the air. She slowly climbed the stairs, past photos of old boats, each wooden step creaking a warning that she was coming. When she reached the upper level, there was another door with a nameplate bearing the inscription *Mr. Wallace, Harbormaster.* Hayley knocked lightly on the door and entered. Compared to the dark staircase, this room was bright, sunlight pouring through a large window that looked out on the harbor.

The harbormaster turned to face Hayley as she entered. A pair of binoculars hung around his neck and he wore some kind of dark blue uniform.

"Miss Risso," he said. "What troubles you to come all the way up my creaky stairs?"

"There's a body on the beach," Hayley blurted.

Mr. Wallace moved his head to the side as if he had misheard. "What kind of body?"

"A dead body."

"A whale?"

"No, not a whale." Hayley took a breath. "The body of a person. On the beach."

His eyebrows dropped in disbelief. "Are you sure, lass?"

"Yes, I'm sure. There's a man lying dead on the beach."

"You're certain it's a man?"

"Yes!" Hayley said, exasperated.

"And you're certain he's dead?"

"Of course I'm certain. I wouldn't be here if I wasn't certain. The man is lying facedown, half-buried, not moving, with a large hole in his stomach. I'm certain he is dead."

Mr. Wallace's eyes narrowed and his lips tightened as if he feared the dead body was a close relative. He removed his binoculars and moved to his desk, flattening the crease on a large book that was already open.

"Where is this body?"

"Five minutes walk beyond the harbor wall, heading toward the cliffs."

Mr. Wallace made notes in the book. "Can you describe the man?"

"There's not much to tell. He's black, he's not wearing any clothes, only underwear. That's about it."

"A black man." Mr. Wallace nodded in interest, then shook his head as if troubled. He scribbled some more in his book. "And has anyone else seen this body?"

"No," she said, a little too forcibly. "No, only me." She didn't want to be connected with Fraser Dunbar. The dead body was *Fraser's* friend, the hidden knife was *Fraser's* doing. She wanted no part of any of it.

Mr. Wallace wrote a few lines more and then rose slowly from behind his desk.

"You know, it's not uncommon. We get bodies washed ashore. I've seen a few in my time. Inexperienced crewmen from tankers, fishing boats lost when a storm hits un-expectedly, Sunday sailors getting into difficulties in the currents of the Minch. Aye, it happens. If this is a black man, as you say, then it's probably a poor lad from a tanker who was lost overboard during that big storm." Mr. Wallace stood silent for a moment, as if honoring the dead. "Nothing was reported, though."

"What now?" Hayley asked, anxious to be gone before the harbormaster probed further or shared more stories of the drowned.

"I'll inform the appropriate authorities. Someone should be here shortly to take a look. They will send a police boat from Portree."

"Aren't you going?"

"I cannae leave my window, lass. It's the living that concern me."

Hayley looked through the window at the empty harbor and the equally empty stretch of water beyond. There didn't seem much importance to Mr. Wallace's watching.

"Well, I thought you should know. I have to go now."

"You should probably come back later, guide whoever comes to examine the poor soul."

"I don't think so. The body is hard to miss. And I've seen enough."

If Mr. Wallace was about to argue the point, he thought better of it. "Aye, fair enough. You did the right thing coming to me."

Hayley turned to go. "He seemed like a nice man," she said.

"How could you know that?"

She inwardly slapped herself across the back of the head. An almost fatal error. She was a better liar than this. "I mean he was probably a nice man. I hope he was a nice man."

The harbormaster gave Hayley a sad smile. "Aye, well, the ocean claims the nice and the nasty. You take care, lass. Remember you're on an island. Never take your eyes off the sea or the sky."

Hayley nodded and retreated from the room, wondered if she had been given a warning or the weather forecast. She returned to the jetty and found Fraser sitting on the beach on the far side of the wall. He was throwing pebbles at an old rotting post that protruded from the sand, and missing every time.

"It's done. What now?"

Fraser shrugged. "You best get home."

The girl gave a snort. Home was Texas, and Texas was a long way away. "Fine. What are you planning to do?"

"I'm staying here until Ben returns."

"Fine. That's fine. If he murders you, I'll let someone know."

"Good. Mr. Wallace will do."

Hayley stood there and Fraser sat on the sand, neither looking at the other, the only sound the breaking surf and distant gulls. She wanted to leave, but something held her back, a reluctance to abandon the boy to knife-wielding biologists.

"He seemed nice," she said again.

"The harbormaster?"

"No. Jonah."

Fraser sighed. "Aye." He picked up a few more pebbles and continued throwing them at the wooden post. "Tonight's the ceilidh," he said.

"The what?"

"The ceilidh, *kay-ley*, rhymes with *Hayley*. Hayley at the ceilidh."

He gave a weak smile, but Hayley offered nothing in return.

"My mom mentioned it. Some kind of dancing."

"That's right. Scottish dancing, the Gay Gordons and the like."

"Who is Gay Gordon?"

"There *is* no Gordon. It's not about being gay or not gay. It's the Gay Gordons."

"Gordon's not gay?"

"It's a dance."

She was confused and not in the slightest bit interested. There would be no dancing from her on the island of Nin.

"I'll see you," Fraser said.

It was her cue to leave and she was glad; it removed any responsibility toward dead African men and sad Scottish boys. "Yeah. See you." She picked up a stone and threw it at the post, hit it first time with a whack.

ELEVEN

On a crisp September afternoon in 1942 a German U-boat surfaced off the coast of Skulavaig, a fire in its torpedo bay spreading to all parts of the boat. The crew swam or rowed ashore, waved a few pistols at the gathered islanders, then scattered. Within a week, they had all been captured.

On a dark February morning during the fierce winter of 1963, two small fishing boats from Skulavaig harbor sailed out into a choppy sea and were never seen again. Seven crewmen lost, two of them brothers.

During the scorching August of 1988, a film crew from Hollywood shot parts of a movie in Skulavaig and several tinsel-town celebrities took rooms at the Harbor Hotel. A few locals got work as extras and even though most of the scenes ended up on the cutting-room floor, for a brief moment Skulavaig had glamour.

Dramatic events were few and far between on Nin, but the talk this day was of a dead man washed ashore. Fraser walked along the narrow road from the harbor, finally released from his grounding, officially at least. The early evening air was still warm and he listened to the conversations of the townsfolk, swapping news of murder and mystery. Fraser was going against the flow, everyone else heading toward the Fisherman's Mission and the ceilidh that took place once a month. He wanted to put some distance between him and the harbor, in no mood for the accordion and fiddle he could hear warming up with a lively tune.

A police car passed him, the blue light flashing. Skulavaig had no police station; the nearest was on Skye and that was mainly country coppers. A dead body washed ashore called for a squad from Inverness, especially when the corpse appeared to have a knife wound in the gut. Earlier in the day a couple of uniformed officers had disembarked from a police boat and then the ferry had brought police cars and detectives in suits, and forensic officers in white overalls, who had trudged along the beach with various pieces of equipment. Only in the last half hour had the body been finally removed. From the road above the beach, Fraser had watched a heavy black body bag being carried away and loaded onto the police boat. He had silently wished Jonah farewell, surprised to feel his eyes fill with tears. Who had murdered the shipwrecked man? And why? He could have done more to help. Much more.

He walked away from the town now, gripped by a growing anxiety about the bloody knife that was under his bed. The road curved north, but he cut across the grassland that led to the top of the cliffs beyond the castle. The police had searched the caves and found nothing. Fraser wondered if Jonah had hidden away his few possessions before he was stabbed and his body thrown into the sea. Where were his father's boots? If they were discovered, it could lead back to him. The thought filled Fraser with a sudden panic.

Just before the clifftop, where the ground sloped up, there was a scattering of trees that wasn't quite thick enough to be called a forest. As Fraser approached he glimpsed movement. It was his brother, flitting among the trees like a deer. Fraser ducked behind some gorse and watched. Dunny chose the biggest beech tree and sat down in the shade of its branches.

From his pocket, Dunny carefully removed a stack of scallop shells, his tell shells. He separated them and laid the five of them out in front of him. From his other pocket he pulled his pen. Fraser watched his brother just sit for a while, staring at his shells, the only movement the flickering shadows of the tree, the only sound the distinctive "pee-wit" cry of a lapwing. The grass, long and beginning to seed, swayed in the breeze and there was the distant sound of the sea.

Dunny picked up one of the scallop shells, wrote something on it, then laid it carefully back down and did the same with the second. He wrote on all five shells, then piled them one on top of the other at his feet and leaned back against the tree, looking up at the sky. Only the thin vapor trail of a plane broke the blue, but far to the west the sky was gray, a band of clouds indicating the approach of another storm.

Dunny sat quite still for a few moments, listening to the breaking waves. Then he pulled himself to his feet and lifted his tell shells, headed up the hill toward the cliff edge. Fraser followed, darting behind trees and keeping low to stay unseen.

What are you up to? Fraser said to himself. Dunny had always been puzzling, but in the last few months his behavior had become truly enigmatic. Fraser didn't know his brother anymore.

When he reached the top, Dunny sidled toward the drop, then lay flat and pulled himself up to the very edge of the cliff. He leaned his head over and looked down. Below him was the beach and the boulders, but Fraser knew the cliff face curved inward at the bottom, so the entrances to the caves could not be seen. The tide was coming in and the surge of the breaking waves was another portent of the coming storm.

Dunny now carefully laid his scallop shells out in a line on the grass beside him. He picked up the first one, reached out over the drop, and let go of the shell. He did the same with the second and third, then he stood up, pulled back his arm, and launched the fourth shell into the air. Fraser watched it somersault as it fell, its pearly inside glittering in the sunlight before it vanished below the cliff.

Dunny lifted his last shell and turned to face away from the ocean. He looked in Fraser's direction and held up the shell as if he knew his brother was watching from somewhere. *For you*, he seemed to say. Dunny laid the shell carefully on the grass, then moved away along the cliff path, disappearing down the slope to the beach.

Fraser waited until Dunny had gone, then crept over to the cliff edge. The shell lay on the grass. He kicked it over the drop. The ocean shimmered in the sun. There was a dark line on the horizon that was the mainland, and sailing up the sound, a tanker carrying an unknown cargo to an unknown destination.

Fraser headed back to town, sticking to the road and avoiding the beach. As he arrived at the harbor, he heard a familiar voice say, "Fraser, son, where have you been?" It was his father. "You're going to miss the ceilidh."

"I'm not really in the mood," Fraser said.

"Are you OK?"

"I'm fine."

His dad placed a hand on Fraser's shoulder. "There have been other bodies washed ashore on Nin. It happens. We live by the sea. People drown."

"Aye."

Duncan Dunbar frowned and shook his head. "Though I hear this fellow had a knife in the gut. Drowning was the least of his worries."

"Who told you that?"

"There's talk."

"Has anyone been arrested?"

"I don't think so."

Fraser wondered about Ben, who had been out sailing all day. He must be back now; a light shone from the cabin of his boat. Fraser had yet to speak to him about the knife.

"So are you coming to the ceilidh?" his dad asked.

Fraser sighed. "Maybe."

"Will your American friend be there?"

There was an implication in the question. "Don't ask me." He added for emphasis, "And she's not my friend."

His dad laughed. "I've promised her a Strip the Willow."

"You've seen her?"

"Aye, up at the mission."

"So why did you ask if she would be there?"

"It must have slipped my mind." His dad gave him a knowing smile. "So I'll see you there?"

"If I can be bothered."

His dad put a hand on Fraser's shoulder again and said softly, "Try to be bothered."

Fraser watched him head up the hill toward the Fisherman's Mission and realized there was a bit of him that desperately wanted to follow—to hear a sad lament on the fiddle, to listen to the gossip concerning dead men, to see Hayley Risso and meet her on the dance floor.

TWELVE

Hayley loved dancing, had been to dance class, enjoyed cheerleading, which was dancing and gymnastics all in one, but she'd never seen dancing like this. It was similar to line dancing except everyone moved around in a circle. It was a bit like a barn dance too, though nobody did much whooping and there was no caller coordinating the steps. The band played in a small space beneath the stairs and were led by an old man on a fiddle and a boy younger than her on an accordion, with a drummer and guitarist as backup. Everyone seemed to know the moves, which involved a lot of twirling and swapping partners. There *was* something infectious about it; several times she'd had to stop her foot from tapping.

So far she had resisted all invitations to dance. She had promised Dunny's father a dance later, but that could be dodged. Her mother had entered into the spirit of the evening as the spirits of the evening entered her. Hayley had never seen her drink whisky before. Several whiskies, to be precise. The whole island seemed to be here, although there was no sign of Ben McCaig, or of Fraser.

In the corner of the hall a makeshift bar had been erected and an ancient man with unruly white whiskers poured shots into small glasses. If she'd been asked to draw a picture of an old Scottish fisherman, she would have sketched *him* and then erased it as too much of a stereotype.

The dance came to an end with a sustained note on the accordion, and Sarah Risso twirled off the dance floor to where Hayley sat by herself.

"Have you danced yet, honey?" she asked, gasping.

"Not yet, no."

"Why not? It's fun, it really is. You love dancing."

"I'm not in the mood."

"Nonsense. How can you not be in the mood with this music?"

"The music's terrible."

Her mother laughed. "OK, the slow ones are a bit depressing, but the fast ones are wild."

Right on cue, the ceilidh band announced another tune and dance. Sarah grabbed Hayley's arm.

"Come on."

Hayley pulled free. "No."

"Why not?"

"Because."

"Because why?"

"Because." Hayley sighed and remembered the disaster that was the church teens' spring banquet. For Timmy Melikian to ditch her for Cheryl Gaskill was mortifying enough, but to do it during the first dance of the evening was just downright rude. "Because . . . I don't have anyone to dance with."

Her mom laughed and gave her a hug. "You can dance with me."

Hayley snorted at the suggestion. "No, thanks. Dancing with your mother is way more embarrassing than sitting by yourself."

Sarah laughed again, then something caught her eye as she looked over Hayley's shoulder. "OK, if you won't ceilidh with me, there is someone over there in serious need of a dance partner."

Hayley turned and looked toward the door of the mission. At first she could see only a crowd of townsfolk, but then a figure reluctantly pulled himself farther into the room. He looked around as if seeking someone and his eyes found Hayley's. Fraser Dunbar. The eye contact lasted a moment longer than she intended and then he was lost behind a group of bodies readying for a reel. Her mom was snatched away by an islander, each man, it seemed, wanting a dance with her. Hayley saw Dunny and his mother standing together in the dance line. The boy looked fragile, squashed in among the hefty adults, but he was smiling and confidently took his mum's hands as the first chord was struck. The tune started and the crowd began to move around the dance floor.

She saw Fraser moving toward her and she stared resolutely at the group of dancers, her eyes not following any of the couples, which was a hard thing to do. His hands were thrust deep into his pockets, perhaps to convey a disinterest in dancing. Hayley hoped so.

"How's it going?" he said, loud enough to be heard above the band.

"Fine," she said, adding quickly, "just so you know, I don't intend to dance."

"Just so you know, I wasn't planning to ask you."

"Good."

"Good."

It wasn't silence that followed, not with the ceilidh band in full flow, but the pause was awkward nonetheless.

"How did it go with Mr. Wallace?" Fraser asked.

"It was fine. He called the police."

"I noticed. What have *you* heard?"

"Nothing. I've been in the cottage all day."

It had been a long, boring day, but she had wanted to stay as far from the beach as possible. The only reason she had come to the ceilidh was to get rid of the cabin fever that was setting in. Cottage fever, she called it. They watched the dance for a few minutes, the music too loud, the movement too frenetic for more conversation. The tune came to an end and there was a ripple of applause. The circling dancers stopped. Most remained on the dance floor and there seemed to be a rearranging of partners.

"What have *you* heard?" Hayley's voice was loud now that the band had quit.

Fraser glanced around to see if anyone was listening, but everyone in the hall was talking, drinking, preparing for another dance, or doing all three. The fiddler announced, "Lads and lassies, the Gay Gordons." The band struck up once more and the dancers moved into position to begin.

"They're saying it was murder," Fraser said.

"We knew that already. And we know who the murderer is."

"We don't know that. Not at all."

"It was Ben McCaig's knife."

"That doesn't prove anything."

"You have to go to the police. Tell them what you found."

"Not yet. Not till I see Ben."

Hayley saw panic cross Fraser's face and an image flashed into her head of Ben McCaig behind her, knife raised. She turned sharply. Fraser's mother was upon them and she realized what he had guessed: They were to be coerced into a dance.

"Come on, you two," said Jessie Dunbar, grabbing both their arms. "This is an easy one to get you started."

Fraser and Hayley said in unison, "No!"

Jessie ignored their cries and dragged them onto the dance floor. She squeezed them into the line of dancers and nodded sternly toward Fraser to take ahold of Hayley.

"Let Fraser lead you," Jessie said to Hayley. "Just follow the couple in front."

The rest of the dancers were in position, the men slightly behind the women, holding hands with their partners, who had their arms raised to shoulder height. Everyone faced in the same direction, ready for the off. Hayley grudgingly raised her arms, and Fraser took hold of her hands.

The dance began: four steps forward, turn, back another four steps, still holding hands, turn again, the women now twirling under the outstretched arms of the men, then come together in the classic dance hold and polka around the floor for eight beats, still in a line, then back to the starting position and repeat. During the first progression, Hayley got it mostly wrong, scowling and tripping over the feet of Fraser and the couple in front and the couple behind. She mumbled several embarrassed apologies as Fraser tried to lead her, but she resisted his guidance.

She was better second time around, picking up the steps and relaxing a little, the scowl fading but still no smile. By the fourth progression, she had mastered the Gay Gordons and was practically leading Fraser around the dance floor. In the polka section, when they faced one another, she kept her eyes on the floor while Fraser looked over her shoulder. There was no eye contact, not even by the sixth progression, but Hayley felt his body a little closer to hers; she no longer bent her back in an effort to increase the distance between them. She began to enjoy the mix of movement and music and the feel of his hands in hers.

He caught her smile and said, "You've done this before."

"It's not so hard." Hayley twirled under his raised arm. "I used to go to dance class."

They came together and whirled around in the polka and Hayley realized she was actually enjoying herself. She hoped no one had noticed. The people of Skulavaig, and especially her mother, were not to think for even one moment that she was glad to be here.

On the other side of the dance floor, she now saw Ben McCaig. He threw his head back as he laughed, clutching a woman close as they danced; he seemed oblivious to Fraser and Hayley, oblivious to everyone else in the room. If this was a man who had knifed someone in the gut that very morning, he was as cool as they came. There was no twitch of the eye, no bloodstained fingers, no guilty glance from face to face. Ben McCaig was having a rare old time.

And as Hayley paused to ready herself for the next progression, she realized Ben's dance partner was her mother.

"No way," she said aloud.

Her mom and Ben were twirling around the dance floor, bodies close together, having far too much fun. Hayley had not been dragged all the way from the States to this wet place, with wetter boys, just so her mother could have fun. She wanted to go over and confront her mother, but the Scottish boy held her tight. They continued to progress around the room, Hayley watching her mom, and Fraser watching Ben. Her mom and Ben watched only each other.

"It's disgusting."

Fraser said, "I know."

"What are they doing?"

"They're supposed to be dancing the Gay Gordons."

"Well, Gordon may be gay but Ben certainly isn't."

"It's not that kind of gay."

"Clearly."

Fraser and Hayley polkaed around the floor one final time and the music came to an end with a triumphant chord. There was hearty applause and the circle of dancers broke up, heading for some liquid refreshment. The fiddle player announced a short break and the musicians made for the bar and drams of their own.

Fraser released her and stood awkwardly, arms by his side. What was the tradition now, Hayley wondered? Did she thank him for the dance, fetch a drink, kiss him? She was neither thankful nor thirsty, and she certainly wasn't going to kiss him.

"I need to talk to my mom," she said.

"I need to talk to Ben," Fraser said.

"Yes, ask him about his intentions."

"How do you mean?"

"With my mom. What are his intentions with my mom?"

Fraser gave a scoffing laugh. "I think it's more important to ask why his bloodstained knife was beside a dead man."

"Yes, find out that too."

She went to find her mother, knew she had to say the right thing; it couldn't sound selfish or unreasonable.

"Mom," she said coldly as she arrived.

Ben lifted two empty whisky glasses. "I'll get us a refill. Would you like something, Hayley?"

"No," she replied sharply.

"OK." Ben shot Sarah a sympathetic glance and headed for the makeshift bar.

"I saw the way you were dancing," Hayley said.

"And how was that?"

"You were touching. You were together."

"That's the nature of the dance. *You* were holding Fraser."

"Not the way you were."

"And how exactly was that?"

"As if . . . as if you were enjoying yourself."

"I *was* enjoying myself. I'm allowed to enjoy myself."

"Not like that. Not with some random guy. You're married to Dad."

Her mom took her hand, said softly, "It's time to move on, Hayley. I have to try to live my life again."

"No." Hayley said it again, forcefully. "No!"

If her mother moved on, then gone was the last hope of her mom and dad getting back together. Hayley knew that only her mom could save the marriage and that when her mom lost interest, the marriage was over.

With sudden, crushing clarity Hayley realized that the marriage *was* over.

She moved away, toward the door of the mission, heard her mom call her name but didn't stop. She had danced a

Highland dance and that would do for this evening, would do for this entire trip, would be enough for a lifetime. She walked through the door into cool air and a darkening sky.

An empty police car remained by the harbor, the *Moby Dick* bobbed in the swell, and the only sound was the hubbub of voices from inside the mission and the incoming tide breaking against the jetty. On the beach, there was a line of dark, churned sand where many feet had trodden before examining and removing the body. The police tape was gone, the sea already surging over the spot where the body had lain and washing away the evidence of murder.

Hayley walked a few paces along the beach, then stopped. It was beginning to get dark and the wind had picked up, flurrying the sand. She turned back toward the harbor and caught her breath as a shadow crossed the sand ahead of her. A man was moving along the bottom of the harbor wall, his body pressed against the old stones. For a moment Hayley thought it must be a policeman, but there was something in the way he moved that she recognized.

She fell flat on the sand and became driftwood, then carefully raised her head to watch the moving figure. He didn't want to be spotted either, crouching behind the wall and carefully peering over the top of the jetty. And then she recognized him. At first she didn't believe it, thought it not possible, but there he was. His build was unmistakable, his borrowed clothes distinctive, his skin dark black.

It made her think about the old story from Vacation Bible School about the man spewed forth from the mouth of a great fish, restored to life. The man called Jonah.

THIRTEEN

"*Where* did you find my knife?" Ben asked.

"Beside the dead man on the beach," said Fraser.

"And where is it now?"

"It's under my bed. In a shoe box."

"Are you an idiot? Seriously?"

This was a new side to Ben: angry and incredulous at the same time.

"I thought I was . . . I thought it might . . ."

"Thinking doesn't seem to be your strong point, Fraze." Ben took one of the whiskies he held and downed it in a single gulp.

"I thought the knife made you look guilty."

"Well, of course it does. My knife in the belly of a dead man makes me look guilty. But so does my knife stashed away under your bed. That makes me look doubly guilty."

"You're right. I'm sorry."

Ben contemplated the other whisky but decided against it.

"Does anyone else know about this?"

"Just the American girl."

"Great. Teenage girls are *so* good at keeping secrets."

"She won't tell."

"I hope not. If she does, we're both in it deep. And I'm not talking about water this time."

"Aye."

"You're certain it was my knife?"

"Aye."

"And you found it beside the dead man washed ashore?"

"Aye."

"And now it's in a shoe box under your bed?"

Fraser nodded and hung his head, all out of *aye*s. He had thought he was doing the right thing, thought Ben would be grateful. Hayley had advised him to leave it alone, but he hadn't listened.

"Do you think I did it?" Ben asked.

"No."

"That I gutted the man?"

"Of course not."

"And what about your American friend?"

"She's not so sure."

"Nice."

Ben stood for a moment pondering the empty dance floor. He looked at Fraser, gave a sigh, and looked away, said, "Tomorrow morning, first thing, you take my knife to the police and explain the exact circumstances of how you found it."

"But—"

"No *but*s."

"But—"

"Fraser."

"What will happen to you?"

"Nothing will happen to me. I'll be questioned, but clearly someone has climbed onto my boat and lifted my knife. Just because it's mine doesn't mean I'm guilty."

"The police might not see it that way."

"Well, the alternative is the American girl blabbing and the police searching your bedroom and finding my knife. Then we will both have explaining to do."

"I'm in trouble either way."

"You are. And it serves you right."

Ben shook his head scornfully and Fraser knew he had lost his trust. He had likely lost his place on the *Moby Dick* as well, lost the chance of further adventures, lost his bright future as one of the world's preeminent whale scientists.

"Leave me alone now, Fraser."

This was the moment to rescue the situation, to save his position as seasonal voluntary assistant researcher, to make Ben see that not all the Dunbar boys were ridiculous. There was one thing that might do it.

"I saw an orca last night. Several of them, round by the caves."

Ben laughed dismissively. "I doubt it, Fraser."

"I did. Just along from the harbor."

"It was probably a basking shark."

"It was an orca. I know what an orca looks like."

"And I know that you don't get orcas in this part of the ocean. Farther out, perhaps, but not here."

"It was orcas. Dunny saw them too."

"And he'll confirm your story?"

"You know he won't." The plan wasn't working. Ben was more irritated than before.

"If you saw something, it was a basking shark. Trust me."

"No, it was . . ."

Ben had gone, striding across the dance floor toward Hayley's mother. Fraser stood for a moment feeling foolish, then moved to a dark corner and leaned against the wall. The whole town was crammed into the room, he was surrounded by laughter and chatter, but he felt alone and miserable. He was alone and Jonah was dead.

"Jonah's alive," said a voice.

He turned and Hayley was beside him, panting slightly, eyes shining.

"Jonah's alive," she said again. "I saw him by the harbor, hiding behind the wall. It was definitely Jonah, there's no way I made a mistake, I know it was him, definitely him . . ."

"Whoa!" Fraser held up his hand. "Hayley, take a breath."

The girl took a deep lungful and said quietly, "It was Jonah."

"Are you sure?"

"I saw him."

"But *we* saw him, dead on the beach."

"No, we didn't. His face was buried in the sand."

"But how many people with black skin are there in Skulavaig? I sure haven't seen any."

"At least two."

"So who is the dead guy?"

Hayley shrugged. "It can't be coincidence that they both are in Skulavaig, by the ocean, at the same time."

"I knew Ben wasn't a murderer."

"Well, someone is still dead."

In the clamor of voices and laughter and clinking glasses, Fraser thought he could hear his heart thump against his ribs. He had helped Jonah, fed him, trusted him. Was *Jonah* the murderer?

"We have to go to the police," Hayley said.

"We can't."

"Why not?"

"Because we might be accomplices to murder."

"Hardly."

"No? I helped hide a man and gave him food and clothes. Now he may have murdered someone. And I was on Ben's boat; I knew where he kept that knife and now it's under my bed." Fraser gave a long sigh. "I think we're in trouble."

"What do you mean *we*? It's not my sweatshirt and socks he's wearing."

"No, but you were with him on the beach last night. And you found the body and told no one except me."

The color drained from Hayley's face. "What do we do?"

"We find Jonah."

"And then what?"

"Get some answers."

"Is that before or after he stabs us?"

"I have the knife."

"That's OK, then. After all, he's only a large grown man. No match for a girl and a skinny Scottish boy."

He thought himself toned not skinny, but this was not the time to argue. "Why is Jonah sneaking around the harbor? Why not lie low in his cave?"

"Maybe he hasn't finished his murderous rampage yet. Maybe he's looking for anyone who knows he's on the island."

"This is Nin, not Texas. We don't do serial killers on Nin."

"We have to go to the police."

"No, not yet. *We'll* end up in jail and Jonah will disappear."

"What, then? We have to tell someone."

"No. We have to sort out this mess ourselves."

"And how do we do that?"

"I told you, we find Jonah."

"That's the worst idea. That's like those horror movies when someone goes into a dark basement by themself to investigate a strange noise and you're thinking, *No one would do that.* That's you, Fraser. You're looking for trouble."

Trouble is already here, Fraser thought. In the last few years, Nin had become an island that people left, but recently five people had arrived: Ben, Hayley, her mom, Jonah, and the dead man. All of them brought secrets and mysteries to his small town and all of them seemed connected to each other, *through him.*

Fraser felt as if he was standing in the eye of a perfect storm, the furious wind spinning around him, destroying his calm life. And that was fine; calm meant boring. He *liked* this furious wind that blew in strangers and dangers. The thrill of it made his whole body tingle.

"Come on," he said to Hayley over his shoulder as the ceilidh band retook their positions. He heard the American girl mutter, "Not in this lifetime," as he dived through the door out into the night.

FOURTEEN

Hayley was staying where she was. Let Fraser Dunbar be the hero and get himself killed in the process.

She sat down and watched the dancers begin another Highland reel. Her mom and Ben McCaig were dancing together again. She tried to feel more outrage, but the truth was that her mother could dance with whoever she liked. The truth was that her dad had walked out on them both and was gone for good.

Her eyes began to fill and she resolved not to let a single tear graze her cheek. Fraser would be gone by now, so she stood up and headed for the door. She was going home— not to sunny Texas but to a cold cottage where she slept on a sofa bed and listened to the wind rattle the windows and make the fire in the hearth flicker and crack.

Outside, the quietness was disconcerting. It was like being the sole survivor in a post-apocalyptic world. She half expected a zombie to make an appearance. She sat on the weathered stones of the harbor wall with her back against an old bollard and stretched out her legs. The sea was beginning to roll and big waves were breaking against the headland.

At the sound of voices, she turned her head. Two police officers were strolling toward their empty patrol car. They were talking quietly, but their conversation drifted on the breeze blowing in across the harbor. Hayley was hidden by the bollard and they made no effort to guard their words.

"Who told you this?" one of the officers said.

"It was that detective from Inverness, McKinnon, I think his name is."

"Big, redheaded laddie?"

"Aye, that's the one. Wouldnae stop moaning about the sand in his socks." The second officer laughed.

Hayley faced the sea and listened.

"So it wasnae murder, then?"

"It seems not. According to the pathologist, the victim died from drowning."

Hayley stifled the urge to squeal and jump up. Instead, she pushed herself farther down behind the bollard and listened all the more intently. She heard the clunk of car doors being unlocked remotely.

"So what about the slash to the gut?"

"It was done postmortem."

"Something in the sea?"

"No, it was a knife wound."

"Why would somebody stab a dead man?"

Car doors opened.

"I guess that's what those detectives up at the hotel are going to have to find out tomorrow. Assuming they're not too hungover."

"Are they blootered?"

"Getting there. I tell you, I've never seen such a bunch of—"

The car doors slammed and the voices were gone. Instead, Hayley heard the engine start and the car pull away from the harbor. She peered carefully from behind the bollard and watched the police car drive up onto the main road and away. Silence once more descended on the harbor, except for a distant tune from the ceilidh band and the murmur of the ocean beneath her.

Hayley turned back to face the sea and tried to digest this piece of information. Both Ben and Jonah were in the clear, at least as far as first-degree homicide was concerned. But who was the man dead on the beach and why had he been stabbed after he'd drowned? If anyone knew the answers to those questions, it was probably Jonah. In the morning the police would begin to interview the islanders, so they had to get their story straight. She had to find Fraser.

Hayley got to her feet and stood on the harbor jetty, looking three hundred and sixty degrees, straining into the dark. There was no sign of anyone.

Where would Fraser go to find Jonah? The answer was obvious.

The caves.

FIFTEEN

It was high tide and Fraser walked on a narrow strip of sand as he strode toward the cliffs. A man was dead, which made this a sad situation and potentially dangerous. It was possible that Jonah could jump out from behind a rock and slit his throat. It was dangerous, yes, but more than that, it was exciting!

The sky was black and the wind was rising. The dark cliffs loomed above his head. Fraser was a silhouette against the ocean and he knew Jonah would see him coming.

He walked on, every muscle in his body tense, almost tasting the adrenaline. At the big cave he called out, "Jonah."

There was no reply, no movement.

"It's Fraser. Are you there? Jonah."

Fraser heard only the sound of breaking waves and his own slow breaths. It was foolish to imagine that Jonah would have returned here, not if he was fleeing the scene of a crime or planning to commit another. Fraser stood and stared at the dark, empty cave.

A deep voice behind him made him jump.

"I am far from home, but it is the same sky, the same stars."

Fraser spun around. Jonah stood on the beach, his feet lapped by surf, his eyes looking above. He was fed now and rested; he seemed bigger, his back straighter, his voice more confident.

"We thought you were dead."

"You seem unafraid of the dark and the dangers that lie there."

"Am I in danger?" Fraser asked, his mouth suddenly dry.

"Do you think you are?"

"Maybe."

"From me?"

"Maybe."

"You thought I was dead?"

"The body on the beach."

"You thought it was me?"

"He looked like you."

"He was a fellow traveler."

"You knew him?"

"His name was Solomon. Another name from the Good Book, though he was not a good man."

"Is that why you killed him?"

Jonah moved up the beach. Fraser took a step backward, then another.

"I did not kill anyone, Fraser. The dead man drowned and was washed ashore."

"How do you know that?"

"Because two nights ago, he and I jumped into the water at the same time."

"And what about the big hole in his belly?"

"I know nothing of that."

The man took another couple of steps up the beach and Fraser took another step backward. He wanted to run but he wanted to stay, to find out the truth. He picked up a piece of rock that had broken from the cliff face and held it in the air.

"Don't come any closer."

Jonah took another step. "You would not be the first to throw stones at me."

"Stay there. I mean it." Fraser knew he shouldn't have picked up the rock; he was a hopeless thrower. He should have run, but he was a hopeless runner—not fast, anyway, and speed was needed here, not stamina. He was back to the rock.

Jonah took a step closer and another Bible character came to mind: Goliath. Fraser was the boy, David. He took a breath, drew his arm back, judged his aim.

"No, Fraser!"

Hayley was running toward them, puffs of sand kicking up from her heels.

"No!" she screamed again.

Whether it was surprise or panic or confusion, Fraser did the exact opposite of what he intended. His brain told him to drop the rock; his reflexes did something else altogether and without thinking he launched it straight at Jonah. With a dull thud the rock hit him on the side of the head.

Jonah looked surprised, swayed for a moment, then fell to one knee. He gripped the sand with one hand and his head with the other. A trickle of blood ran down the side of his face.

"What have you done?" Hayley asked, gulping for air.

"He wouldn't stay where he was."

"Jonah is not a killer," Hayley said. "No one has been killed."

Jonah sat on the sand, looking dazed, and breathed slowly as if trying to contain his rage. "A bigger stone and you may have killed *me*."

"Sorry," Fraser said. "I didn't mean to throw it." He gave an inadvertent laugh. "I can't believe I actually hit you."

"The body on the beach," Hayley said. "He wasn't murdered. He drowned."

"I have already told him," Jonah said. "But still he throws the stone."

"I heard two police officers talking," Hayley continued. "They said the body was already dead when it washed ashore. The knife was stuck into it later."

"That body was a man called Solomon," Jonah said to Hayley. "I have told the boy already."

"I don't understand any of this," Fraser said.

Jonah carefully touched the side of his head. It wasn't a deep cut, but the blood still flowed. "Then I better help you understand, before you pick a bigger stone."

"I'm sorry," Fraser repeated. He offered Jonah a handkerchief from his pocket and the man held it against his head.

"Come, and I will tell you what you want to know."

Jonah lifted himself from the sand and walked to the bottom of the cliff. He was about to pull himself up the boulders toward the cave when he froze and pressed himself flat against the rocks. He motioned for Fraser and Hayley to get down. For a few seconds the two of them stared dumbly at Jonah, then, straining his eyes in the gloom, Fraser spotted a figure only a couple of hundred feet down the beach, coming straight toward them.

It was too late for Fraser and Hayley to hide; they were halfway between the cliff and the sea. Fraser watched Jonah squeeze himself between the rocks. He shook his head, placed a finger to his lips.

The stranger emerged from the dark; it was Willie McGregor. Fraser wondered why he was wandering around so late, then realized Willie would be thinking the same of him. He frantically thought of a reason to be on this stretch of beach. Whale watching, except there were no whales; beachcombing, it was too dark; stargazing, that was a possibility, even though the sky was clouding over.

He turned to Hayley but before he could say a word, she threw her arms around his neck and kissed him on the lips.

He wouldn't have suggested that in a million years. But it was a thrill right up there with watching orcas and sailing lobster boats in storms: He was being kissed by a girl, was kissing her back, and, it seemed to him, making a decent go at it.

"Oh, excuse me," he heard Willie say.

Fraser and Hayley unlocked their lips and turned to face him.

"Sorry, Fraser. Sorry, lass. I dinnae mean to disturb you," Willie said.

Hayley wrapped an arm around Fraser's waist. "That's OK. We were just enjoying the night air."

The kiss had taken the breath out of Fraser. With a gasp he asked, "What are you doing out here, Willie? The ceilidh can't be finished yet?"

"No, it was just getting a bit noisy, that's all. I thought I would take a walk."

There was a pause and Fraser could sense only the touch of Hayley's arm around his waist. He gingerly placed a hand on her back.

"I'm Hayley," she said breezily.

"Aye, lass, I saw you and your mother at the dance. How are you enjoying Skulavaig?"

"Oh, it's wonderful. Especially now." She gave Fraser her most loving look, batting her eyelashes and wrinkling her nose as she squeezed him around the middle. Fraser tried again to breathe.

Willie laughed. "Well, dinnae stay out too late. There's a storm coming."

He turned and headed back the way he had come. They watched him until he had disappeared around the curve of the coast and their part of the beach was empty again.

"Great," Fraser said. "Now the whole town will think we're together."

Hayley unwrapped her arm from his waist. "I think it'll do more for your status than mine."

Fraser snorted at such conceit, tried to forget momentarily about the kiss. There were far more pressing problems to overcome.

"Jonah can't hang around here. It's only a matter of time until he's discovered."

"Where can he go?"

"Where does he want to go, that's the real question."

Jonah had disappeared into the blackness of the cave, but it was Fraser who was in the dark.

SIXTEEN

Hayley clambered up to the cave, sensing the dark rolling in with the tide. She could still taste Fraser's lips. She had kissed quite a few boys in recent months—too many; she was getting a reputation. Scottish lips tasted much the same as Texas lips, a little saltier. Was that the sea or just her imagination? The kiss had been a ruse, nothing more, but it *had* been quite nice.

Jonah stood at the cave entrance. "I did not realize that you were dating."

In unison, Hayley and Fraser said, "We're not." Hayley felt her denial was a little more insistent.

"Who was that man?" Jonah asked.

"Just one of the locals," said Fraser.

"What was he doing?"

"Taking a walk. He didn't see you."

Jonah peered out cautiously, scanning the beach. Fraser squatted on the floor, and Hayley stood by the entrance, ready to run if she had to.

"How did you get here?" Fraser asked.

"As I have said already, I swam."

"All the way from Africa?" asked Hayley, astonished.

Jonah laughed—a deep, throaty laugh that echoed from the cave walls. She had yet to hear him laugh. It made her like him even more.

"Only the last part." His gaze moved out beyond the cave and he sat in silence, contemplating the ocean.

Hayley checked her phone but there were no messages, no missed calls. Her mom was probably having too much fun to even notice she was gone. The time said ten o'clock. She was surprised at how late it was, wondered what had happened to the hours. She imagined that in this far corner of the world, time washed in and out with the tides. Minutes and hours spilled in with the breaking waves and made the days so long. Each hour of daylight had another one added by the pounding surf. Later, as the tide receded, it sucked time back into the water and made the night last mere moments, a brief passing of darkness before the next tide brought in the next endless day.

Jonah was talking again. "I have been traveling north for a long time, up through Africa to the Mediterranean and from there to Europe—Italy, I think. From Italy I have traveled here."

"How do you get from Africa to here?" Fraser asked. "How do you organize such a thing?"

Jonah pinched his lips together. Hayley thought, *He's still wondering if he can trust us.*

"I did not organize anything," he said eventually.

"There are others who did that for me. For the right price, of course."

"There is a name for people who do that," Fraser said.

"I can think of many names for those people."

"So what is the right price?" Hayley asked.

"All that I have."

"Human traffickers!" Fraser exclaimed.

Jonah went quiet again and Hayley thought about the journey he had undertaken. Her geography wasn't great, but it was much better than it had been before the summer. In Texas she had examined a map of Europe to see where Nin was located and had been horrified to discover how much on the edge of everything it lay. There would be no day trips to London to take in a show, no jaunts to Milan for the fashion, no popping over to Paris for coffee and cake. Her mother had promised her only a trip to Loch Ness to see a monster she was certain didn't exist.

"You sailed to Scotland?" Fraser said.

Jonah took a breath and released it slowly, his eyes wrinkling, forehead rumpling as if remembering was painful. "Not directly, no. I think we stopped in Spain and France. For our last journey, Solomon and I boarded a small boat, which sailed for a day and a night. The weather became very bad. I had no idea where we were and I was afraid. We were supposed to change boats and land somewhere. It was not supposed to be this island."

"I was out in that storm myself," Fraser said. "It was not a night for sailing."

Jonah nodded grimly. "When the boat change did not happen, we were told to swim for the land. Solomon and I refused."

"It would have been crazy to try," Fraser said.

"One of the men had a gun. We had no choice. I shook Solomon's hand and together we jumped into the water. We were not given life jackets. I swam for my life and eventually crawled onto the beach just over there. I hoped London was not too far, but it seems I am farther away than I hoped."

Hayley thought back to the night Jonah had come ashore, the same night she had stood on a clifftop with Dunny. She had no idea there had been so much going on down below her. She wondered if Dunny knew, if that was the reason for his tears and wailing. Was he crying for the drowning man or the dying whale?

"I knew I saw someone swimming," Fraser said. "You called for help, but we never came."

"I did not see your boat," Jonah said quietly. "I did not call for help."

"Oh," said Fraser.

Hayley watched the realization cross Fraser's face: If it wasn't Jonah calling for help, it must have been Solomon. And Solomon had drowned. Fraser's face seemed to crumple and she felt his agony.

"I never saw my traveling companion again after we jumped. Then today I discovered his body washed ashore."

There was silence for a while until Fraser asked, "Did you knife him in the belly?"

"I did not."

"Who, then? And why?"

"The first question I cannot answer. As to your second, why a drowned man would be cut open, that much I know."

Before he could say more, the cave was filled with the out-of-place sound of a musical ringtone. Hayley watched Fraser delve into his trouser pocket and pull out his phone. He pressed the button and held it to his ear, nodded a lot but said nothing except "Hello" at the start and "Right, then" at the end.

"What is it?" she asked as he finished the call.

Fraser sighed, his shoulders sagged. "It's Dunny. He's gone missing again. He was at the ceilidh but now he's disappeared. They want us back."

He paused, seemed peeved.

"Well, they want *you* back. You found him last time. They need you to find him again."

SEVENTEEN

Dunny.

The mute boy.

The town curiosity.

His brother.

For most of his life, Fraser hadn't given much thought to why Dunny was the way he was; he was family. They played together sometimes, walked together to the small Skulavaig primary school, ate dinner around the table with Mum and Dad. It was only when Fraser moved to high school and stayed during the week in the school hostel, when he made friends with boys with normal little brothers, that a distance formed between Dunny and him.

Dunny became an embarrassment. Even on Skye, everyone knew of him. Fraser wondered if they had heard of him in Inverness. Maybe even in Glasgow.

And come the new term, Dunny would be going to high school with him. Fraser would have to protect him and explain him and defend him from the jibes, the looks, the bullying that would inevitably come. If his brother wouldn't speak up for himself, Fraser would have to become the voice of Dunny.

Was it any wonder he resented his silent brother?

"Is it any wonder?" he said aloud.

"What did you say?" Hayley asked, trudging beside him on the sand as they headed back to town.

"Nothing."

The beach was completely dark now, the dwindling light finally masked by black clouds gathering in the sky. The wind was picking up. Ahead, the harbor glowed with streetlights and house lights.

"Where do you think he is?" Hayley asked.

"I wish I knew."

"You're really pretty clueless about most things, aren't you?"

Fraser stopped and looked at her. "Why do you have to be so annoying?"

Hayley looked affronted. "Why do you have to be so grouchy and serious and . . . and . . . ." She searched for a third adjective. "And sad."

That one hurt. Their kiss seemed a long time ago.

"It's not my fault Dunny's disappeared again," Hayley said.

They walked again in silence until they reached the harbor wall. A crowd of people milled around, spilling out of the mission. For a moment, Fraser thought his parents had organized a search party but then he heard singing and laughter. The ceilidh had obviously just finished. There was no sign of his mum and dad.

"What now?" Hayley asked.

"I'll try his phone."

"How does *that* work?"

"It's just texting. It's the way we communicate. Not that he writes much. Even less since he started those stupid shells. And I'm not doing that."

"Text him, then."

"My mum tried already. It's as if he doesn't want to be found."

Fraser pulled out his phone anyway, wrote *Dunny, where R U* and hit send.

"What about Jonah?" Hayley asked.

They had left in a hurry, with a promise to return tomorrow.

"We make sure that the police don't find him. Or anyone else."

"Why are you helping him?"

"Because I didn't help Solomon. And look what happened to him."

"You need to tell your mom and dad."

"I promised Jonah I wouldn't. *I* can do this, I can help him. We both can."

Fraser searched the faces of the people at the harbor, looking for someone who might be involved in people trafficking. In summer the island could be full of strangers—day-trippers or holidaymakers or yacht people.

"Jonah can't stay in the cave forever," Hayley said.

"We have to get him off Nin and on his way to London."

"How do we do that?"

"It would be easier if we had some money. Have you any money?"

"A few nickels and dimes. And ten pounds of British money. One brown bill. I like the way your bills are different colors."

In his head, Fraser calculated how much money he had. There was money in his savings account, but that would mean a trip to the bank on Skye and that would arouse suspicion. On hand he had about twenty pounds in loose change.

"I don't have much either. We can maybe muster thirty pounds between us."

"And what will that get us?"

"It might cover the train fare to London."

"And where do you catch this train to London?"

"Inverness, I suppose."

"And how do we get Jonah to Inverness?"

"How do we get Jonah off the *island*? He can't just walk onto the ferry. With the murder, the police are probably checking every single person leaving this island."

There was a beep from his pocket. He checked his phone and said with surprise, "Dunny's replied."

"Not so silent after all," Hayley said.

He read the message aloud. It was short and didn't make sense.

"On boat. Whales."

They both looked at the only vessel out there: the rusting lobster boat, bobbing gently and tied to the harbor wall.

"Is Dunny on Ben's boat?" Hayley asked.

"He could be hiding there."

"Wouldn't Ben find him?"

"Ben is probably in the pub." Fraser wondered if Hayley's mother was there too.

"Well, we better get your brother."

Together they walked along the harbor wall toward the *Moby Dick*. Hayley asked, "What did Dunny say about whales?"

"Nothing. Just the word *whales*."

At the boat, Hayley asked, "Are you going aboard to search it?"

"I best not. Not without Ben being here."

"Why will he care?"

Fraser remembered Ben's angry face and harsh words at the ceilidh. The boat was his home and it didn't seem proper to go sneaking around without permission.

"Best not."

"Fine," the girl said. "I'll do it."

"No." He grabbed hold of Hayley's arm.

She tugged it free. "I'll go if I want."

"Just let it be. Please."

"Why should I?"

"Because . . ." It was hard to find the right words to

describe how he felt. "Because he's *my* brother. *I* need to find him this time."

Hayley looked set to continue the argument but then threw up her arms in defeat. "Well, *someone* will have to go aboard and find him."

"Let me call him first. If he's down below, he'll hear me."

With sarcasm Hayley said, "Yeah, that will work. Shout his name."

"He's mute. He's not deaf."

Fraser leaned over the harbor wall. "Dunny!" he called down to the boat. "Dunny, it's Fraser. Are you in there?"

They waited in silence for a moment and from the corner of his eye Fraser noticed the locals by the harbor looking in his direction. *Just the Dunbar boys*, he could almost hear them whisper.

"Dunny," he shouted again. "Come out."

There was the sound of banging and a commotion from below deck. The cabin hatch began to rise. Fraser gave Hayley a smug smile.

Ben McCaig's head popped out. He looked up at the jetty, seemed flustered and annoyed and not completely sober.

"What are you playing at, Fraser?"

In that moment, Fraser knew for definite his whale-spotting trips were over. He tried to say something, but despondency washed over him and choked the words in his throat. There was the brief thought that perhaps this was how his brother felt every day.

"We're looking for Dunny," Hayley said by way of rescue.

Ben pulled himself onto the deck. "And why the . . ." He paused, glanced down into the cabin. "And why on earth do you think he might be here?"

"We got a text message from him. He said he was on a boat. There's no other boat."

Ben contemplated the sky and sighed, as if the heavens themselves were conspiring against him. "Well, I can assure you he is not on board mine."

Fraser found his tongue. "Can we check?"

"Of course you can't bloody check. I've told you he's not here; that's enough."

From the cabin below came a woman's voice. With an American accent.

"Is that you, Hayley?"

Sarah Risso pulled herself through the hatch and onto the deck. Her hair was disheveled, her face red, and she too looked slightly drunk.

Well, well, well, thought Fraser. He understood now Ben's reluctance to have his boat searched. And his conviction that Dunny wasn't aboard.

"Mom!" Hayley exclaimed.

Fraser looked at the girl. Her mouth hung open and her eyes were wide. Her face worked its way through various emotions: aghast, angry, embarrassed, confused, disappointed.

"What are you doing, Mom?" Hayley asked.

Sarah took a moment before replying. "Ben and I were having a nightcap."

"Did you not drink enough at the ceilidh?"

"It's not your job, honey, to set the limits on my alcohol intake."

"Well, clearly somebody has to."

Sarah was about to reply, but Ben got in there first.

"That's quite enough, Hayley."

Hayley looked outraged. Her mother ignored her. "What's happened to Dunny?" she asked.

"My brother's gone missing again."

Ben crossed the deck to the wheelhouse. He opened the door, took a quick look inside, and declared, "He's not in here." His face took on a worried look, as if he had had a sudden idea and was troubled by it. "Have you checked the dinghy?"

He headed toward the back of the boat, and Fraser followed along the top of the jetty. They both saw the empty space at the stern beside the rusty ladder.

"It's gone," Fraser said.

"What's gone?" Sarah asked.

"The dinghy," said Ben. "It's a small inflatable that I keep for emergencies. It's tied to the hull here."

Fraser said, "The paddles are gone as well."

"Has Dunny taken it?" Sarah asked.

Ben kicked a few old lobster creels out of the way. "He's missing, and so is my dinghy."

All four looked out to sea, which was beginning to roll in the gathering wind.

"Oh, God," Sarah said.

"Would he do this, Fraze?" Ben asked.

"I've no idea. I've no idea what Dunny is capable of doing. This, probably, aye."

"Why would he take off in the dinghy?"

It was suddenly crystal clear to Fraser what his brother was doing, what his cryptic text meant. Dunny had waded into the ocean the previous night and now he had set sail for a similar purpose.

"He's gone to see the whales."

"What whales?"

"The ones we saw last night. The orcas."

"Enough with the orcas," Ben said. "There were no orcas."

"There were," Hayley said. "Killer whales. Big black-and-white things. Dunny saw them first."

"I doubt it." Ben rubbed his forehead, looked at the ocean. "But suppose for a minute they *do* exist and they *are* out there. Would Dunny take my dinghy to find them?"

"I think so," Fraser said.

"So where is he?" Sarah asked.

Fraser voiced the thought they all were having. He pointed beyond the harbor, toward the ocean, which was dark now under the night sky. "Out there somewhere. And he's not the greatest swimmer."

"We should tell your parents," Ben said.

"We should tell the coast guard," said Sarah.

"No," Fraser said to them both, looking down from the jetty. He imagined the taunts and snickers that would come his way on the first day back at school. He saw the photograph that would be in the local paper, the wet and bedraggled Dunny after his rescue. "No. We don't want to make a fuss. We don't know exactly where he is yet."

Sarah ignored him, asked Hayley, "Who was the coast guard man you told me about, honey?"

"Mr. Wallace."

"Let's find him."

"No," Fraser said once more.

"Your brother is out there in a small boat by himself. We need to tell the coast guard."

"No, Sarah," said Ben. "Fraser's right. Not yet. If the coast guard gets involved, we'll have lifeboats and helicopters and it becomes a whole other thing."

"We need lifeboats and helicopters. Dunny has drifted out to sea in your rubber boat."

"Maybe."

Fraser now had a picture in his head of Dunny being winched aboard a Sea King helicopter with the whole town watching and jeering. He couldn't shake the image that was going to be his downfall, his everlasting shame. Brother of Dunny "Dinghy" Dunbar. He only vaguely heard Ben say, "We have the *Moby Dick*."

Sarah scoffed. "You're not taking this boat anywhere in your condition."

"I'm fine."

"You're drunk."

"Just a little."

"Enough to sink yourself and take Dunny with you."

"Nonsense."

"If you try to sail this boat, I will call not only the coast guard but also the police. I'm sure driving while intoxicated applies to boats as well."

"Fraser can steer."

"Don't be ridiculous."

"He's old enough. He's done it before. Right, Fraze?"

Fraser had taken the wheel of the *Moby Dick* on two occasions, both on calm, bright seas, for only a couple of minutes each time.

"Sure," he said hesitantly.

"Come on, then. Let's find that daft brother of yours."

The suddenness of the change in his fortunes was startling. Not only was Ben asking him back on board the *Moby Dick*, where he thought he'd never set foot again, but he was asking him to pilot the boat. And even if it was just to get them under way, it didn't matter, they were going sailing. He swung himself onto the ladder attached to the jetty and shimmied down onto the deck.

"I'll see you when I get back," Ben said to Sarah.

"I don't think so. I'm staying right here." Sarah smiled and said, "I like you, Ben, but I don't trust you."

"That's harsh."

"It's a persona you cultivate, so don't get offended."

Ben smiled and turned to Fraser. "Right, Fraze, let's get under way. You're skipper now."

He winked and Fraser could smell the whisky on his breath. As Fraser headed for the wheelhouse, he heard a thump and turned to see Hayley sprawled on all fours, having jumped onto the deck. She pulled herself to her feet and rubbed the palms of her hands.

"I'm not staying here by myself while you three go sailing into the sunset. And a second sober person is probably a good thing."

Hayley's mother seemed about to argue the point but thought better of it. Ben opened the wheelhouse door and ushered them inside. As the four of them crowded inside the small wooden structure, Ben took his place behind the wheel.

"I thought Fraser was steering," Sarah said.

"How about I start her up and guide her out of the harbor." He gave a half smile and added, "If we sink here, it's not too far to swim to shore."

Sarah said, "We don't need jokes, Ben, not those kinds of jokes, not when Dunny's out there in that little boat."

"Right enough" was Ben's apologetic reply.

He started the engine of the *Moby Dick* and Fraser heard the familiar cough and splutter of aged pistons and rusty crankshafts. He had come to love this sound, for it heralded the swell of the ocean, the salty smell of deep water, and the possibility of a fin or a spout that signaled a whale. He didn't hear batters and clangs and a boat engine that could quit at any moment and leave them bobbing helpless on a choppy sea.

Ben guided the lobster boat away from the harbor wall, out through the breach in the stones into open water. Fraser peered through the wheelhouse window and wondered how they would find Dunny, assuming he was out here.

"So which direction are we heading, Fraze?" Ben asked.

Fraser hadn't a clue. How could he know which way his strange brother would paddle a small inflatable in search of whales?

"North, I suppose."

Ben offered him his place, said with a slight slur, "She's all yours, skipper."

Fraser looked at the small circle of polished wood with spokes rubbed dull by the weathered palms of old fishermen. He peered ahead of him through the window at the rolling sea that was even blacker than the sky. It was his job now to steer this small boat through the giant ocean to find a tiny dinghy. His job to find a brother who couldn't, or rather wouldn't, shout out for rescue if a wave was taking him under.

He stood in front of the wheel and grasped the wood. He could feel the throb of the engine and the roll of the sea beneath his fingers.

It was his boat now.

EIGHTEEN

Hayley peered through the wheelhouse window and saw only sea spray and whipping waves. If Dunny was in the water, she would never spot him from here. She looked at Fraser. His eyes were focused intently on the ocean and his knuckles were white where he gripped the wheel. He looked a little scared, but also older and more confident, and she conceded to herself that in any other place, in any other situation, she might like such a boy. But this was Fraser Dunbar, so the whole notion was ridiculous. She told herself again, *The whole notion is ridiculous.*

"I can't see anything from here," she declared. "I'm going outside."

"Stay where you are," her mom said.

But Hayley had the advantage of righteous indignation. She had caught her mother and Ben McCaig *doing it.* Or if not *it,* then something else, definitely doing something.

"We won't see Dunny from here. We need to be on the deck."

"The deck is dangerous. Tell her, Ben."

Ben said, "There are life jackets behind you."

"Oh, that's a great help."

"They will be if you fall overboard." Ben gave a tipsy smile.

Hayley grabbed a life jacket from the hook on the far wall. It was faded orange and stained from years of fishermen's armpits. She pulled it over her head and tugged open the wheelhouse door. She heard her mom say, "Well, I'm coming with you," but she didn't wait.

Out on the deck the wind was so strong she felt a stab of panic as she pictured Dunny in his small rubber dinghy. She moved unsteadily to the front of the boat as it dipped and rose in the swell. The deck sloped up at the bow and she grabbed hold of the rusty rail. The water beneath her was dark and choppy. She scanned the expanse of sea ahead, but there was no sign of a small dinghy or a small boy. The worst thing would be to discover the dinghy but find it empty.

To her left the dark form of the cliffs loomed into view. Fraser was sailing the boat north along the coast to where they had spotted orcas the previous evening. They were heading toward Jonah and his cave.

"Can you see him?" asked her mom.

For a moment Hayley thought her mom was asking about Jonah. She reminded herself that no one knew about him except Fraser, Dunny, and her.

"There's no sign of anything. No dinghy, no Dunny."

"That's maybe a good thing. Maybe he's not out here at all."

Hayley stared at the water, sighed, and said, "But you know he is, Mom."

They stood in silence, each braced against the roll of the boat, pulling back their hair out of their eyes. Silence was simply the absence of speaking. The wind was moaning, the water slapped against the bow of the boat, and the engine throbbed beneath their feet.

"Should we talk?" her mom said at last.

"There's nothing to talk about."

"I think there is."

Hayley said nothing more, so her mom said, "Well, I'll talk and you listen."

Hayley gripped the rail even tighter and tried to focus on the rolling waves, but her vision was blurry. She willed the tears not to spill down her cheeks.

"I'm sorry you saw what you did tonight. Things just happened between Ben and me. Things got a little out of control. Whisky and heartbreak are a lethal combination."

They gazed out over the choppy waters.

"I know you don't approve of Ben and me being together. To be honest, I am not seeking your approval. But it would be nice to have your understanding."

Hayley said, "What's to understand?"

"You have to understand that I can't wait forever for your father to come back to me. It's not going to happen."

"It might. You don't know that for sure."

"I do, honey."

"He might come back."

"He won't." Sarah added quietly, "I don't want him back."

Hayley felt a sob rupture in the back of her throat, but she held her breath and let it escape slowly through her nose as she clenched her lips.

When it had passed she said, "How can you say that?"

"Because it's the truth. Our marriage is over."

"You want Ben instead?"

"I don't want Ben. Ben is just ... me dipping my toe back in the water. He's a nice guy, a sexy guy, but he's not a replacement for your father. I don't want another husband. He's just a little fun, that's all. Or at least he was going to be before you and Fraser interrupted."

"You mean nothing happened?"

"No, nothing actually happened."

"But it will."

Sarah sighed and said, "No, probably not. The moment has passed. This wind sobers you up."

There was no more talk for a while. Hayley faced the wind and let it gust over her, felt a lifting of worries from her shoulders, as if the wind was catching something, if only the anger she felt toward her mom, anger that was selfish and irrational. Tonight had been whisky and cuddles, and maybe a little more, with another guy. Her dad had *settled down* with another woman. That was a world of difference.

And the island of Nin was a different world.

Hayley lifted one hand from the rail and placed it on top of her mom's where it gripped the rusty metal. They didn't look at each other, said nothing, but words were not necessary. They stood there, searching the ocean, and then there was a shout from the wheelhouse. It was Ben, leaning from the door.

"Any sign?"

"Still looking," Sarah said above the wind. Ben disappeared back inside. "He doesn't trust Fraser in charge of his boat."

"Quite right," said Hayley. "The boy is useless."

"That's a bit harsh. Fraser is smarter than you think. It's Ben that shouldn't be trusted." Hayley's mom gave her a smile. "All men, in fact."

"Now *that's* harsh."

"Perhaps. But you stick with quiet Scottish laddies."

"No, thanks."

"He *is* kind of cute."

"I don't think so. *Ben* is cute. Fraser is just . . . just a boy. An island boy."

"He's a nice boy. You could be friends at least. You should make the effort to at least be friends."

"Maybe . . ."

Hayley did a quick review of the last few days: exploring a ruined castle, meeting Jonah in the cave, watching orcas, finding a dead body. In all their exploits, Fraser had been right there, with her. They had danced a Highland jig together; they had even kissed.

Oh, my God, thought Hayley. *We're friends already.*

But there was no time to analyze that bombshell.

"What's that over there?" her mom said.

She was pointing to the left of the boat at the stretch of water between them and the shore.

"Where?" Hayley asked.

"Right there." Sarah was pointing frantically, as if jabbing her finger would help.

"What do you see?"

"I don't know. Is that a fin?"

Hayley looked again, scanned the ocean as the boat dipped and rose. The dark water was flecked with breaking whitecaps, but there was one whitecap that remained when the other waves had broken. It was a white patch beneath a dark fin, the dorsal fin of an orca.

"I see it," Hayley cried. "That's a whale."

Her mom leaned out over the water, seemed to doubt herself now. "It's just a wave."

But Hayley knew it was not. "It's an orca. I've seen them before."

The fin disappeared beneath the water and the whole ocean was lost behind a wave that rolled under the boat and sent the *Moby Dick* down into a trough. When it rose again, both the fin and the head of the whale could be seen clearly, the black and white standing out against the gray of the water, lit again by a full moon that appeared between scudding clouds.

"My goodness, that's a killer whale," said Sarah.

"We call them orcas, Mom."

"Whatever it is, honey, it's swimming in front of our boat." Sarah's fascination turned instantly to horror. "Oh, God, what if Dunny's close by? It could attack him."

"Orcas don't eat people," Hayley said, and then wondered if that was true.

The whale circled as the boat moved closer and then it turned and pushed on, a surge of ocean slipping from its sleek back.

"What's it doing?" Sarah asked.

A thought came to Hayley that seemed ridiculous and yet made sense in this strange part of the world.

"I think the whale wants us to follow it."

NINETEEN

Piloting a small boat in a growing storm was much harder than Fraser imagined. He wondered if he was turning the wheel or if the wheel was turning him. Each time the boat dipped into a trough he clung to the old wood, and when it rose again to the crest of the wave he hung on even tighter.

Yet this was nothing compared to the stormy sea of two nights ago, the night when everything began. He felt another surge of admiration for Ben McCaig's sailing prowess, wondered again why it wasn't Ben guiding the boat tonight. As if to answer the question, Ben moved unsteadily across the wheelhouse to stand beside him, the smell of whisky on his breath.

He laid a hand softly on the wheel, as he had done a hundred times already this evening, and nudged the boat slightly to starboard. "Just keep her pointing straight north," he said. "Mind the compass there."

The large compass was mounted on a plinth of oak, its magnetic arrow jittering left and right around the ornate *N*.

"It's hard to keep her straight in these waves," Fraser said.

"A firm hold and a gentle touch is all you need." Ben laughed. "That might work with Hayley as well."

Fraser scowled slightly and asked, "Did it work for her mother?"

"It might have done. We were somewhat interrupted."

"Aye, just as well. Besides, blame Dunny, not me."

"If we find him out here in my dinghy, I'll do just that." Ben took a step away from the wheel. "And you have your own piece of madness to sort out."

Fraser knew he was talking about the knife under the bed.

"The girls are pointing," Ben suddenly said. "They've spotted something."

"I can't see a thing."

Ben lurched across the wheelhouse. "Didn't we promise to never go sailing again in a nighttime storm?"

"I'm sure we did. You promised Willie McGregor and I promised Mr. Wallace."

Ben grabbed an old telescope from a shelf, an ancient thing that might once have belonged to Columbus himself. He pulled open the door, and a rush of wet air whistled in.

"This isn't good," he said. He stepped outside and the door slammed shut behind him.

Fraser was now truly skipper of the boat, sailing the *Moby Dick* alone as the wind blew and the seas rolled. All he had to do was keep heading straight north. Ben had assured him there were no hidden reefs to puncture the hull and little chance of a collision with any other vessel. The waves were not yet high enough to tip the boat over. All he had to avoid was running aground. Fraser looked through the window to his left. The shoreline and the cliffs behind the beach were a good way off. He glanced again at the compass; he looked at the bow, where Ben stood beside Hayley and her mother, all three staring ahead at the ocean, Ben through the lens of his antique telescope. If Fraser needed it, help was close at hand.

This wasn't so hard. He could do this, sail the *Moby Dick*, be captain of the ship. He took a deep breath and tried to relax his shoulders, loosened the grip on the wheel. This was what he was born to do. He would sail the seven seas in search of whales and adventure and good-looking girls. Skulavaig was to the stern, the world ahead, and he would remain behind the wheel of this small boat and not relinquish his hold until he was far across the ocean and squinting into a tropical sun.

And then Ben was beside him, demanding that he move and give him the wheel.

"There are bloody orcas," Ben said, his voice a mix of disbelief and excitement.

Fraser took a step back, his bubble burst. He was first mate again.

But the whales were back.

"I was wrong to doubt you, Fraze."

"You saw them?"

Ben nodded. "We're following one. It's swimming ahead of us and Hayley thinks it's leading us somewhere. And I'm drunk enough to believe her."

"Leading us where?"

"Where do you think?"

And then Fraser understood. "To Dunny?"

"Go see for yourself."

Fraser went to the door and stepped outside. He edged along the deck beside the wheelhouse, looked over at the sea and saw it froth. This was not an ocean for small dinghies and small boys. He moved toward the bow, staggering left, then right, as the boat pitched. Hayley and her mum clung to the rail.

"It's an orca," Hayley shouted above the whistling wind.

"Ben told me. He's believes us now."

"It's leading us to Dunny."

"Or it's trying to escape us chasing it."

"No. It keeps circling around and waiting for us to catch up."

Fraser scanned the ocean, and the unmistakable form of an orca cut through the choppy water, its head lifted high as it seemed to check the location of the boat. Its dorsal fin was tall and straight: a mature male, the leader of the pack. It moved left of them, past the boat, but this time it didn't circle back around. It swam toward the shore.

"It's changed direction," Hayley said.

Her mom turned and indicated frantically to Ben in the wheelhouse. Fraser looked and Ben was grinning with his thumb up. He must be able to see the whale through the window. The *Moby Dick* arced to port.

For a couple of minutes the boat sailed slowly toward the coastline, the cliffs looming larger as they drew nearer. This was not a heading that could be maintained indefinitely. Orcas were intelligent creatures but Fraser doubted they understood about rocks and thin hulls.

"Where are we going?" he shouted, as if he was asking the orca itself.

He searched the sea ahead and his question was answered. Bobbing in the waves like a flimsy piece of flotsam was the small dinghy. And sitting in it was his little brother, his white hair blowing in the wind. The oars were gone and he gripped tight to the sides of the small craft. Around the dinghy swam the orcas. It was an amazing sight. And crazy. What had possessed his brother to do such a thing? And what were the whales doing?

"There he is," screamed Hayley.

"Are they attacking him?" Sarah asked.

"No," said Fraser. "They must just be curious. They won't harm him."

But he heard doubt in his voice. What did he truly know about the predatory instincts of killer whales? They had that name for a reason.

Sarah ran back to the wheelhouse and a moment later the throb of the engine faded to a gentle put-put. The roll and pitch increased with the decline in forward motion.

"What now?" Hayley asked.

The gap between boat and dinghy decreased. There were five orcas swimming beside Dunny, including the large male that had guided them here. The *Moby Dick* dwarfed the little rubber boat, but Dunny had not looked up once or acknowledged their presence.

"Dunny!" Fraser shouted.

His brother's eyes remained firmly on the whales, watching each one as it glided past. He seemed oblivious to the fact that the dinghy was being tossed around and water was sloshing over him.

"What is he doing?" Hayley asked.

"Dunny!"

And then, as if it wasn't remarkable enough that Dunny was adrift in a dinghy, at sea, in a storm, in a crowd of whales, Fraser witnessed something truly astounding. One of the smaller whales swam right up to his brother, parallel with the dinghy, and seemed to pause, to hold itself alongside for a moment. Dunny relinquished his grip on the little boat with his right hand and reached out and touched the whale. He stroked the orca's back.

"Did you see that?" Hayley cried. Fraser could only nod. "He patted that whale. Like a dog!"

"I saw."

Now it was Hayley's turn to shout, "Dunny!"

The gap between fishing boat and dinghy was only a dozen feet or so. They were looking down on the boy, and Fraser feared they might run him over. The whales, aware of their approach, must have sensed that their time at the court of King Dunny was over, for one by one they slowly submerged under the choppy waves and were gone. Dunny was now just a little boy in a dinghy without oars, being tossed in a stormy sea. He looked up and for the first time seemed to notice the lobster boat. He looked first at Hayley and then at his brother, and his face turned from a contented smile to one of frowning misery. His mouth opened and, though Fraser could hear nothing above the whistle of the wind, Dunny's lips seemed to form a word.

No.

The boy stood up in the dinghy.

"Don't stand up," Hayley shouted.

But it was too late. The waves rolled under the dinghy, tipped the small boat over, and Dunny fell into the sea.

As Fraser waited for his brother to appear from under the waves, five seconds became a lifetime. And in the midst of the dread and panic and despair that welled up in him, he asked himself: Had Dunny fallen, or had he jumped?

His brother's head popped onto the surface and his arms were thrashing and splashing and he was gasping and coughing and spitting . . .

"He's drowning!" Hayley said.

Fraser was struck immobile. There were orcas in the water with very large teeth. And if Dunny wasn't about to be eaten, he was surely about to drown. His brother was not a great swimmer. Fraser held on to the rail and watched his brother go under and then pop back up, go under again, then pop back up. Fraser had to rescue him, but his legs wouldn't work; he had to call for Ben, but his tongue wouldn't shape the words; he had to move, but his fingers wouldn't give up their grip on the rusty metal.

Why wasn't his dad here, why did *he* have to rescue his brother? He was only fourteen; he wasn't a whale scientist, he wasn't an explorer, he wasn't captain of the boat.

A movement at his side made him turn his head and he saw Hayley refastening her life jacket. Her jacket and boots and sweater lay in a pile on the deck. Then she climbed on top of the railing, took a deep breath, and threw herself into the water.

There was a splash and a scream from the wheelhouse, and then only the rolling ocean, nothing more. The whales were gone. Dunny was gone. And Hayley was gone.

TWENTY

The water was cold. It sucked Hayley's breath from her and for a few long seconds she wondered if it was ever coming back. Then her body made an involuntary gasp, she coughed and spluttered and tasted the salt of the sea. As she rose and fell with the ocean, she kicked her legs and moved her arms, but this wasn't swimming. Her bulky life jacket restricted any kind of movement, although it was keeping her alive. The sea was too cold and too heaving to allow anything more than floating and keeping her head above water. And then Hayley remembered why she was here: Dunny.

She looked around her and there were only waves and the *Moby Dick* looming large above her. The whales were gone, or were they just circling below, waiting to attack? Walls of water led up to a circle of light far above her head and for a moment she fancied she saw her mom and Fraser Dunbar looking down into the well and shouting words she couldn't hear. It was a lonely place at the bottom of this hole in the sea. The beginnings of a scream gathered itself at the back of her throat, the beginnings of terror and the loss of control. She watched her arm rise above the waves and knew she was only a pounding heartbeat away from frenzied thrashing at the water. And then something touched her arm and held on; when she looked, Dunny was there beside her and he was grinning.

Hayley grabbed hold of him and together they rose out of the trough. As the wave crested, with the two of them on top, they were momentarily as high as the deck of the *Moby Dick*. Her mom stood there, a frantic look on her face, flanked by Fraser. Ben was desperately searching the stern of the boat, for a life belt maybe.

Hayley waved. It seemed a silly thing to do, as if she was warming up for a high school swim meet, with her mom sitting in the bleachers. Her mom was shouting something, encouragement, presumably, to swim in her direction.

Hayley tried, but she had too much to contend with: the swell, the cold, the bulky life jacket, the tight hold she had on Dunny. She was a strong swimmer—she had been going for state finals—but this wasn't swimming, this was survival. She floated in the water, concentrated on keeping their heads above the waves, hoped the *Moby Dick* would come to them.

Then there was movement and a splash and suddenly Fraser was there, bobbing beside her. He tried to speak, but the air had been wrenched from his lungs. Hayley saw he wasn't wearing a life jacket.

How does this help? she thought.

"Come on," Fraser shouted finally, offering no advice on how this might be achieved.

Hayley slapped the water a few times but made no forward progress. The boat was only a few feet away, with Fraser in between, but it could have been moored on Mars for all the hope she had of reaching it. She was tiring already, her arms heavy, her legs encased in concrete and dragging her down. The cold water numbed her brain as well as her body. Panic again swelled within her, matching the swell of the ocean. It was not drowning that troubled her but the fact that her mom would have to watch her drown.

And then she was moving and the *Moby Dick* grew closer very fast. She thought at first it was a wave that was carrying her along, but then she saw it was Dunny pulling on the back of her life jacket. For a moment it seemed that something was pulling Dunny. They swept past Fraser, who looked bluey-pale and astonished. A wave lifted them up and they rode it all the way to the hull of the boat, smacking against the ladder. Ben hung there, an arm reaching out. Dunny released his grip on Hayley and she grabbed on to the ladder. Ben took hold of the top of her life jacket and hauled her up and out of the water as she shakily found a rung with both feet. Water poured off her and a sudden more intense cold hit her as the wind sliced through her wet clothes. At the top, just before she collapsed on the deck in the arms of her mother, she looked down at the sea. Dunny clung to the bottom rung but he was looking down, not up. And beneath him, beneath the water, Hayley thought she saw movement, a dark shadow of something big and alive just beneath the surface. She looked again and it was gone.

TWENTY-ONE

Fraser floated in the water and watched first Hayley and then Dunny climb the ladder to safety. Dunny waved toward Fraser, hand signals that Fraser couldn't interpret. *Speak to me*, he thought, *for once in your life*. Dunny had stroked past him with Hayley hanging on, but Fraser couldn't swim like that; he didn't know Dunny could swim like that. He kicked for the *Moby Dick*, swam for a few seconds and a few strokes and looked up. The boat seemed farther away. He kicked again, tore at the sea, sucked in air and spat out water. He paused, bobbed perilously in the rolling waves, looked again. The gap had not been narrowed. It was only a short distance; on land it would have been a couple of strides, but in the cold water it suddenly felt impossibly distant. Ben still hung from the ladder, shouting encouragement. Fraser kicked and pulled again, kept going until the pain in his muscles made him stop. When he looked, the boat was farther away.

Oh, crap, he thought.

It was the tide or the wind or the swell or a combination of all three, but Fraser saw that the *Moby Dick* was going in one direction and he in another. As he floated, helpless now, he watched Hayley's mom appear on deck with a life jacket. She handed it to Ben, who launched it in his direction.

It fell short.

It was only then that Fraser realized he wasn't wearing one.

Oh, crap, he thought again.

Ben pulled himself onto the deck and disappeared in the direction of the wheelhouse. Fraser swam a few weary strokes, but the life jacket was drifting out of reach faster than the boat. There was a bang and a clatter from the *Moby Dick*—the engine firing up. Ben was coming to him. The bang and clatter stopped. A few more seconds of feeble bobbing and the banging started up again. It faded just as quickly. The old boat was having trouble starting. Fraser knew what this meant: Ben would have to go down below into the engine compartment behind the small cabin. He would have to hammer a few things and take a wrench to a few others things. It would take ten minutes at least. Fraser didn't have ten minutes.

The boat drifted still farther away. Fraser wasn't scared and it surprised him. He was glad that Dunny was safe, miffed that it was the American girl who had saved him again, or at least had made the first move to save him. In truth it was Dunny who had done the rescuing. Now Fraser was the one in trouble and there seemed no one able to save *him*.

He rose and fell with the waves, moving his arms and kicking his legs to keep himself afloat. He admired his calm demeanor, his lack of panic, as if he was watching someone else struggle in the water, as if it was some other boy whose head was only just above the surface. He could sense fear lurking around the corner but for the moment he was thinking clearly and rationally. He was about to drown. It was the sad, inevitable result of jumping into a stormy sea without a life jacket.

The boat drifted farther away. He moved in the same direction, just not as fast. He could still see Dunny, Hayley, and her mother on the deck but couldn't tell if they were moving or shouting or perhaps only weeping. He hoped somebody was weeping. There was no sign of Ben, but the engine of the *Moby Dick* remained silent, so Ben had to be down below, whacking it with a hammer.

Fraser was barely able to keep himself above the water. Both he and the boat were drifting toward the shore. He looked in the direction of the beach and the cliffs. They were drifting toward the shore!

It wasn't that far. He might not be able to reach the boat, but he could work with the tide and the waves and swim to land. With a sudden surge of energy that came with hope, he kicked his legs, hauled his arms in and out of the water, focused only on swimming and breathing. For every two strokes forward, the swell bounced him back one but he made progress. After a couple of minutes, which felt like hours, he looked up. The shore was closer—not much, but closer. He saw a dark shadow move beneath him, remembered there had been whales in the water. He kicked out again, not to swim but to scare. The shadow disappeared, had probably been a figment of his water-logged imagination.

His world narrowed to this small patch of salty sea. He could hear only his breaths, see only gray water. The waves became friends and foe. One wave would pick him up and push him forward. Another wave would move him back or break across his face, making him gasp and splutter. He looked again. The cliffs were not so distant but not yet close. He could have walked there in a minute, run it in seconds, but swimming was so much harder. The water felt thick and was in constant motion. The wind was in his face. His legs were made of stone but ached like flesh. He couldn't feel his arms, knew they must still be moving or he would be underwater by now. He pushed himself on, his breathing labored, his arms still stroking but to no real purpose. He groaned with the effort and coughed out seawater. The waves were spiteful; the friendly ones had deserted him. He was pushed back two strokes for every one forward. He kicked again, but there was no response. A breaker rolled over his head and he only just managed to come out the other side.

So close and yet so far. He had given it a go, had tried his best—it had just been beyond him. Weariness washed over him with the next breaking wave and he knew he was done. Hayley would get a medal and her picture in the paper. He would get a wreath of flowers thrown from the beach and a mention at school assembly. Fraser began to cry. He didn't want it to end this way, but he had nothing left in him. He wanted to see his mum and dad again, wanted their protective arms around him. He wanted to see his brother again, would have given Dunny a hug and apologized for being such a poor older brother. He wanted to see the whales again. The whales had been amazing.

He felt himself slip slowly under the water.

TWENTY-TWO

Hayley clung to the rail of the boat. Her shivering was painful; she had never been so cold. Her wet clothes stuck to her flesh like jagged ice and every gust of wind was an electric shock. But she wouldn't move. Her mom had pleaded with her to go below and get warm and dry, but she refused to budge. Not while Fraser was still in the water. Her mom was pacing the deck, yelling at Fraser, yelling at Ben down below, yelling at her for being wet and cold.

She watched the gap between the boy and the boat grow bigger. She shouted at him and urged him to swim harder, but the gap only increased. Then she watched him turn and head for the shore and she shouted at him some more to keep going. Her mom ran to the cabin hatch and disappeared below. Dunny stood beside her and though he also shivered, he didn't shout. He shifted his weight from side to side, he rubbed the rail with his hands like he was polishing the rusting metal, his head was moving up and down and left and right, but he made no sound. Hayley wanted to shout at *him*, to snap him into life, to force him to give encouragement to his brother. If Fraser could hear his brother shout, it might help him. But Dunny said nothing and together they watched Fraser slow down, tread water, and begin to flounder.

She opened her mouth to shout again but knew it was pointless. The wind was too strong and Fraser was too far away. She started to cry and when she looked, Dunny was crying as well. No sobs or wails, just tears that ran down his cheeks and mingled with the sea water and rain. *At least he will cry for his dead brother*, she thought, and when she looked again, Fraser was gone.

The engine of the *Moby Dick* banged and rattled and kicked into life, but it was too late. Hayley stared at the spot on the ocean and saw rolling waves and breaking whitecaps and sea spray. It was a malevolent sea and a nice Scottish boy had been no match for it.

And then she saw an arm. It burst from the water as if hauling itself out by grabbing at the sky and beside it was a second arm. It took her a moment to realize that the second arm was different from the first, and that they were not connected to the same body.

Fraser's face appeared above the waves, his mouth sucking at the air. In the water beside him, holding him and pulling him and saving him was Jonah. Beside her, Dunny began to wail, a joyful wail like someone on a roller coaster might make, and he clapped his hands together in applause. Hayley raised her arms into the wind and gave a cry of jubilation.

Fraser was saved.

TWENTY-THREE

Fraser hoped he was swimming but knew he was not. He flapped his arms and legs and let himself be carried toward the shore. Jonah's swimming style was awkward, he half drowned Fraser in the effort, but together they made slow progress toward the shore. It seemed a long time of splashing and spluttering and struggling but eventually, Fraser felt his knee touch something solid and they were being rolled over by the surf breaking up the beach. The man and boy dragged themselves the last few feet out of the water and lay panting on the wet sand as the swash flowed around their bodies.

"Are you well?" Jonah asked between gulps of air.

"Aye. Thank you."

They lay on the beach some more, refilling their lungs, regaining their strength, and Fraser listened to the angry pounding of the surf just a foot away and the groan of the wind. Nature seemed annoyed that he had escaped. He began to shiver violently and then Jonah was on his feet, offering him a hand. He pulled himself up and his legs were feeble and shaky, but he stayed standing.

"Come, you must get warm," said Jonah. "I will light a fire."

Fraser looked out to sea and it was dark and black clouds hung low. The *Moby Dick* lay offshore; it seemed to be moving in a slow circle, but all he could see was a faint light from the wheelhouse. He waved but knew he wouldn't be seen.

"Come," Jonah said again. "We must get dry, then you will go home."

Together they walked up the sand toward the cave and the realization slowly came to Fraser that he had nearly drowned. The shivering increased and he felt the beginnings of a sob, partly of relief, partly of shame that he had almost ruined the lives of both himself and his family. His eyes misted over but he stifled the sob, swallowed it back down, and wiped his face with his wet hand.

Jonah helped him up the rocks and into the cave. He had rolled some larger rocks together at the cave entrance and behind there he had built a fire, its glow hidden from view. The fire had been doused but embers still smoldered and the aroma of something cooking hung in the air.

Jonah sparked the fire into life again by adding new twigs. Flames soon filled the circle of stones, and Fraser peeled off his sodden shirt, trousers, shoes, and socks and laid them on a rock beside the fire. He sat in his underpants and allowed his body to warm. Jonah said nothing. He had waded into the sea in only his jeans, just as he had emerged from it two days earlier, and they were steaming from the heat of the fire.

After a while the shivering stopped and Fraser felt exhausted but not sleepy, his body spent but his mind buzzing.

"You saved my life," he said at last.

Jonah looked at the flames and said, "I know how it feels to be swimming in a storm."

The fire flickered in the wind that was blowing outside. It sucked out the smoke and Fraser reckoned there was not a warmer, cozier place on earth.

"I was trying to save my brother."

"Yes, I could see. He climbed onto the big boat. You saved him."

"I didn't do much."

"It was enough. He is saved."

"It was Hayley."

"You worked together."

"She saved him."

"No. I think it was . . ." Jonah paused, looked beyond the cave, but the sea was black.

"What?"

"I think it was the whales."

The fire crackled and the wind moaned and Fraser felt a tingle that was not just the warmth of the flames.

"You saw them? You saw the whales?"

"I saw the small boat first and then your brother.

The waves were tossing him up and down. I was about to swim out and help, but then I saw them." Jonah stoked the fire and shook his head, as if still astonished by what he had witnessed. "We call them *leruarua* in our language. Last night you called them orcas. It was the same whales. I feared for your brother in his small boat with such large whales. But then the creatures swam close to the boat and I saw the most amazing thing."

Jonah paused, stared again beyond the fire, beyond the cave, beyond the sea, it seemed. Fraser waited a moment to hear this amazing thing, but when the man said nothing more, he offered one of his own.

"Dunny touched the whales."

A bright smile erupted on Jonah's face. "Yes. Your brother touched *leruarua*. He stretched out a hand and stroked their backs and touched their fins."

"I saw it too."

"When the big boat appeared, the whales were gone and your brother fell into the water."

"I think he jumped."

"The storm was growing. I was surprised he did not fall in sooner."

"I think we spoiled his fun."

"He was in danger, even if he did not realize it."

"He didn't need our help and he didn't want it."

"You saved him. He is safe now."

"You saved *me*. I was the one needing to be saved."

They sat in silence for a little while beside the fire, and Fraser drank some rainwater that Jonah had in a plastic bottle.

"Here, eat," Jonah said.

From behind him he lifted an old bicycle wheel missing its tire. Jonah had bent it into shape to allow a handful of small fish to be placed above the smoldering charcoal of his fire.

"You caught fish?" Fraser asked.

"I did. It would not be fair to depend on you bringing me food every day."

"How did you catch them?"

"I found an old piece of fishing net among the rocks. If it is placed at high tide in the cove along the beach from here, you can gather a few small fish as the tide goes out. It is similar to how they fish the flooded lakes of South Africa."

"What kind of fish are they?"

"I do not know."

"How do they taste?"

"The fish from home taste better. Here, try one."

Jonah placed the fish that were already cooked above the fire, allowed them to warm for a few moments, then picked one from the rack. He placed it on a large leaf and handed it to Fraser. Fraser examined the scrawny thing lying on the leaf. It still had its tail and eye, an eye that gazed accusingly at him, saying, *Don't you dare.*

Fraser tore into it. Jonah took one for himself and said, "Be careful of the bones."

It had a bland, greasy taste but nearly dying had made Fraser ravenous. The eye seemed to follow him as he twisted the fish to find the smallest bits of flesh. When he had finished, he wrapped the bones in the leaf and took another that Jonah offered.

As he ate he remembered something that was bothering him. "You said you knew what happened to the man Solomon. Why he was stabbed."

It took a while for Jonah to answer, as if he was reluctant for Fraser to share the burden, or the danger, of knowing.

"The money to make this journey from Africa to Europe is paid in two installments, half at the beginning and half upon arrival. Most people who are smuggled into Britain have a relative waiting with the final payment. The man Solomon had another way to pay."

He stopped and Fraser leaned forward, wanting to know more.

"He had swallowed a small diamond."

"A *diamond*?"

Jonah nodded. "He told me this one night while we were traveling. I believe the person who cut him open was looking for it. Certainly, there is no diamond there now."

Fraser had a sudden image of Jonah rooting about in the inner parts of a corpse. "You searched?" he asked.

Jonah shuddered and Fraser could tell it hadn't been a pleasant experience.

"We had agreed to help each other when our journey began," he said at last. "His diamond would have helped."

"Do you have one of your own?" Fraser nodded toward Jonah's stomach.

Jonah smiled but shook his head. "It will not be so easy for me to make my second payment. And there are people looking for me and expecting their money."

"What's your plan?"

"The plan was to get to London and then . . ." He shrugged. ". . . disappear."

"What will happen if they find you?"

Jonah sighed. "They may kill me and send evidence back to Lesotho as an example to others of what happens to those who fail to pay. More likely I will become a kind of slave. They will own me."

Fraser felt cold again, despite the fire. Hiding in caves no longer seemed such a lark. "Why not go to the police?"

"I could, and I would be safe for a while, but eventually, I would be sent back home and these people would be waiting. I need to stay and I need time. There is someone I am here to find in London."

Jonah paused in his tale and Fraser could feel his eyes getting heavy. The crackling fire and the breaking waves were a lullaby. He knew he should head for home and let everyone know he was alive. He pulled his mobile phone from his damp trouser pocket but it wouldn't turn on. His shirt was practically dry, so he put that on and repositioned his socks closer to the fire. Jonah pulled on the old sweatshirt, socks, and boots Fraser had given him.

"Of course," Jonah said, "there is one way I can get to London without being hunted by men looking for money. The reason why I have been hiding in this cave since I washed ashore."

"If people think you're dead," Fraser said, understanding.

"Exactly. If they think I drowned like Solomon, then perhaps they will leave me alone."

"Where are these people?"

"I do not know. It could be that man who was on the beach."

"No, that was Willie McGregor. He's not a people smuggler."

"Does he own a boat?"

"Aye, a big yacht."

"Then he might be."

Fraser whistled through pursed lips at the possibility.

"If I stay here in this cave for a few weeks, then they might think me dead. Then I can leave."

"But the place is full of police now," Fraser said.

"And that is the problem. They will search this cave again, I am sure."

"So who cut open Solomon and stole his diamond?"

"I assume it is one of the men to whom we both owed money."

Fraser gave a small gasp. "But that means there is someone on the island already."

"And now he is looking for me." Jonah patted his stomach and laughed. "All he will find are very small fish bones."

"We have to get you away from here."

"It will not be so easy."

"I have some money. It isn't much but it might buy you the train fare to London."

"I cannot take your money, Fraser."

"You have to. I owe you."

"You owe me nothing."

"You saved my life."

"You have done more than enough already. You have been my friend."

They sat in silence again for a little while and watched the fire and listened to the wind.

Fraser asked, "Who is it you have to find in London?"

"My brother."

"You have a brother in London?"

"I have not seen him for many years. I have an address but I do not know if he is still there."

"Your brother will look after you?"

Jonah grinned. "My brother does not know I am coming." His smile faded. "He has not spoken to me for many years."

"I know how that feels," Fraser said.

"I come from a large family, I have many brothers and sisters. We own a small farm but the money it makes cannot support us all." The man's face grew sad. "My eldest brother and I argued when we were still young. I did things and said things . . . I regret them. He left Lesotho, came to this country for a new life. We lost contact with each other. But now I have heard that he is in trouble and needs help. I have to find him."

"London is a big place."

"That is why I need time. It will be good to see my brother again. He will be a man now. We were just boys when he left. I have to make things right again."

"If you need time, you could stay here for a bit, get a job on one of the lobster boats, get a proper house."

Jonah laughed. "I might miss my cave. But it is a nice thought." He sighed now. "I cannot stay. My brother needs me. Just as Dunny needs you."

"I haven't been much use so far."

"Do not underestimate the bond of brothers."

"I hope you find him."

"First I have to escape the people who are looking for their money."

"Take my money, use that."

Jonah laid a hand gently on Fraser's shoulder. "You are a kind boy, Fraser. But the money I owe is much, much more than a train ticket to London. I will be working for these men for a long time to pay it off. It is better that they think me dead."

They sat on the warm rocks, and Fraser wondered how he could help make this man's hopes come true. He owed him his life and getting him to London would never be repayment for that, but it was a start.

"We need to tell Ben."

"Who is Ben?"

"He's a scientist. That's his boat out there." Fraser looked out at the ocean but all was black. "We need a boat to get off the island."

"You think I should sail to London?"

"You could, I suppose, but Ben will know a better way."

"And this man can be trusted?"

There was no other way of getting Jonah off Nin. "We have to trust somebody."

Jonah sighed and rubbed his chin. Finally, he said, "If you trust this man, then I will trust him also. Will he help?"

"I'm certain he will." Fraser reached for his trousers drying on the rocks. They still felt damp as he put them on. "I better get back. My parents will be worried."

"Yes, you should return home. Talk to this man, ask him for help."

"You won't be much longer in this dark place."

"I am not ungrateful; the cave has served me well. But I will be glad to be leaving it."

Fraser pulled on his socks; they were warm and dry and felt nice around his toes. He slipped on his shoes, was tying the laces when he heard the sound. It was faint at first but quickly grew louder. A deep, repetitive rumble.

Jonah got up and moved to the cave entrance. "What is that?"

Fraser knew exactly what was making the sound. It was a helicopter. Searching for him. He joined Jonah at the mouth of the cave and looked out toward the sea. From the silhouette of an approaching Sea King helicopter, a bright light swept over the water. The helicopter circled the spot where Fraser had begun to struggle. As the light passed over the waves, it picked out the shape of the *Moby Dick* rolling on the ocean. It was still out there, looking for him.

"They do not know you are here," Jonah said.

"They think I'm still swimming out there." Fraser felt a sudden stabbing guilt that he had sat so long by the fire.

Jonah said quietly, "I am sure by now they think that you are drowned."

He imagined his parents' reaction to the news of his death, wondered if there would be tearing of clothes and gnashing of teeth; more likely the repressing of emotions that was the island way. But he was alive, not dead, and that brought its own troubles. He pictured his father's face when he learned of Dunny and the dinghy and skippers full of drink. He saw his mother's expression when she heard about swimming in storms and stroking whales.

"I kind of wish I *was* dead," he said.

TWENTY-FOUR

Hayley stood on the bow of the boat and decided this was her worst day. Ever. She was hypothermia cold, her wet clothes lay in a pile down in the cabin, and she was dressed in the most ridiculous combination of towels, some of her mother's things, and a pair of old oilskins that reeked unpleasantly of sea life. None of the items warmed her in any way. She was also nauseous. The roll and pitch of the boat was relentless and although she hadn't actually vomited yet, she knew it was coming. To top it off, worry was gnawing away at her insides: There was no sign of Fraser Dunbar or Jonah.

At first she had been convinced he had been saved, but she hadn't actually seen him or Jonah reach the shore. Her mom was crying and Ben had a drained, sickly look to him. They thought Fraser had drowned. Dunny stood still and quiet, with an untroubled face, as if he knew everything was fine. She had said nothing to her mom or Ben about Jonah.

Ben had called the coast guard while they sailed in endless circles. It seemed pointless; they couldn't see anything in the dark and the storm, but Ben had said their boat was acting as a marker. She saw the light of the helicopter long before she heard it. When it appeared overhead it was deafening, and as the light swept across their small boat they had to turn their faces to the deck and close their eyes. From the wheelhouse Ben was talking to someone on his phone and she wondered if it was the helicopter pilot.

The helicopter swooped across them once more, the light picking out the tops of surging waves and dark heaving water. The vision frightened her and it was hard to imagine she had been swimming there a little earlier. The thought made her shiver more intensely and her mom put an arm around her shoulder and gave her a vigorous rub. All that did was make the wet oilskin jacket cling to her body.

The helicopter looped around and headed back toward them. It flew over their heads and continued on toward the land. The beam of its light picked out the cliff face, giving the impression of a jagged wall of rock looming large above the small boat. Hayley hadn't realized how near to shore the *Moby Dick* had sailed in its effort to find Fraser. The light focused now on the beach, and the helicopter hovered in the same spot, just a dark shadow against the cliff with its powerful beam and a red blinking light on the tail. The throb of its rotors was earsplitting.

Dunny stood beside the wheelhouse, dressed in a combination of oilskins and ill-fitting clothes that belonged to Ben. He had his eyes focused on the dark sea, ignoring the thundering helicopter overhead. Hayley looked at him and wondered if he truly appreciated the possible result of his reckless dinghy ride.

She clung to the rail and closed her eyes. When she opened them, the helicopter was in the same place, the noise just as loud and the light just as bright. She closed her eyes again but it made the rolling of the boat seem worse and her stomach began to heave in time with the waves. The helicopter was still hovering over the same bit of beach, its light still trained on the same section of sand.

"Has it spotted something?" she shouted to her mom.

"I'm not sure. Maybe."

Hayley could hear a change in her mother's voice, hope instead of despair.

"Is it Fraser?"

"I'm not sure."

She looked back toward the wheelhouse and watched Ben wrestle with the wheel, his eyes not on the sea but on the land. She looked at Dunny, who also stared now at the beach with a gentle smile on his pale, wet face. What did he know to make him smile? Her mother squeezed her shoulder and she looked again at the sand just beyond the breaking waves.

A boy stood on the beach, picked out in the beam of light, waving his arms as he looked up at the helicopter. Fraser.

Hayley's mother exclaimed, "He made it," and began to cry again. Ben blew a horn that resonated above the thump of the helicopter and sounded fit for an ocean liner, not a lobster boat. Dunny clapped his hands together and whooped once at the ocean.

Hayley gripped the rusty rail, leaned out over the bow of the boat, and threw up what seemed like everything she had ever eaten in her life.

TWENTY-FIVE

It was like being abducted by aliens. A bright circle of light surrounded Fraser's body and he had to shut his eyes to narrow slits as he looked up. The whirling blades made the air a solid object, buffeting his body and kicking up sand, which stung like a swarm of wasps. The noise was exactly what he would expect when a large helicopter hovered above his head. He could make out the words COAST GUARD on the side of the aircraft.

He waved again and gave the thumbs-up sign. A crewman leaned out of an open door in the side of the helicopter. Fraser feared the man was about to winch down onto the beach and insist that Fraser come with him. He didn't need rescuing; he had been rescued already.

Fraser turned and pointed down the beach. The lights of the town could be seen in the distance. It wasn't a long walk. Fraser mimed walking and waved again at the hovering helicopter.

"I'm fine," he shouted, knowing there was no chance of his words being heard. He gave one final, exaggerated wave off and then stood beneath the light and the noise and willed the helicopter away. It worked. The light clicked off and the helicopter rose slowly in the air until it was higher than the cliffs. It turned its nose away from the ocean and headed inland. It took a minute before the noise of its rotors faded completely, another minute before Fraser's eyes adjusted again to the dark and he could pick out the cliff face and the sea and the line of the beach heading back toward town.

It suddenly seemed very quiet, despite the gusting wind and the waves crashing against the shore. He looked toward the cave but knew Jonah would be hiding in its depths, out of reach of a curious coast guard. He must have doused the fire too. Out to sea he saw the silhouette of the *Moby Dick* turn slowly away from the coast and head south, back to the harbor. He started to walk fast along the sand and then began to run. His body ached from his swim, but he kept moving, working out in his head what to tell his parents. It was his brother's fault, of course, all of it: It was Dunny who had sailed off in the dinghy, but Dunny would stand silently and watch him get the blame.

By the time he reached the harbor, he had slowed to walking pace, too tired to run. He was also wet again, though not plunge-beneath-the-ocean wet. This was rainy-wind wet, a state of affairs so common in Skulavaig that he barely noticed. As he climbed up onto the harbor wall, he braced himself for bodies rushing toward him: his weeping parents, television camera crews, townspeople jostling for a look, the helicopter crew ready to pose for pictures, his school friends with banners and bunting . . .

The harbor was empty. There were no people, no cars, no boats, no whales. Light spilled from the hotel, but the mission was closed and dark, the ceilidh long finished. He had the curious sensation of being massively relieved and deeply disappointed at the same time. He stood for a few seconds being buffeted by the wind and wondered, once again, if anyone had noticed he was gone.

A voice came from the harbor wall opposite. "I told you to stay in your bed when there's a storm."

Fraser looked across and saw Mr. Wallace, who had just emerged from the harbormaster's office. He wore a bright orange survival suit with a life vest around his neck and he carried a pair of binoculars. Fraser walked down the jetty and they met by the road.

"You were reluctant to ride in the helicopter," the harbormaster said.

Fraser looked at the orange suit and life vest. "Were you in it?"

Mr. Wallace smiled. "No, I'm a sailor, not a flier. I wear this gear when there is a rescue under way. Just in case."

In case of what? Fraser wondered. In case the harbormaster stepped off the jetty when peering through binoculars in the dark?

"I was fine," he said.

"Aye, the pilot said you seemed to be OK. We decided to let you walk back and I would meet you here. The helicopter is needed for more important things than giving daft laddies a ride home."

"I didn't need rescuing. There was no need for a helicopter."

The second part was true at least. If it hadn't been for Jonah, he would have been at the bottom of the sea long before the helicopter arrived.

"Ben McCaig gave the impression you were in serious trouble."

"I was fine."

For a moment Mr. Wallace seemed ready to say something stern but instead his face relaxed and he said, "Let's go up to my office, lad, and get you warm and dry. I need to write a report and you have a few questions to answer. Your dad will be over in a minute. I didnae call him until I knew you were safe. All of you."

"What did you tell him?"

"Not much." The harbormaster gave a grim smile. "I'll leave that pleasure to you."

They walked together up the slope to the Fisherman's Mission. Inside, there was quiet and warmth, and Fraser noticed his ears hurt from the wind and he was shivering from the cold. The room was scattered with the remains of the ceilidh: chairs and tables and empty glasses.

"The old boys will clean up in the morning," Mr. Wallace said.

Together they climbed the stairs to the harbormaster's office, past the pictures of wrecked fishing boats on the wall. Fraser looked at every picture. Now he knew what the crew of each boat must have felt as they succumbed to the waves. His stomach churned at the thought.

They entered the office and Mr. Wallace pointed to the sofa. He went to stand by his large window and Fraser sat down. The room was warm and it made his body tingle.

"Are you wet, lad?"

"I'm OK."

"You must have been soaked when you came out of the water."

"The wind dried me a bit."

"Were you not chilled to the bone?"

"I was cold but I kept moving, warmed myself up."

Fraser doubted if any of this would convince Mr. Wallace, but he couldn't speak of fires and warm caves.

"What happened to your promise, that you wouldnae sail again at night?"

Fraser knew this was coming. He had stood in this very room and made assurances that there would be no more midnight sailings. He glanced at the clock on the wall. It said one minute past midnight.

"This was different. We went out to fetch Dunny."

Mr. Wallace nodded gravely. "Ben McCaig told me that on the phone. Your brother was out there by himself in a dinghy?"

Fraser said quietly with his eyes to the floor, "Aye."

"Why, lad, why this sudden desire from the Dunbar brothers to pit their wits against heavy winds and heavier seas?"

Fraser kept his eyes down and shrugged, wondered himself about his brother's motives. "I can't speak for Dunny. And Dunny won't speak for himself."

The harbormaster shook his head and turned to peer out of the window. Downstairs the door banged and then the stairs creaked as someone ascended slowly. Fraser's heart beat faster and saliva disappeared from his mouth as he awaited the anger and disappointment of his father. With excruciating slowness the office door opened and Willie McGregor appeared. Fraser sighed with relief but knew it was only a temporary reprieve. His father was on his way.

"Where's my boat?" Willie asked.

"It isnae your boat anymore," Mr. Wallace replied, turning from the window.

"I saw the helicopter. And then I saw this lad, back here without the boat he sailed out in." The fisherman moved to the center of the room and stood with his legs slightly apart, as if bracing himself against the swell. "I should never have sold McCaig my boat. The man is not a sailor."

"The boat is fine," Fraser said.

"He sails out in the dark, hunting whales, he says; trying to impress the lassies, more like. The boat's tough but she's old, she willnae take a pounding. And then the boy's back and the boat isnae and there's a bloody great helicopter flying overhead."

"The boat is fine, Mr. McGregor," Fraser repeated forcefully. He looked at the man, with his thick silver hair, his suntan, and the gold chain around his neck. Is that what a people trafficker looked like? He was always around, on the beach, in the mission, on his big yacht. All it took to be a smuggler was a boat, and Willie had a nice one.

"I watched you sail away, lad. So how come you're here and my boat isnae?"

Fraser had no idea how he would explain all this, where he would even start. Certainly with Willie in the room, there would be no talk of castaways. He stared dumbly at the floor until the harbormaster spoke for him.

"Unfortunately, Fraser went for a swim."

Willie McGregor tutted. "I knew someone would fall overboard with McCaig as skipper."

"Not quite." Fraser sighed. "I jumped in."

"Och, away with you. Why would anyone jump into that cold water?"

"I was trying to save Dunny."

"Why was he in the dinghy in the first place?" Mr. Wallace asked.

"He was whale watching."

The harbormaster frowned. "Suddenly, the Sound of Whales is full of whales. Where's your brother now?"

"He's back on the *Moby Dick*."

Willie McGregor shook his head and tutted again. "I ask you, why did McCaig ever give her that ridiculous name? What was wrong with the *Mary Sue*? You dinnae name boats after fictitious leviathans. Is it any wonder there's always a storm?"

"And why did *you* not get back on the boat?" the harbormaster asked.

"I couldn't reach it. I couldn't swim fast enough."

"But you managed to swim to shore?"

"Aye." Fraser could see how close his story was to falling apart. If he was forced to speak of Jonah, Mr. Wallace would report it and Jonah would be found and sent back to Lesotho. Or if Willie McGregor *was* the trafficker, he would get to Jonah first, which would be even worse.

"The ocean knows, you see," Willie continued, still on his previous point. "You cannae just change the name of a boat to something daft about whales and then be surprised when the ocean doesnae like it."

"It's a good name," Fraser said defensively. "Ben studies whales." He had helped him paint the name.

Willie McGregor was not to be persuaded. "Dinnae talk to me about whales. I come from a long line of whalers; it wasnae always lobsters that my family pulled from the sea. There was a time when the McGregors hunted big beasts, up into Arctic waters no less."

The fisherman walked to the window and stood beside Mr. Wallace. He stared out, beyond his own reflection, beyond the dark night.

"My great-grandfather was the last of them. It was a good business to be in, but there were too many boats killing too many whales. My grandfather moved to Skulavaig for the lobsters when the whales grew scarce. In all my years in the boat, I saw only a handful, even out there in the Sound of Whales."

"Well, they're back," Fraser said. "All kinds of whales. That's why Dunny went out in the dinghy tonight. He was having a close encounter with a pod of orcas."

The fisherman shook his head. "I've never seen orcas in these waters."

"We've seen them a couple of times. Ask Ben. He didn't believe us either, but he saw them tonight."

"And exactly how close was this encounter with the whales?" asked Mr. Wallace.

"You couldn't get much closer. He was floating amongst them in his wee dinghy." Fraser took a breath, wondered how this next bit would sound. "He was stroking them as they swam past."

"Och away!" Willie said.

"It sounds incredible, I know, but that's how it was. Dunny has these encounters with whales. He has some kind of connection with them. I can't explain it."

And as he thought about it, and voiced his thoughts, things became clearer, it all began to untangle. He thought about his brother's strange songs on the beach or his clifftop wanderings or the trips they had made on Ben's boat.

"Dunny finds whales. All kinds: orcas, pilot whales, minke, even a sperm whale."

"A sperm whale?" Willie said disbelievingly.

Mr. Wallace nodded. "McCaig did say to me that he had recorded a sperm whale."

"Aye," said Fraser. "And Dunny was there. He's always there."

Fraser stared out of the window, out into the night, crushed by the revelation. Every time he had sailed with Ben and found something interesting, Dunny had been there. He had thought *he* was Ben's lucky charm, but it was Dunny who brought the luck, not him. Why had he never thought of it before? Perhaps he hadn't wanted to. When it was just him and Ben, nothing. When Dunny was on the boat or on the beach or on the clifftop, there were whales.

"Maybe young Dunny has a nose for whales," Mr. Wallace said with a smile. "We've all got our talents, even the quiet ones."

Willie faced Fraser with an excited gleam in his eye. "Tell me exactly what you mean, lad, when you say your brother can find whales."

Fraser wondered how much to tell the man. He promised himself he would say nothing that would lead to Jonah. "Dunny just seems to know where they are," he said carefully. "Like tonight. He knew there were orcas out there, so he took Ben's dinghy and rowed out to see them. He didn't care about the storm."

The fisherman turned back to the window and faced the ocean, but Fraser could see from his reflection in the glass that he was looking inward, hunting a memory.

"In the old days, the old whaling days, there were occasional laddies just like your brother. Laddies who could find whales. They were a rare breed and there was a Gaelic name for them. *Gairmies*. Every whaling boat from Dundee to Newfoundland wanted a *gairmie* on board."

Mr. Wallace nodded. "I've heard of these boys," he said.

Fraser asked, "What did they do?"

"*Gairmies* were strange fellows. Out at sea they could find you a whale, but back on land they were usually a bit peculiar. I remember my grandfather telling me about a laddie that sailed with his father. The lad gained the unfortunate name of Cursing McKendrick. He would shout obscenities at passing womenfolk and curse God in the street. But the town endured his outbursts because he could find a whale. In those days whales meant money. There was a lot more money in whales than in lobsters."

Willie moved back into the center of the room. "I suppose today Cursing McKendrick would be treated for that condition—what do you call it? The one that makes you swear though you cannae help it."

"Tourette's," Fraser said.

"Aye, that's it."

Once again, Fraser felt an obligation to defend his brother. "You're saying Dunny is peculiar?"

"Not peculiar, lad, just . . ." The fisherman searched for a word that wouldn't offend. "Just different."

Fraser knew Willie meant peculiar. "Dunny doesn't speak, that's all."

"Aye. And is that not a bit different?"

After a moment of tense silence, Mr. Wallace asked, "You reckon Dunny's a *gairmie*?"

Fraser scoffed. "It isn't much of a talent, is it? There's no whaling boats sailing out of Scotland these days."

"No," said Willie. "But he would make a better whale scientist than McCaig."

Fraser said nothing, for he could see the truth in it. The thing *he* wanted to be, the job he wanted to do, Dunny could do a whole lot better. It was a galling thought.

"So how do these lads find the whales?" the harbor-master asked.

"That's the very thing, you see," said Willie. "Some folks thought of *gairmies* as whale finders. If you put them in a boat, they would lead you to whales. But that's not really what the word means. There's not an exact translation into English. *Gairmie* doesnae mean 'finder' . . ." The fisherman paused. "It means 'summoner.'"

There followed only silence, save the blowing of the wind. From Willie's disappointed look, it was clear he expected a better response.

"Can you not see the difference?" he said. "With a *gairmie* on board, the boats didnae go to the whales. The whales came to them."

Fraser sat back in the sofa and felt a weariness enclose him along with the sagging cushions. He tried to make sense of Willie McGregor's story. If such a thing as a *gairmie* existed, it meant that Dunny was no longer flawed; now he was gifted in an extraordinary way. Deep down, Fraser had always known that his brother had some kind of gift; he just hadn't expected it to be this one. Perhaps his own interest in whales was just Dunny's gift being channeled through him. Perhaps when Dunny summoned the whales, he summoned his older brother as well.

The harbormaster said, "When the whales came to the *gairmies*, they were being summoned to their deaths."

"Aye," Willie said. "Slaughtered in their thousands. You can see why there's not been sight nor sound of a *gairmie* for over a century."

Fraser got up and looked out of the large window again, toward an ocean almost as devoid of whales as it was of whale summoners. He realized what became of the *gairmies*. They must have recognized what their gift was bringing: the very destruction of the creatures they summoned.

And now Fraser understood the true nature of Dunny's gift. His brother was not always silent; there was not always an absence of communication. Dunny chose not to speak, but in some mysterious fashion, by some method that Fraser would never understand, Dunny had his own way of communing and connecting with other souls. Not people, though. Only whales.

The question now was, why had the whales returned to the Sound of Whales? Had they been summoned by Dunny? If so, to what purpose?

And Fraser saw danger in Dunny's connection with the whales. If his brother was so in tune with the comings and goings of the beach and the ocean, then Willie McGregor might reckon Dunny would know of other visitors to the island. Which, of course, he did.

TWENTY-SIX

The lobster boat eased itself gently through the gap in the stone walls, into the haven of Skulavaig harbor. The wind howled and even in the harbor the boat rolled and dipped as Ben McCaig guided it against the wall. Hayley could see the relief on Ben's face now that he had sailed the *Moby Dick* safely home. Her mother stood slumped against the back wall of the wheelhouse, exhausted from the stress of watching Fraser Dunbar drown and then come back to life. Dunny stood by the wheelhouse window, a vacant look on his face but with a shape to his mouth that might have been a smile.

Hayley too was exhausted; it was only the cold that kept her awake. The adrenaline that had made her jump into the churning ocean and kept her swimming and glued her to the rail as she searched for Fraser, that chemical had slunk back into whichever gland had produced it, leaving a fatigue that hung on her shoulders heavier than the wet oilskins she wore.

"Quite an adventure," Ben said, turning off the engine. The pistons stopped clanging, the propeller ceased turning, and the howl of the wind grew. "Enough for one night," he added.

"Enough for a lifetime," said Sarah.

"I'll tie up the boat," Ben said.

He relinquished his hold on the wheel and opened the door of the wheelhouse. The gust of wind made Hayley shiver.

"Let's get you home," said her mom.

They followed Ben out onto the deck and Sarah helped Dunny out as well. Ben climbed the ladder onto the jetty and tied a large rope around a bollard.

Sarah asked, "You're not sleeping on the boat tonight, are you?"

For a moment Hayley thought her mom was offering him a bunk in the cottage, but then she added, "The sea's too rough. You should take a room in the hotel."

Ben gave a wry smile as if his hopes had been raised for a second and then dashed. "I'll be fine," he said, "I'm too excited to sleep and I've my notes to write up. There's a whole scientific paper here. The boy and the whales."

Sarah nodded, then carefully climbed up onto the sea wall, with Ben holding out a hand to help. Dunny followed and then Hayley. The stone jetty felt strange beneath her feet. It wasn't moving up and down, it didn't twist and drop, she didn't have to brace her legs to balance and hold on to something to stop her collapsing in a heap. She understood now why sailors kissed the solid shore after a long and perilous journey at sea.

"Well, good night, then," her mom said to Ben. "Thanks for what you did."

"It's Fraser and your daughter you should thank," he said. "They're the ones who got wet."

Sarah looked at Hayley and said with a smile, "I'll thank her just as soon as I've killed her."

Ben laughed and said to Hayley, "Go get warm and dry." He climbed back down onto the boat and added, "You too, Dunny."

Sarah said, "I'm sure his parents will pay to replace your dinghy."

"It might wash ashore. Besides, we saw orcas off Nin. That's compensation enough."

"Good night," Sarah said again.

Was that wistfulness in her mother's voice, Hayley wondered. She took a last look at the small boat that had been her savior and almost her undoing. What would the girls on the swim team make of her dip in the ocean?

As Sarah and Dunny arrived at the mission, the door opened and out stepped Dunny's parents. Jessie Dunbar grabbed her youngest son and clasped him tightly. Then she held him at arm's length and Hayley heard her voice carry across the harbor.

"You must never do that again, do you hear me?"

Dunny nodded mutely. His father placed a hand on his head and gave the deepest and most desperate of sighs.

Hayley could only marvel at the understanding and

forgiveness displayed by the Dunbars. She supposed it came from a lifetime of dealing with Dunny. They always seemed calm, collected, almost resigned to their boys' antics, both Dunny's *and* Fraser's. Not *her* mom; she lost it at the slightest disobedience, the smallest mischief. With just cause, Hayley supposed—a lot of rules had been broken in Texas in the past few months.

"Home," Duncan Dunbar said before turning to the open door of the mission and calling, "Come on, Fraser."

Jessie squeezed Sarah's arm. "Thank you," she said sadly.

When Fraser appeared, Jessie bundled her sons together, and with their dad following a step behind, they walked toward their house. Fraser glanced over his shoulder and gave Hayley an apologetic smile.

Hayley waved weakly in return as he disappeared up the road. She wanted to run after him, to grab him, to ask him a hundred questions, to hear his adventures, to hug him tight and tell him how glad she was he had made it. She wanted to do this, but instead she stood there watching him go and wondered what had changed that made her want to hug him rather than hate him.

I am numb with cold, she told herself. *Exhausted. I am not myself.*

Who would be after tonight?

"Bed," she heard her mother say. Nothing sounded finer. Even a bed that was a couch in a drafty cottage in a sodden town on a windswept island. Bed was all she needed. Sleep and warmth and a new day, without whales and storms and Scottish boys. But as she trudged up the path from the harbor, she knew that in this part of the world it would be hard to avoid all three.

TWENTY-SEVEN

Fraser awoke with an ache in every limb. It was Sunday morning and the clock by his bed told him it was just before seven. In Skulavaig the Sabbath was strictly observed and it drove him mad. He didn't have a problem with God as such, he just resented the fact that life ground to a halt, as if his little town wasn't dead enough at the best of times. Still, he had it good compared to some; he only had to attend the morning church service; he was allowed to skip the evening one, although his mother attended both and often took Dunny with her. He was also allowed to watch television, unlike some of his classmates, who had to pack away their game consoles, phones, even their soccer balls. In some parts of the Western Isles a kick-about on a sunny afternoon was barred on the Sabbath.

In Skulavaig the shop would be closed, so would the Fisherman's Mission; even Mr. Wallace would be absent from his window for a few hours. Ships dared not flounder off the west coast of Scotland on a Sunday. Ben usually had the good grace to stay in harbor on the Sabbath, although Fraser had never seen him at church. Ben McCaig was a scientist and for him the wonders of the universe needed no creator. Fraser thought that at least the orca must have been designed by something higher.

He pulled himself up to a sitting position in his bed and tugged his curtain fully open. There had been no punishment for last night's swim; it had been a misguided attempt to help, that was all. He had simply been made to promise that next time he would fetch his father. Not that there would be a next time. Dunny's promise had been to *never ever* do anything like that again, to which he had agreed with a nod. Once more, Fraser felt his brother had escaped lightly, as if not speaking somehow also affected his ability to think, reason, reflect. Fraser knew his brother could do all three just fine. Dunny's actions were rarely random.

Church was not until ten and, despite the escapades of the previous night and the fatigue he felt, he was certain his whole family would go to morning service. It was their usual Sunday routine, but today they would also be giving thanks to God for his safe deliverance. Fraser knew he would give his silent thanks to a brave man stuck in a cave a long way from home. The thought made him even more determined to help Jonah get to London, away from Skulavaig and the men who hunted him.

Fraser pulled his tablet from the floor and switched it on. He did a quick Internet search and discovered that a train left Inverness for London at 6:47 every weekday morning, arriving in London just after three o'clock. He checked the price and nearly dropped his computer when he saw it was one hundred and twenty pounds. He didn't have anything like that amount of money. He had enough for the bus fare to Inverness, but that was about it.

All was not lost, however. Cash wasn't necessary to book a train ticket, just a bank card. He didn't have one, but his mum did. He was allowed to use her debit card number to download music and games; it would work just as well to book a train ticket. In a few days' time his mother would come and find him and demand to know why he had paid ScotRail one hundred and twenty pounds, but that was a problem for later.

Fraser quickly typed in the necessary information and the card number. He booked a one-way ticket from Inverness to London leaving on Tuesday morning. That gave him two days to plan Jonah's escape. When the booking site asked for personal details, he realized he didn't know the man's last name. He had never asked. He typed the name Jonah Dunbar and hit the send button. Jonah was now family.

The next challenge was getting him to Inverness. There was a bus twice a day that went from Kyle of Lochalsh to Inverness. Jonah could get that bus tomorrow and bed down overnight in Inverness somewhere. The problem was getting off the island. Catching the ferry would be foolish; there were men looking for him, someone on the island, maybe even Willie McGregor. There were also police officers in Skulavaig investigating Solomon's death, and they would ask questions of anyone leaving who wasn't a local islander. No, there was only one safe way to the mainland and that was on Ben McCaig's boat.

All he had to do was persuade Ben to help.

Fraser dressed and sneaked quietly from the house. It was seven forty-five and the rest of his family was still sleeping. He walked down the road to the harbor, his feet sliding on asphalt still slick from the previous night's storm. The sun was veiled behind morning mist, but the early light was warm and held the promise of a lovely day. The *Moby Dick* lay becalmed in the harbor; there was not a breath of wind to ripple the water. He needed to talk to Ben but that could wait until later. It wasn't yet eight o'clock—too early for the scientist, even at his best. With a hangover, only a few hours' sleep, and the fact that it was Sunday, Ben wouldn't stir until midday.

Fraser would go and see Jonah first and explain his plan. He had put some cheese and cold meat in a bag with some bread for Jonah's breakfast. He passed Ben's boat, which showed no signs of life, crossed the jetty, and jumped down on to the sand. Some police tape was still stretched across a section of the beach, but the tide had come in and gone out and washed away any evidence of a crime scene. The body had been removed and Fraser still had Ben's knife under his bed. When Jonah was safely on the train to London, he would present it to the nearest available police-man and await the wrath that would surely descend upon his head. But he couldn't think about that now.

Fraser looked along the beach toward the cliffs with the caves. The morning mist hung over the sand and seeped out across the water, so only a small strip of ocean could be seen; then it was just hazy brightness. Much farther up the beach he spotted movement, a figure way ahead. Only for a few seconds and then it was lost in the mist. There was a distinctive gait to the man—it *was* a man—and Fraser recognized his build. He wondered again why Willie McGregor would be wandering the beach. He was beginning to have a bad feeling about the fisherman.

Fraser quickened his pace, hoping to outflank Willie and get to the cave first. It was time to get Jonah on his way. His plan was only half-formed and relied on the good grace of Ben McCaig, but it was the only plan he had and it needed to be set in motion now. He was hurrying up the beach, when out of the mist another figure emerged, sitting on the sand, just above the gently breaking surf.

Dunny!

His brother had again sneaked from the house unheard. Fraser moved toward him and asked gruffly, "What are you doing here?" as if Dunny was going to answer for once.

Dunny turned slowly. His face wore the look that said, *I know things you don't and even if I could speak of them, I wouldn't*. Then he went back to gazing at the mist-shrouded ocean. *If only he would say something*, Fraser thought for the millionth time, or maybe he *was* talking, but just to the whales. A *gairmie*, that was the word: a boy who summoned whales. Fraser searched for a pod of whales that might be chewing the fat with Dunny, having a chin-wag, a natter, some chitchat, a *right good blether*. The sea was flat and empty, but there could have been whales farther out, hidden by the mist.

"After last night's madness, you shouldn't be back out here. Does mum know you've left the house again?"

Dunny faintly shook his head, and Fraser sighed in deep exasperation.

"I can't keep rescuing you when you get into trouble."

His brother gave him a look that said, *You rescued no one.*

Fraser stared out across the water but couldn't see what his brother could see, couldn't hear what his brother could hear.

"Are there whales out there?"

Dunny didn't answer.

"I mean right there, right now? Are you . . . are you talking to them?"

He felt stupid for asking, hated himself for pandering to the idea.

"Get yourself home, Dunny." His brother didn't move. "Get back to the house." He grabbed the boy's arm and pulled him roughly to his feet. Dunny yanked himself free and frowned at Fraser.

Fraser pointed back down the beach. "Home. Now!"

Dunny had always been compliant, had always done what Fraser told him to do. For a moment Fraser thought

this was about to be the great rebellion, the sibling upris-
ing that often came after years of torment and demands.
Instead, Dunny reached into his pocket and pulled out
a limpet shell. He held it out to Fraser.

"I don't have time for this, Dunny."

Dunny pushed the shell into Fraser's hand. Fraser took
a quick look at it. On the surface was written, *Watch*.

"Watch what?"

Dunny shook his head. Did he mean, watch out? Fraser
shoved the shell into his pocket.

"Get yourself home."

Dunny moved away and Fraser started running along the
beach toward the cave. He had to overtake Willie. When
Fraser reached the rocks, he slowed his pace to a fast
walk. The morning mist was thicker here, a proper haar
trapped in place by the high bluff. From the top of the
beach, you could hear the breaking waves but not see them.
The base of the cliff was pockmarked with small caves and
big clefts. Willie could have wandered past or could be
hidden away, watching and waiting. Fraser reached the
cave. He looked around him, but there was nothing to
see in the haar and he hoped he too was hidden from pry-
ing eyes. He scrambled up the fallen rocks to the cave
entrance and stood at the opening, peering into the dark.

Jonah was very careful; there was nothing that would
give him away: no footprints in the sand, no discarded fish
bones. There was only the blackened ring of stones with
the remains of a fire, but every cave had one of those.

A voice from the back said, "Good morning, Fraser."

"Sssshhhh!" said Fraser in reply.

Jonah emerged from the shadows. He gave a bright smile but his eyes were tired. "What is wrong?" he asked quietly.

"That islander we saw the other night, he's back on the beach."

"Is he looking for me?"

"I don't know." Fraser paused, thinking it through. "Willie McGregor has a fine-looking boat. Perhaps he was meant to bring you ashore." Fraser peered carefully around the cave entrance and scanned the beach, but the mist had settled over the sand and nothing could be seen. "It's time to get away from here."

Jonah sighed. "As I said, I have nowhere to go . . ." He gave a wry smile. "And no way of getting there."

"You have." From his pocket Fraser pulled out a twenty-pound note and a slip of paper and handed them to Jonah. "This is how you can get out of this cave and out of Skulavaig."

"What is this?"

"It's your bus fare to Inverness and your train ticket to London."

The man shook his head, looked embarrassed. "I cannot accept this, Fraser. It is too much."

"You saved my life. And you deserve this chance. Let me help. Please."

Jonah considered for a moment, turning over the ticket and the note in his hands. "I will repay you. Someday, I will return to this island and repay you."

"Don't worry about that. We have to get you *off* the island before you can return to it. I brought some food for you too. I have to go to church and then I'll find Ben."

"You are a good friend, Fraser Dunbar."

Jonah tightly grasped Fraser's hand with both of his, seemed to want to say more but choked.

"It isn't wise to stay here," Fraser said. "Not if Willie McGregor is roaming around. He's bound to check the caves." He thought for a moment, then said, "Come on."

He slithered down the rocks outside the cave and waited on the beach for Jonah to join him. The man followed, carrying the bag of food and his bottle of water. Fraser put his finger to his lips. The breaking waves could be heard but not seen; only a thin strip of sand was visible in the mist, and the top of the cliff face disappeared in the haze.

"Where are we going?" Jonah whispered.

"To the castle."

The man laughed. "From a cave to a castle."

"I wouldn't get your hopes up; it isn't much of a palace."

Fraser carefully led the way back along the bottom of the cliff, staying tight to the rock, ready to dive for cover should Willie McGregor emerge from the fog. They reached the steep path up the cliff and began to climb. About halfway to the top they stepped out of the mist into clear air bright with sunshine. Fraser told Jonah to wait while he scurried to the top and searched for signs of life. It was empty except for some flapping gulls that seemed unable to decide whether to land or stay airborne. Fraser went back down for Jonah and together they moved along the clifftop toward the castle.

"I have been up here once," Jonah said. "But I saw your castle and thought someone might be living there."

"Not for a hundred years."

As they walked, Jonah pulled some shells out of his pocket. "I found these on the sand below the cave."

Fraser looked at the scallops, remembered watching his brother drop the shells from the clifftop. "They're probably Dunny's; they're his tell shells."

"There's a word written on one of them. It says, *Come*."

Fraser snorted. "That was yesterday. Maybe he wanted help paddling the dinghy."

"You mock Dunny but he sees things the rest of us do not."

More than you imagine, Fraser thought. He was not yet ready to speak of *gairmies*.

"Do not lose your brother, Fraser," Jonah said. "Like I lost mine."

"You'll find him again."

They approached the ruined building, and two empty windows high up in the walls were like black eyes watching them come closer. The stones of the castle were mottled gray with dark mortar in between. No stone was the same size or shape and it was a marvel of early construction that they all fitted together, creating a smooth facade. The roof of the keep was gone, the upper section collapsing, nothing much remaining of its ornate chimney and the circular windows that had protruded from each top corner.

"That's it," Fraser said, pointing to the dark entrance.

"Are there ghosts?"

"I'm sure of it," he said with a smile.

Jonah looked around him at the shell of the building with light pouring in from high above but the ground level all shadows and dark corners and alcoves. "In Lesotho the spirits of the dead are our guides through this earthly world. We do not fear them."

"It's not the ghosts you have to worry about. Keep an eye open for anyone snooping around. There is a good hiding place over here if you need one." Fraser crossed the rough floor and pointed to a narrow crack in the wall. "It's a bit of a squeeze, but get in there and there's a space between the two walls. You can follow it round and there's a window high up to climb out of in an emergency. But just keep out of sight and you will be fine. I'll be back as soon as I can."

"Thank you again."

"You'll be fine," Fraser repeated, trying to convince himself that this plan might work.

"Of course I will. Look at me." Jonah spread his long arms wide. "I am a king in his castle."

The image that Fraser saw as he turned to leave was far from regal; there were no robes or crown or court. Just a tired man far from home who needed the help of an island boy to finish his long, long journey.

TWENTY-EIGHT

Hayley pulled her quilt up to her chin, wallowing in the warmth, savoring the sleepiness. Previously this bed settee, as the natives called it, had been uncomfortable, the room drafty, the cottage cold and creaking, but now it was the coziest place in the world and Hayley had no intention of going anywhere today. Not unless her mom told her they were off to catch the ferry that would take them to the bus that would carry them to the train that would take them to the airport to catch a flight back to civilization. Beneath the duvet she curled her toes and hunkered down.

From the bedroom she heard the sound of her mother's voice. She was talking on the phone.

"I know it's the middle of the night," her mom said.

She was talking with someone back in the States.

"I'm close . . . yeah, I'm sure of it . . . there's someone on the island . . . I'm checking boat registrations . . . it's a big yacht . . ."

Her mom was investigating. Hayley recognized the

tone of voice: blunt, persistent, demanding. But what was she investigating?

"It's here . . . I just need to probe a bit deeper . . ."

Hayley felt herself drift deliciously off to sleep again.

"Call it what you like, it's people trafficking, pure and simple . . ."

Hayley was awake. She sat up in bed, listened again, but now there was silence. The bedroom door opened and her mom appeared.

"You're up," Sarah said. "How do you feel?"

Hayley collapsed back onto the mattress. "Tired."

"Well, of course you're tired. Very nearly drowning has that effect. It tires you out."

Hayley stared at the ceiling. "I know, Mom, I've said I'm sorry."

"And this is a girl who wanted to quit the swim team last semester."

"OK, I get it."

Sarah went back into her bedroom and Hayley sat up again. Her mom was investigating people trafficking. What did she know about the individuals involved? Who did she suspect? Did she know already that Jonah was on the island?

When her mom reappeared, Hayley asked, "Who were you talking to on the phone?"

Sarah gave her a quizzical look. "Just one of my sources back in the States. Why?"

"No reason." There was a pause as Sarah collected some of her things. "You're investigating people trafficking?" Hayley asked.

"You were listening?"

"They're thin walls."

"I'm investigating people trafficking and forced migration and . . . and you know all this already."

"Why here? Why this island?"

Sarah pondered for a moment, then said, "Get dressed and I'll show you."

Twenty minutes later, Hayley was dressed and following her mother along the coast road through Skulavaig. A low wall ran above a beach that was different this side of the harbor. There was no sand here, just rocks and shingle and breaking waves that made a harsher sound, as if the ocean had to try harder to wash up the pebbles. The road was quiet, the town was quiet, though there were people on the move, heading to church.

"Where are we going, Mom?" she asked one more time. Her mom had been deliberately evasive.

"We're almost there."

The coastal road curved around, houses on one side, the sea on the other. Hayley saw a large church building that faced the ocean. It was made of red stone like the cliffs and had a tall steeple with a cross at the top.

"Oh, you're kidding me," she said. "We're going to *church*?"

"We've a lot to be thankful for. And we need a little guidance. But that's not why we're here."

At the church, Hayley read the sign on the wall: CHAPEL OF ST. NINIAN. "But we're Southern Baptist, we're not Catholic."

They walked up the steps to the door.

"The service doesn't begin for half an hour. There's something I want to show you."

"Have you been here before?" Hayley asked.

"I have. And keep your voice down."

The foyer of the church was chilly and their footsteps rang on the stone floor. Candles flickered and there was the sweet smell of incense. In the nave the floor was tiled in an intricate pattern, with pillars on either side and pews that ran the length of the long hall. Sarah walked down the nave and Hayley followed, noticed several people sitting with heads bowed and a few with faces raised, admiring their surroundings. At the end of the nave were steps up to the chancel, with a table and pulpit for the priest. And on the far wall, impossible to miss, was a large colorful mural. A man with robes and a beard stood holding a cross to the sky. Behind him was green land and blue sea, and above his head swooped a mighty eagle. It was all gilded in gold so that it sparkled in the candlelight.

"Who is that?" Hayley asked.

"That is St. Ninian. The island of Nin is named after him."

"And who was St. Ninian?"

"He was a missionary in the fifth century who helped convert Scotland to Christianity. He was supposed to possess special powers. Today people come here on a pilgrimage, especially if they're ill or dying. Ninian was reputed to have the power to heal."

Hayley felt something jolt in her stomach, like a lung had dropped or a kidney exploded. "Oh, God, Mom, what's wrong with you? Is that why we're here?"

Sarah laughed and then said, "No, that's not why we're here. I'm fine." She saw Hayley's panicked look. "Seriously, I'm fine. I'm sorry, I didn't mean to imply that I needed healing."

Hayley wasn't completely convinced. "So why *are* we here?"

Sarah took a seat on a pew with a red cushion.

Hayley sat down beside her, asked again, "Why are we here, Mom?"

"I wanted to show you the mural."

"I meant, why are we here on this island? It can't only be to get away from Dad. There are a million secluded places on the planet we could have gone, places with hot tubs and hot boys and cable."

"I told you, I'm researching my book."

"About people trafficking?"

"That's part of it."

"So why here?" Hayley was fishing but she had to do it carefully. "Why is Nin so interesting?"

"My book is about people who leave their home and

travel on long journeys to distant lands where they are not made welcome."

"Illegal aliens, you mean?"

"Yes, though my book is more about what it means to be alien, not just what it means to be illegal. There are hundreds of thousands of people right now who are being trafficked around the world. My book is their story."

Hayley thought of Jonah in his cave, wondered, did her mom know he was coming?

Sarah continued, "One of my contacts during his journey reported seeing a picture on a wall of a saint and an eagle. It took me a while but I finally tracked it down." Sarah nodded at the mural. "As strange as it seems, one of the journeys to England passes through Skulavaig."

But to Hayley it didn't seem strange, not now that she had met Jonah, a man on a similar journey. There was a connection here, this was not coincidence, and Hayley imagined how excited her mom would be to actually meet and talk to someone in the process of journeying, a man who was almost there. And yet she had made a promise to Jonah to tell no one of his presence on the island.

Sarah said, "I'm here to discover why this island is involved in people trafficking. And maybe, if we know more about it, we can do something about it."

They said nothing for a few moments. Hayley heard true silence for the first time in a long while. No creaking roof beams, no breaking waves, no wind, no seagulls. She thought of Dunny.

And she tried to make sense of all that her mother had told her. Her mother would be investigating people trafficking not for drama and scandal but because she could change things for the good. That was how her mom operated; she wrote about issues where she could change things, make a difference.

How, then, could she not tell her mom of another man come to Nin, this one close by, this one still journeying. But she had made a promise to Jonah.

What to do?

Hayley's head hurt from thinking about it.

What to tell?

"Let's go," her mom said. "Before the service begins."

The church was filling up with worshippers. Hayley followed her mom back down the nave and they passed the Dunbar family sitting on a pew. Her mom said hello and Hayley caught Fraser's look of astonishment. She avoided eye contact, worried her face might reveal her dilemma. They went out through the foyer and squinted in the bright sunlight as they left the church.

Her mom looked at the shimmering ocean. "It's so peaceful and pretty compared to last night."

"Every day is like this. It's a storm, then sun, then a storm, then sun."

"Shall we go for a walk?"

"I suppose."

"Which way?"

Hayley looked to her right. The coastal road led to the marina and she had never been to that part of the island. She looked left. The road wound back to the beach and cliffs and there, somewhere, was Jonah with his story. Her mom had never been to *that* part of the island.

"Which way, honey?" her mom repeated.

Hayley stared at the ocean and gazed at the sky and tried to decide.

TWENTY-NINE

The voice of the priest echoed around the church as Fraser shifted again on the pew, trying to get comfortable. It was hard enough to concentrate on the sermon at the best of times. Now he had the vision of Hayley Risso coming down the aisle with a troubled look and her eyes to the floor. Why had she been in church and what was she up to now?

He couldn't answer those questions stuck in here. And he still had to find Ben and arrange Jonah's escape. None of that was going to happen if the priest didn't bring his interminable sermon to an end. Fraser looked at his family sitting to his left. His mum was listening intently and nodding occasionally. His dad was nodding as well, but only when his eyelids closed and he jerked himself awake. Dunny sat with his head cocked slightly, his bottom lip jutting, as if he was calculating some great mathematical equation in his head.

What was he thinking? What did he know? What did the whales know? What were the whales telling Dunny?

Fraser smiled at the thought and suddenly the congregation were on their feet and his mother was pulling him up for the closing prayer. At last. When the service was finished, the parishioners moved as one for the exit, but she lingered for a chat with the priest, holding on to Dunny's arm. Fraser's dad sighed and sat back down.

"I'll be back for lunch," Fraser said to his mum, then darted for the door.

"Come back, please," he heard his mother say, along with a stern, "Fraser," from his dad. He pretended not to hear, skipped in front of a couple of stragglers and fell out of the door into the sunlight. He had escaped.

He jogged down the narrow streets of Skulavaig, his footsteps echoing on the empty road. On a Sunday morning, there was a slow movement of people to and from church but there was no other reason to stray from your home. Everything was shut, the ferry didn't run, cars stayed parked, even the nine-hole golf course was closed. Fraser had always thought this madness; everywhere else in the world, golf courses were busiest on a Sunday.

When he reached the harbor he discovered to his dismay that the *Moby Dick* was gone. He stood and stared at the empty water enclosed by the old stones, a floating rainbow of oil the only indication that Ben had been here. Ben was the most important part of his plan to help Jonah and without him the plan couldn't get started.

"Gone to the marina," said a voice from behind him.

Fraser turned to see one of the old fishermen standing by

the mission, waiting for it to open. Even the mission was supposed to stay shut on a Sunday, but a blind eye was turned to the few who sneaked in for a game of darts and a sly dram.

"Thanks," Fraser said and went back up to the road. He glanced at his house, thought that perhaps he wouldn't be home for lunch after all.

The marina was a twenty-minute walk along the coast road. Fraser half walked, half jogged past the nice houses that looked over the water. He saw a couple of policemen by front doors, questioning the islanders. It made him quicken his pace. The houses petered out and the road narrowed until it was a single track. The land was boggy and speckled with small pools of water. Long gashes in the ground were the scars of peat cutting. Small, white-washed cottages lay scattered across the bleak landscape.

A couple of cars passed him. Visitors to the island; locals would have stopped and offered him a ride. He reached an old sign that said MARINA and followed the rough road down the hill to the water. In a small bay were a series of long, metal jetties. A solitary building, marked MARINE CHANDLER, stood at the side. Four yachts were tied up against the jetties, including Willie McGregor's big one, and the *Moby Dick* nudged the far end of the farthest pier. The boat chandler was one of the few businesses that opened on a Sunday, along with the hotel and the churches, but this morning, there was no sign of life.

Fraser walked down the jetty, his feet clanging on the

metal, the sound echoing around the sheltered bay. Ben appeared from the cabin of the *Moby Dick* as Fraser reached the boat.

"What are you doing here?" he asked, looking at the shore as if expecting to see parents or American girls or harbormasters.

"I need to speak to you."

"You've walked all the way from town just to speak to me. Can it not wait?"

"No, not really."

Ben stood by the gunwale but didn't invite Fraser aboard.

"After last night I thought you'd have had your fill of boats and oceans. You should be in your bed recovering."

"I don't have time for that. This is important."

"Well, I don't have time either. I'm busy."

"Doing what?"

"Things. I'm doing things. None of your business."

Fraser watched the scientist sigh and squeeze his forehead, reckoned it was a hangover making Ben grumpy. It couldn't be him personally, not now, not anymore, not when there had been orcas. "I need your help," he said.

Ben sighed again, said, "Come on board."

Fraser hopped onto the deck, stood there hesitantly, wondered how to begin.

"What kind of help?" Ben asked.

"I need your help to take a friend of mine to the mainland."

"Why?"

"Because there's no other way of getting there."

"Are you and Hayley eloping?"

"It's nothing like that! This is serious. My friend needs to get off the island without anyone seeing him."

"And why is that?"

Fraser took in a large gulp of air and then came out with it. "His name is Jonah. He's from Africa. He's here illegally. He saved my life and I promised to help him. He's heading for London but he needs to get off the island. There are people looking for him. I thought you could take him in your boat."

He took another gulp and they stood in silence as Ben digested the information.

Eventually, Ben said, "Is he connected to the dead guy?"

"Aye, they knew each other."

The stunned look on Ben's face became a frown.

"Was it your friend who stole my knife?"

"I don't know. I don't think so. Maybe."

"And you want me to help him?"

"I promised. He saved my life."

"How?"

"Last night. He pulled me from the ocean."

"Jesus. I thought you swam to shore."

"No. I would have drowned. And we wouldn't be standing here this morning. I'd be dead and you'd be in jail, drunk in charge of a boat."

"Bloody hell." Ben contemplated the ocean. "How long have you known about this man?"

"A few days. Since he swam to shore."

"And you didn't think to tell me."

"It wasn't my place to tell."

"Who else knows about him?"

"Just Hayley. And Dunny."

"And where is he now?"

"In the castle on the cliff."

Ben gave a wry laugh. "Bloody hell."

"He was in one of the caves at first but there are folk snooping around, so I thought he best move somewhere else."

"Who's snooping?"

"Willie McGregor, for one. I don't trust the man, he's up to something."

"Willie is always up to something. Him and that bloody harbormaster. Thick as thieves, those two."

Fraser gave a slight gasp at the thought. Was it possible that Mr. Wallace was also involved, that people trafficking off the west coast of Scotland was an inside job? What better cover for smuggling in people than a harbormaster keeping watch from his window and seeing nothing.

"Why does he want to go to London?"

"He has a brother there. They had a falling-out ages ago. Now his brother's in trouble and he's trying to help."

"That sounds like a sob story to me."

"No, he's telling the truth."

"You know him better than me."

Fraser knew hardly anything, but that didn't matter. "Will you help?"

Ben pondered for a moment, frowned slightly, but then smiled and shrugged. "Sure, why not? I owe you one. I never believed you about the orcas."

Fraser felt a giant weight lift instantly from his shoulders. With Ben helping, he could keep his promise. "Thank you, Ben. But I can't bring him here, he'll be seen. The harbor is too public as well. There are policemen wandering around."

Ben pondered again, said, "There's an old jetty just beyond the castle. You could bring him there."

"Can we sail this afternoon?"

"Best wait until tomorrow. That will give us a full day to get there and back. I'll be at the jetty in an hour and your African friend can bunk down on the boat tonight."

"That would be brilliant." Fraser gave a deep sigh. The plan was coming together.

All they had to do was avoid the bad guys, whoever they were, for one more day.

THIRTY

"This is spectacular," Sarah said as they walked along the cliff path. She was looking out across the water as it glittered in the sunlight. "You should have brought me up here earlier."

"Usually I'm trying to stop the wind from blowing me over the edge."

Hayley felt sick. This was a big act of betrayal and she had barely convinced herself she was doing the right thing.

Jonah wasn't in his cave, so they had climbed up here. Ahead was the castle, its stones glowing in ruined majesty. Perched on the cliff, spotlit by the sun, it was like a picture from a fairy tale, and if a dragon had flown from the hole in the roof, it wouldn't have seemed odd.

"Impressive," Sarah said as they approached.

"It's creepy."

"That's what I like about it."

As they reached the old walls, Hayley moved cautiously to the entrance and peered inside. After the bright sunlight it took a few moments for her eyes to adjust. There was a damp smell to the place and a shadowy gloom that made the heart beat a little faster. The walls were rough stone, the floor just rubble and hard, packed earth. The grandeur of torches and tapestries and ornate fireplaces was long gone. Now it was cobwebs and bird nests and moss.

Hayley edged deeper into the ruin. "Jonah?"

The sound startled a bird that flittered noisily out through the roof space and made her jump.

"Are you OK, honey?" asked her mom from the doorway.

"Yes, fine." Hayley took a breath to settle her nerves. "Jonah," she called again, this time bolder. "It's Hayley. Are you here?" She moved farther into the room. The center of the building was brighter than the shadowy edges, light creeping down from above.

"You promised you would tell no one," came a voice from the walls.

Hayley heard her mother give a yelp of fright.

"My mom can help you, Jonah."

Jonah stayed silent and hidden.

"Jonah, my name is Sarah Risso. I'm Hayley's mom. It's only she and I, no one else is here." They waited for a reply but when none came, Sarah pressed on. "I'm a writer and I am writing a book about people on a journey. About people searching for a better life. About people far from home. I'm writing a book about you."

Another moment and then suddenly Jonah was there, as if a shadow became solid and walked. This time both Hayley and her mom jumped in fright.

"Let us talk outside where it is light," he said.

Hayley led the way out into the sunlight and Jonah seemed like a man released from a dungeon after many years. He looked exhausted and dirty and troubled. He blinked in the light and took deep breaths that seemed to take a great deal of effort.

"I'm sorry if I broke your trust," Hayley said.

"You are only a child," he said. "I have forgotten that. Fraser is only a boy."

Sarah was looking at the man in wonder, as if she had only half believed her daughter and was now amazed that a large, disheveled man stood before her. "I will protect your identity," she said. "And I know people who can help."

"I only need to get to London, that is all."

"Can I ask why?"

Jonah contemplated this for a moment, perhaps not sure himself any longer.

"I will tell you my story," he said at last. "The world needs to know why we risk so much and come so far. And in return, when I get to London, you can help me find someone."

Sarah nodded. "All right," she said.

Jonah moved to a low wall beside the ancient keep and sat on top of the ragged stones. Sarah took a seat beside him, and Hayley sat on the grass, the sun on her face. She had been in the castle only a minute, yet the warmth and the light felt like unexpected gifts. Jonah had been living

232

in the dark for days now and she understood the weariness that seemed to cling to him tighter than Fraser's ill-fitting sweatshirt.

"I have a brother in London who I have not seen for many, many years. I pray that he is still alive. I have to find him and help him. In what way I do not yet know. That is why I am here."

Hayley asked, "Why did you not get on a plane and fly here?"

"I tried," said Jonah. "But the British government refused me a visa to enter the country. They said I would not return here. So I have come . . ." Jonah gave a grim smile. ". . . by less orthodox means."

"So what now?" Sarah asked.

"Now I wait. Fraser has a plan."

Hayley saw her mother suddenly look uneasy and shake her head slightly. "Fraser is just a boy. You said so yourself."

"Yes, but he has a plan and no one else does. If I could do something myself, I would, but I am on an island and cannot get off it without help."

"And what about the people who brought you here?"

"I wish them to think I drowned."

Sarah looked at her watch, took out her phone and swiped a couple of times, sat thinking for a moment, then put her phone away.

"Sit tight for now, Jonah," she said. "I will try to help. Do not do anything impulsive and don't let Fraser talk you into anything rash. Let *me* try to help."

For a moment Jonah said nothing, rubbed his stubble-covered chin with his hand. He gave the slightest of shrugs and said, "OK."

Hayley peered into the man's eyes and thought she recognized a look. It was the one her dad gave when telling her only what he thought she wanted to hear. Was Jonah simply humoring her mom or did he really trust her? Why would he trust any of them? Hayley thought, *He was right not to trust me.*

"I'll come back later when I know more," Sarah said.

"It is a beautiful day," Jonah said. "I will sit in the sun and think of my brother."

"Don't get caught."

"It is not a worry. I have my lookout."

Jonah looked behind him at the castle and Hayley followed his gaze up to a rectangular hole in the wall that was once a window. For a second, there was a face there, then it was gone and just black emptiness remained. But she knew who she had seen.

"He follows me sometimes or I see him watching. He never comes close but he will warn me if someone approaches. He is a very good shell thrower."

"Dunny is everywhere," Hayley said.

Jonah laughed and offered his empty hands. "And nowhere all at once."

She scanned the castle walls, but there was no sign of Dunny. Or his brother. They were just boys, she reminded herself. And she was just a girl. Her mom could do things, could fix things that were beyond her and the Dunbar boys. That's what she would tell Fraser when he learned of her treachery. She pictured his broken face and hoped she was back in America before that ever happened.

THIRTY-ONE

From his vantage point high on a collapsing wall, Fraser watched the receding figures of Hayley and her mum. He waited until they were out of sight before he carefully climbed down, in the process dislodging a large stone that tumbled to the ground and broke into pieces.

"Are you still throwing rocks?" Jonah asked from below.

"Sorry," Fraser said, jumping down. He looked at the smashed stone, looked at many more scattered across the floor, wondered how much of the castle he and Dunny had destroyed in their playing through the years.

"We have to go," he said.

Jonah didn't move, tried to smile but it was more a grimace. "The girl's mother said she could help."

"No." *His* was the only plan that could work. "They're not to be trusted."

Fraser had returned from the marina and headed straight for the castle. He had spotted Sarah Risso from a distance, talking with Jonah, had feared policemen and coast guards and customs men, but there had only been Hayley. He had sneaked into the castle from the rear, had listened from the shadows as Jonah told his tale. He had also heard Sarah Risso's offer of assistance and had bristled at the implication that he was just a boy, not old enough to have ideas, not old enough to help.

"The lady suggested I wait here," Jonah said.

"Aye, well, the lady is probably away to fetch a policeman."

"Would she do that?"

"How do we know?"

"*Hayley* would not do that."

"Hayley is a traitor and a turncoat," Fraser spat. "She told her mum about you when she promised she wouldn't. Her word means nothing now."

The scale of Hayley's betrayal filled Fraser with a raging despair. There had been several occasions when he had badly wanted to tell his dad—when he first discovered Jonah, when he found the dead body, when he was pulled half-drowned from the ocean—but he had always resisted, for his new friend's sake. Now Hayley had told her mum, just like that. He was done now with American girls and their soft lips and broken promises. He would do this alone.

Kind of alone.

"Dunny, come on," he shouted. "I know you're here and I know you can hear me, so show yourself. Now!"

Fraser heard a scraping in the shadows, a shifting of stones, and he knew that Dunny was climbing out of whatever hole he was hiding in. When he appeared, silhouetted in the doorway, some of the anger and frustration Fraser felt toward Dunny began to crumble like the old stones that surrounded them. His brother was the one person he could trust.

"Let's go, Dunny. We need to get Jonah somewhere safe."

Fraser turned to Jonah.

"You can bide tonight in Ben McCaig's boat; you'll be safe there, and tomorrow he'll take you to the mainland. Then it's a bus to Inverness and the train to London."

"The lady was going to help me find my brother," Jonah said.

"She can still do that, once you're safe in London."

Fraser started to walk fast along the cliff path, checked that Jonah was following. This was going to work, he was going to make it happen, just as he had promised days before when he first encountered a shipwrecked man in a cave.

Something whacked off the back of his neck and sent him stumbling onto his knees. He clutched his neck and felt it sting, looked at the ground and saw a scallop shell lying there. He turned. Behind him Dunny was standing, his arms by his side, his face scrunched up, trying, it seemed, not to cry.

Fraser lifted himself to his feet, rubbed his neck, and checked his fingers for blood, but there was none. "What the hell are you playing at, Dunny?"

His brother gave a vigorous shake of his head.

Fraser moved at speed back down the trail, past an astonished Jonah. "What is your problem, Dunny?" His brother gave a look of such pleading despair and shook his head again. "Speak to me, Dunny." He took ahold of Dunny's shoulder and shook it. Fraser was tired of the silence and the shells and the sorrow. "Enough of this *nonsense*. You can speak fine, you just choose not to. If there is something bothering you, then tell me what it is. I want to hear it. From your lips. In words."

Fraser folded his arms and stood there on the path in the shadow of the castle, looking at Dunny, waiting. Dunny lifted his hands and squeezed his fingers into his palms, screwed up his face as if he was trying to force out a word, trying to express something important. His breaths were irregular, his dark eyes filled with tears now.

"Tell me, Dunny."

His brother's head dropped onto his chest, his arms fell to his sides, he stood there for a moment, defeated, and then he turned and ran.

"Let's get going, Jonah," Fraser said. He didn't have time to psychoanalyze his brother.

"Dunny wants to tell you something, I think."

"Then all he has to do is open his mouth and speak." Fraser sensed Jonah's disapproval. "There's an old wooden jetty on the other side of the cliffs. Ben said he can get his boat alongside. We can't go back to town; policemen are going door-to-door, asking about Solomon, and the harbormaster might be watching from his window."

At the end of the clifftop, there was no path down, just a series of steps and rocky crags.

"It's a bit of a climb," Fraser said.

"Lesotho is mountain country. I can climb."

Together they carefully made their way down the sandstone bluff, in some places clinging to the rock face by their fingertips and stretching a leg down to the next ridge. They helped each other, until they both jumped the last bit onto the sand.

Fraser wiped his forehead, sand grains sticking to sweat. "That was fun."

"I think you have a little Sotho in you. You are welcome among my people."

"Thanks. And you can be an honorary member of my clan, the clan Dunbar." Fraser smiled and added, "You would look good in a kilt."

They walked along the beach and the fine white sand began to be pockmarked with pebbles and large slabs of red rock.

"Look over there," Fraser said, pointing to the top of the beach. "There's Ben's dinghy. It must have washed ashore."

"Can we use it?"

"We don't need to. Ben and I can collect it later."

As the coastline curved, the last of the cliffs faded to flat. Around the bend of the beach was a wooden jetty, rotten and broken in places, with gaps between timbers that were covered in sea moss and barnacles. At the far end was the *Moby Dick*, bobbing gently in a calm sea. Ben was sitting in the stern with his legs over the side, leaning back, eyes closed, enjoying the sunshine.

"There it is," Fraser said. "Your ferryboat to freedom."

"I have been on one of those before," Jonah said. "It did not end well." He stared for a few seconds at the lobster boat. "This small boat does not seem to be in good condition."

"Aye, she's old. But wait until you see her ride a wave."

"I truly hope I do not have to."

Fraser looked up and down the beach. They were doing this in broad daylight and anyone could have been watching, but it was a risk they had to take. No guts, no glory, he told himself.

Ben saw them coming and stood up to greet them. At the jetty, Fraser went first, pulling himself up onto the old timbers. They creaked and the whole structure swayed slightly, but he made it to the end and jumped the gap onto the boat. Jonah followed, arms stretched out like a tightrope walker. When he reached the boat, Ben offered a hand and pulled him aboard.

"You must be Jonah," he said, shaking his hand.

"I am." Jonah nodded slightly. "And you are Ben and I thank you for your help."

"It's not a problem. I owe Fraser one; he introduced me to some orcas."

"I have seen the whales myself. There are many things about Scotland I will never forget and the whales are one of them. I would stay if I could, but now it is time to go."

"Are you berthing here tonight?" Fraser asked Ben.

"No, I'll moor in the harbor as usual. If your friend stays below, it'll be fine. I'll take him to the mainland in the morning. I'll stick to the usual routine, sail about ten once the ferry's been."

"Can I come?"

"Of course you can."

Ben moved to the wheelhouse to start the engine, and Fraser led Jonah through the deck hatch down to the cabin below. The small space was little more than a bunk and a narrow galley with an opening that led through to the engine. The wood of the cabin was warping, the metal struts were rusting, and it smelled of fish, despite repeated scrubbing.

Jonah sat on the bed and Fraser sat on the floor. The engine began clanking and the boat began to move.

"You have your train ticket and your money for the bus and food," Fraser said, his voice loud against the pistons. "Is there anything else you need?"

"You have supplied more than enough. I just need to get to London."

Fraser knew it was just a short ride to the harbor, not like tomorrow, when they would have to cross the Sound of Whales and then sail back, one crewman lighter. Jonah's island story was drawing to a conclusion, but there was still much that could go wrong. At least now he shared the burden with Ben McCaig, and Ben knew how to get out of a fierce storm or a tight fix.

They reached the harbor and the pitch of the engine changed and the boat slowed.

"I'll see you in the morning," Fraser said.

"Thank you, my young friend."

Fraser pushed open the cabin hatch and clambered onto the deck, had a look to see if anyone was watching but there was no one around and nothing moved. Sunday in Skulavaig. He sighed as he realized that after tomorrow his town, his island, his life returned to normal. Ben would still have his boat and Hayley would still be in the cottage, but the excitement would be over. Until, at least, the next storm or the next tide brought something else his way.

THIRTY-TWO

Hayley pushed open the door of her mother's room and saw that it was empty. She checked the bathroom and small kitchen but there was no one there, and in this small cottage, that was it. Her mom wasn't home.

Monday morning was sunny and warm and busy. There was the noise of traffic, just a few cars, competing with the shrill squawk of the gulls. There were people moving around, there were boats out in the sound, there was life again. She would Skype some friends later if she could get a connection, but it was the middle of the night right now in Texas. She pictured her house sitting empty in the dark, imagined opening her bedroom window and feeling the sticky air and hearing the cicadas chirping.

Hayley wondered where her mom had gone. There were no messages on her phone, and the clock said just after nine. From the window she could see Fraser's house. It filled her with dread, but at some point she would have to tell him that she had blabbed.

She washed and dressed and left the cottage, wandered along to the other harbor where the ferry docked. Already a line of cars had formed to depart the island and she noticed the two police cars among them. The investigation was at an end and she wondered if they had discovered anything about the dead man. It was strange and exciting that *she* knew almost everything. Her mom wasn't in the café, so she strolled back to the old harbor, in no hurry, for she had nowhere to be and all the time in the world to get there. She knew she was delaying her encounter with Fraser.

Where was her mom? She had said she was going to help Jonah. What was her plan? She'd been vague, maybe deliberately. And what were Fraser's intentions?

As she turned the corner at the top of the harbor, the picture became a little clearer, for there was her mother and she was talking to Willie McGregor. They both disappeared inside the Fisherman's Mission. And upstairs was the harbormaster's office!

She gave a giant gasp as her stomach dropped. Was this how her mom intended to help, by turning Jonah in? And did she have any idea that Willie was probably the people trafficker? Hayley walked quickly toward the mission, wondered whether to fetch Fraser or warn Jonah, but she knew nothing for certain.

She pulled open the door and looked inside. The room was empty. She went in and stood at the bottom of the stairs that led up to Mr. Wallace's office. There were voices coming from above, including her mom's. Hayley began to climb the stairs, but these were the noisiest stairs ever; on only the second step, there was a loud creak that made her halt and hold her breath. The talking continued, so she resumed her ascent, placing her fingers on the steps and creeping up with excruciating slowness. Near the top the voices became more distinct and she paused and listened.

"I know this, Sarah," said the harbormaster. "We know exactly what's going on; we just cannae prove it."

"Not yet anyway," added another voice, which was Willie McGregor's.

"That puts me in a bit of a dilemma." This was her mom talking. "I'm not prepared to divulge too much, but obviously I want to help."

"Tell us where he is, lass," said Mr. Wallace.

Hayley's groan was as loud as the creak of the stairs but she didn't care. Her mother had given up Jonah, had turned him in, and everyone—Fraser, Dunny, Ben, and Jonah himself—would blame her. She was the one who had told her mom and had taken her to the hiding spot. It was her betrayal.

Hayley marched up the remaining stairs and burst into the room, to the obvious surprise of the three adults sitting there. Sarah stood up and was about to say something, but Hayley spoke first.

"You promised you wouldn't tell."

Her mom offered a sympathetic smile. "So did you, honey."

"That was different. I told *you*."

"And you must have known that I would have to do something about it. The man can't live in a cave indefinitely."

Sarah turned to Mr. Wallace and Willie McGregor. "He's no longer in the cave, in case you're wondering."

"The caves," said Willie. "Dammit, I checked the caves."

"But you promised to help him," Hayley said.

"And I am. I'm negotiating with the appropriate authorities about what best can be done for our friend. It has to be done properly, through the proper channels."

"But Fraser has a plan."

"Hayley, honey, Fraser is just a boy. And you are just a girl. I love how you were trying to help, but this is beyond what you guys can do."

"But they'll send him back to Lesotho."

"Not necessarily. Jonah has information that could be of use to the authorities. That will help him."

"He's an African from Lesotho called Jonah," said Willie McGregor.

"It doesn't matter if you know his name," said Sarah. "Or where he's from."

"Of course it does," exclaimed Hayley. "He's one of the men looking for Jonah. He's one of the people traffickers."

Willie McGregor laughed. "Dinnae be daft, lass."

"Jonah hoped people thought he was dead, like Solomon, and he would be left alone. Now they'll be after him for his money."

"And who is Solomon?" asked the harbormaster.

"The dead man on the beach."

"The lad had a name. And you knew all along?"

"Not at the start. Not when I first told you."

"I'm not a people trafficker, lassie," said Willie.

"But you have the big boat."

"Aye, I cashed in my savings and pension and bought a boat. It doesnae mean I smuggle people in it."

"He's not," said Sarah.

"But Jonah was supposed to transfer to a Scottish boat to be brought ashore," Hayley insisted.

"We know this, lass," said Mr. Wallace.

"*His* boat," said Hayley, pointing.

"Not mine."

"Whose, then?"

"That's what I've been investigating," said the harbormaster. "Willie's been helping me out. Your mother has filled in the pieces."

"Whose boat, then?" she repeated.

"Hayley," her mom said with a sigh.

"Whose boat?"

There was a pause and then Hayley knew the answer.

She spun around and made for the door, took the stairs two at a time, ignoring her mother's cry to come back. She ran along the road to Fraser's house and banged hard on his door.

Jessie Dunbar opened it.

"I need to see Fraser."

Jessie could hear Hayley's panic. "Is everything all right?"

"I just need to see Fraser."

"Come in, then," she said hesitantly. Hayley followed her through the door. "He's up in his room."

Hayley climbed the stairs to Fraser's room, pushed open the door, and saw Fraser sitting on his bed, looking at the ocean. The boy turned and said, "Dunny, I told you to . . ."

His words were cut short when he saw it was Hayley. His face flicked from astonishment to puzzlement to resentment.

"What do you want?" he said.

"I need to tell you something."

Fraser snorted. "Don't bother, I already know." He added, "Traitor."

So Fraser knew of her betrayal. It saved her having to confess. "I had to tell her. I thought she could help."

"We didn't need help. If your mum tells anyone now, Jonah's done for."

Hayley couldn't hide a look of guilt and shame. She felt it spreading over her face, and from Fraser's reaction, he saw it too.

"Who has she told?" the boy asked.

"Mr. Wallace." Hayley took a breath. "And Willie McGregor."

"What?" Fraser was dumbfounded. "But . . . but . . . we've been trying to keep Jonah away from Willie, and you've just handed him over. Once they have him, he'll be forced into slavery, or worse."

"No, you don't know the whole story. Mr. Wallace and Willie McGregor, and my mom also, they think it's someone else who is the people smuggler."

"Who?"

Hayley suddenly had a vision of Fraser standing on top of a giant tower of Lego pieces, balancing precariously on one leg, and she was about to kick away the bottom block.

"It's Ben."

There was a silence and stillness while Fraser deliberated, then he was all noise and motion. "That's the biggest piece of dog crap I've ever heard. Really? That's the best they can offer? Ben! They think they've got us fooled. They think we'll believe anything. They're talking complete and utter . . ."

"Fraser," said Hayley, "Fraser!" She grabbed him by the arm. "At least consider the possibility."

"No, it's nonsense."

"Until we know for certain, you shouldn't involve Ben in any plan you might have."

Fraser looked at her, then looked out of his window, down toward where the *Moby Dick* was moored, then back at her.

"What have you done?" Hayley asked quietly.

"Ben's already involved."

He made for the door, was through it and gone before Hayley had a chance to ask, *What plan?* She followed him down the stairs and through the hall, past a confused Jessie Dunbar. She burst out of the front door. Fraser stood there with her mom and the harbormaster and his back was stiff and his hands were clenched.

"It's not true," he said.

"I'm just doing my job, lad," said Mr. Wallace. "I have to look into it, that's all."

"What does it matter if people come to this country? And if someone helps them? Where's the harm?"

The harbormaster sighed. "We cannae just have a free-for-all, open-doors, everyone-welcome policy. We havenae the jobs, or the houses, or the schools for everyone who wants to come. It has to be controlled."

"But Jonah is just one man."

"One of many. And it's not just people that are trafficked; it's drugs and weapons and counterfeit goods. It is organized crime carried out by organized criminals."

"Ben is not a criminal," Fraser said.

"And neither is Jonah," said Hayley, moving alongside the boy. "He's just a man looking for his brother."

Mr. Wallace shook his head. "I dinnae care about the African man. He's just a poor soul far from home. It's the gangs I want, in particular their Scottish contacts. He can lead me to them. I need to know what he knows. And who he knows."

"But once you've discovered that," Fraser said, "he gets sent back to Lesotho."

The harbormaster shrugged. "Maybe. He shouldnae be here."

"That's what I'm going to work to prevent," Sarah said.

Mr. Wallace rubbed a hand across his brow. "What do you think is going to happen, Fraser? How do you think this is going to end?"

Fraser said quietly, "It will end how it is supposed to end."

"There's already been one death. I'm trying to prevent another one."

"That other man drowned. He wasn't murdered, he drowned. His name was Solomon and I could have saved him but I didn't."

"Well, Solomon never got the new and better life he had been promised. I doubt your friend Jonah will, either."

"We have to give him a chance."

"He willnae have a chance if you've told Ben McCaig."

"Ben's not involved."

"But I think he is, Fraser. We've been watching your whale-scientist pal for a while. Someone brings the people to shore. It's not the main men, it's never them; that's when it becomes dangerous, a criminal activity. Up to that point it's a pleasure cruise with African friends. No, they transfer to another boat and that boat lands them in the UK. And that is where McCaig comes in."

"Mr. Wallace has shown me evidence," said Sarah. "A log of his sailings, details of bank deposits. It all adds up. And I feel a fool because I didn't see it."

"Nonsense," Fraser spat. "You're twisting this around just to find Jonah. He is going to get away and it will be *thanks* to Ben, you'll see."

"What have you done?" Hayley asked. "What *is* this plan of yours?"

"Never mind. It's sorted."

"Is Jonah with Ben?"

"I'm saying nothing more in front of him. Ben's not involved, of that much I'm certain."

"What about his knife?"

Fraser gave her a warning look and shook his head, but it was beyond all that now.

"We found Ben's knife by the dead body," she said to her mom.

"Oh, God."

"He wasn't murdered, remember," Fraser said. "The knife was planted."

"Why would Ben cut open a dead body?" Sarah asked.

"I don't know," said Hayley.

"I do," Fraser said. "It was to look for a small diamond that the man had swallowed to pay for his journey."

"So Ben has a diamond?" Hayley asked.

Fraser gave no answer, refused to look at her, his mouth tight, breathing through his nose. For what seemed a long time, the four of them stood on the harbor road in silence. All eyes turned to view the small lobster boat whose rusting hull shone in the sunlight on waters that sparkled like a coral sea.

It was Fraser, suddenly bursting into life, who broke the trance.

"I need to go."

He took off running down the road toward the boat, and Hayley chased after him.

"Is Jonah still in the castle?" she called.

"It's got nothing to do with you."

"Is he still in the castle?"

"No."

"Where is he, then?"

"He's on Ben's boat." They skidded to a halt at the top of the jetty. "But it's fine, see. You're all talking nonsense."

They took three steps down the stone wall and there was the sound of a clanking engine and water stirred beneath the hull.

"Och, no," Fraser said as he began to run down the jetty. Hayley called his name but he didn't stop, sprinting down the old stones as the boat slowly pulled itself away from the harbor wall. "Ben," he shouted. "Ben!"

He arrived at the spot on the jetty where the boat had been moored, seemed to calculate the gap between the wall and the starboard gunwale, was about to make the jump, when his legs betrayed him and he checked himself on the very edge of the wall. "Ben," he cried once more. "Wait!"

Inside the wheelhouse, Hayley could see Ben McCaig turning the wheel, curving the boat around to face the harbor opening. The man refused to look in their direction, even though he must have heard the shout. The boat completed its turn and made for the gap in the harbor wall.

"Where's Jonah?" Hayley asked.

"He's on the boat. Ben was supposed to take him to the mainland today."

They watched the vessel glide slowly between the harbor walls and touch the open sea.

"Maybe that's what he's doing."

"I don't think so. Why would he leave me here?"

Hayley watched the boat sail lazily into a calm sea. Ben McCaig seemed in no hurry to do whatever it was he planned to do. The throttle of the boat was only at quarter speed; he could have been circling and searching for whales.

So that was that. Jonah was caught. All that hiding and sneaking and planning had come to nothing. They had nearly succeeded, but it had all gone wrong right at the end. And then she saw movement at the back of Ben's boat and knew that things weren't quite done yet.

At the stern of the boat, from beneath a pile of old lobster creels, there emerged an instantly recognizable shock of fine, white hair.

Fraser opened his mouth to speak or shout or scream, but all that came out was "I hate my brother."

THIRTY-THREE

As the boat sailed away from the harbor, Fraser felt tears well up beneath his eyelids, a soup of anger and frustration and despair that threatened to spill down his cheeks and add embarrassment to the pot.

"What do we do now?" Hayley asked.

"Dunny can sort out his own mess for once."

"It would be nice if he could, but I don't think he can."

"It can't be me, not every time."

"You're his brother."

"I resign the position."

Hayley gave a sympathetic laugh. "It's a lifetime appointment."

Fraser nodded wearily.

"We should tell your dad," she said.

The boy stood in silence, watched the boat sail farther up the sound, still chugging gently at a leisurely pace. "No," he said.

"Mr. Wallace, then. Ben has kidnapped Dunny."

"No, he hasn't. And we can't." He looked back up the road to where Mr. Wallace and Sarah Risso stood. "They don't know that Jonah's aboard. All they saw was Ben going for a sail and that's his usual Monday morning routine. If we tell anyone, Jonah is doomed."

"He's doomed anyway. We don't even know where Ben is taking him."

"No place he wants to go."

"And what about your brother?"

"If he sneaked on, he can sneak off again."

"You hope."

"If Dunny has stowed away, it's for a reason."

And as Fraser stood there, he thought of his brother wandering the beach and clifftop, how he grabbed Ben's arm by the dead whale, how he wrote on shells and tossed them into the sea, how he watched from castle windows. Dunny was everywhere. And yesterday's scene on the cliff path had been his brother trying to warn him. Dunny knew everything.

Now Dunny wanted to help Jonah. And the only way to do that was by stopping the boat.

Fraser moved down the jetty to where it met the sand, jumped down onto the familiar stretch of beach. The boat was ahead but it wasn't gaining ground, as if reluctant to leave the shelter of the island.

"What are we doing?" Hayley asked, running after him.

"Why do you care?"

"I said I'm sorry, OK. I would like to help."

Fraser pondered for a moment, thought he would give her a taste of her own medicine. He raised a hand, palm out. "Whatever."

She didn't seem amused. "So what are we doing?"

"We're following the boat."

"It's heading out to sea. I'm done swimming out there."

Fraser looked back. "Everyone is done with that. The boat is sticking close to the coast. Dunny's going to stop it."

"How can Dunny stop a boat?" Hayley asked, walking fast beside him.

"He's a creative boy, he'll think of something."

"Then what?

"Then we undertake a daring rescue."

"Of course, because we're Navy SEALs and there's our minisub just offshore."

"I'm ignoring your sarcasm. We do have a boat, remember. The dinghy."

"Didn't that sink?"

"It washed ashore. I know where it is."

"So what's the plan?" Hayley asked.

"It's not quite finalized."

"But it starts with Dunny stopping the boat."

"That's the tricky part."

"You think."

There were ways of doing it, of course: sabotage the engine, snap the rudder, let the anchor drag. His brother certainly wasn't going to tackle Ben by himself, but if Dunny could free Jonah, the man could deal with Ben McCaig.

Fraser looked along the shore to where the *Moby Dick* had made a little distance on them. Its course was beginning to veer away toward the deeper ocean and Fraser knew if something was to happen, it had to happen now. Ben was taking Jonah to a rendezvous with dangerous people and his wee brother was hidden in the stern and sailing closer to trouble with every turn of the propeller.

What could Dunny possibly do? What could any of them do really?

Farther out to sea, in front and to the side of the boat, the ocean darkened, almost imperceptibly at first, like the shadow of a high cloud moving over the water.

The shadow became a ripple, an undulation that sparkled as if glitter floated on the surface.

The ripple became foam, a bubbling of the sea, and the bubbling became a rising of water, the ocean doming as if giant hands were cupped beneath the surface and lifting up a torrent of water.

From deep below, there appeared a dark shape, a blackness against the brightness of the sun-skimmed sea.

The noise came first, a surging blast like the roar of a mighty waterfall, and the dark shape lifted itself above the surface to reveal the black, barnacle-encrusted head of a whale. And the whale kept coming. First its head, then its massive body, with two long fins that projected like wings, and up it rose, its body tapering down to the colossal tail flukes, and even the tail lifted clear of the ocean. For an instant the whale took flight, as if suspended in midair, the fins ready to flap and carry the whale high into the sky, riding the thermals toward a faraway turquoise sea.

The whale twisted slightly and fell back onto the ocean, the concussive slap of blubber on water sending spray in all directions.

"That's a humpback," Fraser said in disbelief.

It was beyond belief: a humpback whale breaching offshore of Nin. He looked at Hayley, who was staring, mouth open, at the black silhouette that floated on the ocean now. The whale released a blast of spume from its blowhole as if to confirm that it was real, not imagined.

Fraser saw that the boat had stopped, the pistons of the engine dying. Ben McCaig might be involved in criminal enterprise, but he was first and foremost a whale scientist. A breaching humpback whale would stop him dead in his tracks.

Dunny had stopped the boat in the most spectacular way imaginable.

THIRTY-FOUR

When she could get her lips and tongue to work, all Hayley could muster was a stunned "Oh, my God."

Now she had truly seen it all. For the briefest of moments a giant whale had flown. The lobster boat sat motionless beside the black back of the whale as it blew vapor from its hole with a percussive whoosh.

"What is that?" she asked.

"It's a humpback," Fraser said again. "Those fins are like no other whale's."

"It . . . it . . ." Hayley could think of no other way to phrase it. "It jumped from the water."

"It's called breaching," Fraser said quietly. "It's unbelievable."

"I definitely saw a flying whale."

"I can't believe it happened here, in these waters." Fraser pointed at the whale. "It's just unbelievable."

"Well, it did happen. So what now?"

Fraser dragged his thoughts away from the whale. "We go get Jonah. We can use the dinghy."

"We'll never reach the boat, not when it starts moving again."

"I don't think it will."

"The whale won't stay there forever."

"I think it might. It will stay if Dunny asks it to."

He moved on and Hayley followed, past the bluff, past the caves. The shore became rockier. Fraser cut left, moving toward the top of the beach, and Hayley saw the gray dinghy a little farther up on the sand. She stopped for breath, looked out toward the ocean and saw the boat just offshore, the whale beside it, barely moving, staying on the far side. The animal was big, longer than the boat, its black body sleek like a submarine. Fraser appeared beside her, dragging the dinghy.

"We haven't any oars," he said.

"Why is the whale still here, Fraser?"

"We'll have to find some driftwood."

"What's going on?"

"We're going to row out to Ben's boat and rescue Jonah."

She grabbed the boy's arm and forced him to look at her. "Why is that big whale swimming beside the boat, Fraser? And why is it Dunny's doing?"

Fraser smiled and said, "You wouldn't believe me if I told you."

"Try me."

"Dunny is a *gairmie*." He paused, as if that was sufficient. Her frustrated frown showed that it wasn't. "A *gairmie* is a boy with . . ." Another pause. "With an unusual talent. A very unusual talent. Unbelievably unusual, in fact."

"Tell me!"

"Dunny can summon whales."

"What?" Hayley practically spat the word.

"He can summon whales; in Gaelic that's what *gairmie* means, a 'summoner.' He calls whales and whales come."

"Don't be ridiculous."

"I said you wouldn't believe me."

"Can you blame me?"

"Well, that's what he is, he's a *gairmie*."

Hayley repeated the word, rolled the *r* like Fraser had done. "So how does he do it?"

Fraser shrugged. "I haven't a clue."

"Does he blow a whistle? Use a seashell as a trumpet?"

The boy laughed. "It's nothing like that. He communicates with them. I've seen it happen, though at the time I didn't realize that was what he was doing. He kind of sings sometimes."

Hayley remembered that first night on the clifftop. "I've heard him sing. It scared me."

Her gaze returned to the small boat and its leviathan neighbor. She could pick out the figure of Ben at the bow.

"There's Ben," she said.

"I see him. I think he's taking photographs."

"Can you see Dunny?"

"No. He's hiding, waiting for us."

Hayley reached into her pocket. "I think your brother left this." She held out a long, thin razor shell. "It was lying on the harbor wall. You nearly stood on it."

"Toss it."

"It's one of Dunny's tell shells. It has a message."

"Not interested."

"At least read it."

Fraser sighed and snatched the shell from Hayley's hand, read it quickly, then read it aloud.

"*Will help.*" He scoffed. "The usual riddles." He dropped it on the sand and stood on it. It broke with a crack.

"Fraser! That might have been important."

"If anyone could understand it."

"It could have been a message for Jonah."

"Well, if it was, he never got it. Come on."

Fraser lifted the heavy dinghy and pulled it with difficulty down the sand. He searched the beach as he moved and eventually hoisted a long, twisted piece of wood into the air and then a second, holding them triumphantly aloft. "Oars!"

Hayley helped Fraser drag the dinghy across the sand toward the water's edge.

"We shouldn't do this," she said, feeling the swash of an incoming wave surge around her feet. "My mom can handle it."

"If we do that, then Jonah is sent back to Lesotho."

"My mom said maybe not. Anyway, Lesotho is his home. We're not responsible for him."

"But I made him a promise."

Fraser dropped the dinghy and it splashed onto the rim of the ocean. He threw the two pieces of driftwood inside and turned to Hayley.

"Are you coming?"

The girl searched the sea and then the sky. The air was calm; the water had only the gentlest motion when a wave rolled slowly to shore. The sun even had warmth to it, its light dappling the water and making it almost inviting.

"You couldn't ask for a better day for a boat trip," Fraser added.

Hayley sighed, knowing once more she had followed this Scottish boy to the place where trouble met the sea. She sighed also because she had strangely never felt more alive, and the more she experienced it, the harder it would be to leave this place. Skulavaig was never supposed to grow on her; this Scottish boy was never *ever* supposed to grow on her.

"I hate you, Fraser Dunbar," she said, climbing into the boat.

"Good," the boy replied with a smile. "I'm not very fond of you, either."

He pushed the dinghy out into the water until the sea was up to his thighs, then he rolled in. The small craft wobbled and Hayley gripped the rubber while holding on to the boy. He pulled himself up to a sitting position and lifted a piece of driftwood.

"It's not bladed like an oar but it will have to do."

He gave the wood to Hayley and took the other piece for himself. Hayley watched him place the makeshift oar through a hoop on the side of the dinghy and dunk the end into the water. He pulled on the wood, and the vessel moved forward slightly and to the left.

"You need to do the other side," he said.

Hayley dipped her piece of wood into the water and tried to copy Fraser's movement. They inched away from the beach, the only sounds the slap of gnarled wood on water and in the distance the blow of air from the humpback whale as it rested beside the lobster boat.

It took a few minutes of splashing and bobbing and turning the wrong way but eventually, Hayley and Fraser found a rhythm and a stroke that propelled them forward and in the right direction across the tranquil water. The whale floated on the other side of the boat, as if it had seen them coming and didn't want anyone else to know.

"So Dunny sings to whales," Hayley whispered, afraid her voice would carry across the water.

"I think he talks to them."

Fraser pulled on his makeshift oar. Hayley pulled. They both pulled. Wood through water. And again.

"Dunny doesn't talk."

"Not all talking needs words."

"Is he . . . telepathic with whales?"

Fraser gave a half shrug. "Aye, I guess that's the word. Something like that."

"But how do the whales understand what he's thinking?"

Fraser gave a small laugh. "More to the point, how does he understand them?"

They kept pulling on their driftwood and the boat grew closer. Hayley looked down into the water. It was dark and deep and she was amazed to think that they had been swimming here, all three of them, in the cold and the wind and the night. Four of them, in fact, for Jonah had swum out to rescue Fraser. She pulled a little harder on her oar, thinking of the man facing a return to the place where his journey began. She thought about her own return to Texas and wondered if perhaps she wanted to stay just as badly as Jonah.

When she next looked up, they were at the lobster boat.

THIRTY-FIVE

His brother had done it, had *dunnyed* it, *dunnying* being defined as "arranging the assistance of a humpback whale to stop a boat." A gift few possessed. Fraser pressed his hands against the rusty hull and accepted that whatever happened from here on in, the way he saw Dunny had changed forever. His wee brother might not speak, but he could summon whales from the depths of the ocean. There was not a boy in Skulavaig or a school friend on Skye or a soul in Scotland who could boast of a brother like that.

"What now?" Hayley whispered.

The dinghy bobbed against the side of the boat, and the deck above looked a long way up.

"We need to get to the stern," Fraser said. "There's a ladder there."

"Then what?"

Fraser turned and smiled. "Think like a pirate."

He used his hands to move the dinghy down the hull of the boat, glancing up every few seconds, expecting Ben to be peering down at them.

"Where's Ben?" Hayley whispered, clearly thinking the same thing.

"He's on the other side, where the whale is."

"And where's your brother?"

"Probably sitting on the tail, talking with the beast."

The dinghy reached the stern of the boat, and Fraser carefully peered around the back. There was nothing to be seen, so he pulled the dinghy up to the ladder that hung down toward the water and tied its fraying yellow rope to the bottom rung. He took hold of the rusting metal and swung himself out of the dinghy.

"Where are you going?" Hayley hissed.

"We can't stay here."

"If you climb up there, you'll be seen."

"If I can get to Jonah, I can free him. Then it's two against one."

"Three."

"Dunny's not much of a third man."

Hayley growled. "I was talking about me."

Fraser looked down and gave her a smile. "Aye, of course."

Slowly he pulled himself up the ladder. The sun was warm, the sea had barely a ripple, and the only sound was the occasional blowhole breath from the whale that lay becalmed against the hull. For a moment, Fraser had the strongest urge to delay the rescue of a castaway and instead go and watch the humpback do its thing. He might only get one chance to see such a whale up close and personal. Then again, he had a *gairmie* for a brother; it might be humpbacks, belugas, and blue whales every other week. Nin would be the whale-watching capital of the world and he would be the world's most celebrated whale scientist.

At the top of the ladder he peered cautiously over the stern gunwale. The deck was empty up to the wheelhouse. Jonah was stowed away somewhere and Ben was at the bow. Fraser had no idea where Dunny was—either hiding or among the whales. He pulled himself onto the deck and lay flat on his stomach. The wood felt warm beneath his face and it had a rich aroma of fish and charcoal, as if someone had been barbecuing sardines. He slithered across the deck toward the wheelhouse. His commando crawl felt vaguely ridiculous, but the dread of discovery kept his elbows working, pulling him forward.

He reached the wheelhouse unseen, sat up with his back to the wooden structure, and considered his next move. That he had got this far, this close, was a miracle, but now he had to commandeer the boat and set Jonah free. *Think like a pirate*, he reminded himself, wishing there was a cutlass clenched between his teeth. He slowed his breathing, tried to slow his thumping heart, but that was much harder. He was more angry than scared. He had trusted Ben completely and had been betrayed. Lied to as well. Ben McCaig was not the man Fraser thought he was. It almost felt like the whales weren't real either.

He crawled along the narrow strip of deck toward the bow, raised himself up and sneaked a peek in the wheelhouse window. Jonah was there, lying on the floor beside the wheel, his arms and legs tied together with thick, ragged rope. His eyes were closed but he sensed the boy's presence and lifted his head. As he opened his eyes, Jonah's face showed a moment's surprise and then a flicker of sudden hope before Fraser ducked back down by the side of the wheelhouse.

All he had to do now was distract Ben, free Jonah, find Dunny, and return Hayley safely to shore, then help Jonah outwit police, coast guard, and customs to get to London. His head hurt from the thinking of it and no plan came, nothing cunning, nothing crafty. He crouched with his face to the ocean and it felt like the whale was waiting for him to do something, anything, that might match the humpback's dazzling efforts.

And as he lay there on the deck, he thought about Dunny's shell and the ridiculous thought came to him that its message was not from his brother but from the whale itself. Then he felt a hand grab the collar of his shirt and before he could turn, he was sprawled across the deck.

"What in God's name are you doing here, Fraser?" Ben McCaig yelled.

Ben's throw had knocked the wind from him, so he said nothing, instead tried to breathe.

"How did you get on board? Have you been here all the time?" Ben paced toward the bow, then turned and paced back. "You can't have been; I saw you on the jetty."

Fraser lifted himself carefully to his feet.

"Did you swim?" Ben asked. "You're not even wet."

Fraser nodded toward the whale. "I hitched a ride."

From his face Ben seemed to think it almost a possibility.

"Let Jonah go."

Ben shook his head. "I can't do that, Fraze."

"Why not?"

"It's complicated. You shouldn't have got involved."

"Where are you taking him?"

"To the place he was supposed to go in the first place."

"You told me you were a scientist. And I believed you. I totally believed you. I wanted to *be* you."

A look of despair crossed Ben's face. "I *am* a scientist. That's what I do. This . . ." He waved his hand around the boat. "This is just a sideline, that's all."

"People smuggling is hardly a sideline."

"It's harmless. I'm a taxi service, nothing more. It's the only way to fund my research. My university grant doesn't come close to paying for a boat."

"You must let Jonah go," Fraser said.

"I can't. He hasn't paid for his passage yet."

"What do you care?"

"Because I *have* been paid. I ferry them to shore and other people help with the onward journey."

"Why Nin? It's an island."

"It's not supposed to be Nin. I drop them on Skye. From there it's across the bridge and on their way."

"Then take Jonah to the bridge and let *him* go on his way."

Ben gave a grim laugh. "If only it were that simple. Your friend will be free to go where he pleases, but first he has to pay what he owes."

"And if he doesn't have the money?"

"That's hardly my concern. I told you, I'm just the taxi."

"I doubt Mr. Wallace will see it that way."

"Wallace? That man is a buffoon. A binoculared buffoon. He has no proof. What can he do?"

Fraser took in the boat with a sweep of his arm. "This is proof."

"Your African friend will be long gone."

"I am proof."

Ben jolted as if he'd been slapped. "You wouldn't do that."

"If you don't let Jonah go, I'll tell the harbormaster everything."

"That's blackmail."

"I call it helping a friend."

"I thought *I* was your friend."

"Aye. So did I."

In that moment Fraser knew that there was an ending here, if not yet an outcome. The carefree boat trips up the sound were over.

"You forget, Fraser," Ben said. "We were both on the boat the night two Africans went swimming. As far as the world is concerned, you are every bit an accomplice."

The word jarred but Fraser saw the truth in it. He had thought of himself as a seasonal voluntary assistant researcher, but *accomplice* fitted just as well.

"Is that why you took me sailing in the storm, so you would have an accomplice?"

Ben gave a bleak laugh and said, "Allow me some credit—I'm not that conniving. No, we were actually going whale spotting. I was meant to collect your friend here the next morning, round the top of Skye. It's actually less suspicious to transfer by day. That night the storm caught us all by surprise."

"It all worked out in the end, didn't it? It's quite convenient for you."

"Hardly, Fraser. None of this is convenient; quite the opposite: It's beyond inconvenient." Ben held up his hands, and his voice took on a tone of reconciliation. "But forget about all this. This is just silly stuff. Look there . . ." He pointed to the water beyond the far deck, and as if prompted, the whale blew out a blast of salty air. "You must have seen it, Fraser. It's a humpback and it's here in the sound, right here. That's much more important. We might not ever get another chance to see this."

He was right, of course, this was the moment, and Ben was almost persuasive. At any other time, the humpback might have won the day, but not now.

The whale made a rumbling sound and Ben moved quickly across the deck, stretched out over the gunwale, and peered down. He motioned for Fraser to join him for a look, as if he had forgotten all about the tied-up Jonah. Fraser glanced back and Hayley's head peeked around the weather-beaten wood of the wheelhouse. Fraser caught her eye and her look implored, *What do I do?*

A new plan formed in Fraser's head, one that required only distraction and a coconspirator. He nodded at Hayley and then at the wheelhouse. The girl nodded in return. He then went to join Ben.

"You're right, Ben, we might never have this chance again. A humpback whale in these waters. In our waters." He stood at the bow of the boat, holding Ben's attention.

"What do you think brought it here?" Fraser asked, knowing already the answer to his question.

THIRTY-SIX

Hayley had to move fast. She snuck around the wheelhouse and opened the door. Jonah was sitting on the floor, offering his shackles. She grabbed the rope at his wrists. It was a tangled knot and the cord was thick and frayed and difficult enough to grasp, even harder to untie. She tugged for a few seconds until the knot loosened a little, pulled some more, fed an end through a loop, then another. She glanced up at Jonah and his eyes seemed to say, *Take your time and it will come.* She tugged and pulled again, felt the knot begin to dismantle, knew she almost had it.

Almost. Ben gave a guttural, nonsensical shout of surprise and she looked out of the window to see him striding toward her, his face a changing mask of bewilderment, dismay, and anger. Hayley knew she was about to be tossed from the boat and right then she decided she was having none of it. This man Ben McCaig was all bluster and shallow charm, and she was a pissed-off Texas girl with a thousand axes to grind. If the wimpy Scottish boy helped, they could take him.

Hayley threw herself at the wheelhouse door. She watched Ben stop, look puzzled and perhaps just the tiniest bit scared, and then she was upon him. She flung her arms around his neck and squeezed and pulled at the same time. She wanted to generate a full-on throttle, but it felt more of a cuddle than anything. She tried to squeeze tighter but Ben grabbed her around the waist and pulled her from him. With the slightest of pushes he sent her sprawling across the deck. She banged her butt hard and the fight washed out of her like a receding wave.

"What are you doing?" he asked, with that same look of bewilderment.

He stood waiting for an answer only for a moment before Fraser jumped him from behind. He wrapped his arms around Ben's midriff and tried to drive him to the floor. Man and boy staggered across the deck until Ben grasped Fraser's head, spun him around, and sent him sliding across the deck.

"What is your problem?" Ben asked, standing over them. "Have you both completely lost it?"

"You can't take Jonah," Fraser said, scrambling up. "We won't let you."

Ben gave an exasperated sigh. "You haven't a choice. The African will be delivered as promised. It has to be done and I'm not going to be stopped by two daft teenagers."

"It won't be us that stops you," Hayley said with a smile.

It took Ben a short second to register what she meant. He turned and met a fist to the chin that lifted his feet from the deck and left him crumpled on the old bleached planks.

Jonah stood over him and said, "I have come a long way and endured many hardships, but I will finish my journey."

"Nice hit," Fraser said, getting to his feet.

"I am not a man of violence."

"Tell that to his face," Hayley said, impressed.

"It is never the answer." Jonah surveyed Ben's horizontal body and shrugged. "It is very occasionally the answer."

Ben lay on his back with his eyes closed and gingerly rubbed his chin. "You've broken my bloody jaw," he mumbled.

"Next time it will be your neck."

With his eyes still closed, he raised his hands in surrender.

"What now?" Fraser asked.

"We have to get away from here," Jonah said.

"Can you sail this boat?" Hayley asked Fraser.

"Aye, I think so."

"So where are we going?"

"London," said Jonah.

"Cool," Hayley said. "I didn't think I would get to see London."

"We're not sailing to London," Fraser said.

"Oh, why not?"

Hayley knew it was a ridiculous idea, but it seemed in keeping with the spirit of the last few days. Why couldn't they sail to London? It was no more ridiculous than men in caves and swims in storms and bodies on a beach and whales close enough to touch.

Jonah reached down and roughly pulled Ben to his feet. "If you do as you are asked, perhaps you will avoid a swim home."

"Lock him in the cabin," Fraser said.

"You can't outrun them," Ben said. "They'll find you. They're not particularly nice people."

"So why work for them?" Fraser asked.

"I told you, it's just a sideline, for money. Everybody wins. No one is forcing these people to come here." Ben looked at Jonah. "It was your choice. I'm helping you get where you want to be."

"I no longer require your assistance, thank you," Jonah said coldly.

The man urged Ben toward the cabin. Hayley looked down at the humpback whale that floated in the water beside the boat. Why was it still here, and where was Dunny, for that matter? A sense of uneasiness grew in her as Fraser pulled open the deck hatch.

"In here," the boy said.

"Down," Jonah said, and Ben climbed down the steps and into the narrow cabin below. Fraser closed the hatch behind him.

"There's a key to lock it in the wheelhouse." He moved in that direction. "We can't sail to London but we can sail to the mainland. From there you get the bus to Inverness and then the train on to London. Exactly the plan as before, except I skipper the boat, not Ben. You still have the money and the ticket?"

"I do."

"You're all set."

"Fraser," Hayley said, her uneasiness taking form. "Where's Dunny?"

Fraser stepped into the wheelhouse and looked, but it was empty. He stood and considered for just a second, then said in alarm, "The cabin!"

At that moment the cabin hatch popped open with a thud against the deck. First Dunny emerged, then Ben, his face set in a determined grimace. In his hand was a large knife—his whale-gutting knife. He held it close to Dunny.

"The mutiny is over," he said. "I'm taking back my boat."

"Dunny, come here," Fraser said with horror.

Ben grabbed hold of the boy's arm and Dunny winced in pain. Ben said, "Dunny stays with me. And let's treat this with the seriousness it deserves."

"You would not hurt a child," said Jonah.

"Desperate men do desperate things. Don't put my desperateness to the test."

"That's your whale-gutting knife," Fraser said.

"That's right."

"But it's—"

"Under your bed? I'm not going to leave it there, am I, in a shoe box, waiting for the police to find it."

"You stole it from my bedroom?"

"I didn't steal it; it's my knife. I took it back."

"Put it down, please," said Hayley.

"I will, I will, just as soon as your African friend is tied up again in the wheelhouse and you two are off the boat."

"That's not going to happen," Fraser said. "Let go of my brother."

Jonah touched Fraser lightly on the shoulder. "Do as the man asks. The trade is fair: I stay, your brother goes."

"He won't hurt Dunny. He's a better man than that."

Hayley watched Ben, and his resolve seemed to waver for a second. The knife began to stoop toward the ground; he seemed on the verge of conceding the fight, when Jonah said, "I will not take that risk. I will do as he asks."

Ben again raised and pointed his knife, his mouth clenched.

"Fraser?" Hayley said, but the boy shook his head, seemed afraid of what Ben might do.

So this is how it ends, she thought. Me and Fraser and Dunny paddling meekly to shore while Jonah is transported into slavery and Ben makes his getaway. This wasn't an ending; this was a fizzling out, a dribbling away, a drying up in the sun. Her whole body heaved with disappointment. This was not the Texas way: In the Lone Star State, you went out guns blazing.

And then she looked at Dunny. Despite a knife to his back, he was completely untroubled. In fact, one of his inscrutable smiles spread across his face, and she heard him make his strange humming sound, a long, low note that rose in pitch and volume. The humpback whale blew, a jet of spume and salty water that cracked the air and rocked the boat before the beast sank beneath the surface, leaving only a mat of small bubbles. Dunny surveyed the ocean and his eyes shone, and Hayley knew there was more to come.

THIRTY-SEVEN

Fraser looked out across water that sparkled in the morning sunlight as if the ghosts of Solomon and a thousand other drowned souls were holding up their diamonds to a shore they never reached. He couldn't remember a sun so warm and an ocean so still, the water no longer broken even by the barnacled back of a humpback whale. As he stared toward the horizon, his eyes focused on a moving speck heading their way.

"A boat," he said, and pointed.

Five heads looked in the direction of the distant vessel, just a dot but growing gradually in size as it approached.

"Fraser," Ben barked. "The telescope."

Fraser hesitated. The teacher-pupil, master-servant relationship no longer applied, not when the sorcerer's hostage was his apprentice's younger brother.

Ben jabbed the knife in Fraser's direction and said, "Go!"

Fraser stepped inside the wheelhouse and gasped in the heat—it was as hot as a greenhouse. He lifted the telescope from the shelf and went back on deck. Ben snatched it from his hand and scanned the distant ship, still pointing the knife toward Dunny.

"Is it the police?" Fraser asked.

"Can't tell, too far away."

"It's the police. Hayley's mom or Mr. Wallace will have called the police."

"More likely a fishing boat." Ben threw the telescope to Fraser, who only just managed to catch it. "But we're not staying here to find out. Into the wheelhouse. Your brother as well."

Ben guided Dunny toward the wheelhouse with Fraser following behind. Ben looked back toward Jonah and Hayley.

"Any silly moves from you two and someone might get hurt."

Once again he waved the large knife and Fraser thought Ben didn't have it in him to hurt them, but this was a different side to him, perhaps a side with murderous intent. Ben wasn't the only problem, however. If the approaching boat *was* the police, then Jonah was just as doomed.

"What's your plan?" Fraser asked.

"We're getting out of here."

"You can't outrun a police boat in this old thing."

"We don't need to outrun them. We just need to get up to Skye and deliver our package."

"Is that all he is?" Fraser asked. "A package to be delivered?"

Ben gave him an incredulous look. "Of course that's all he is. I'm not a tour guide. This is a business transaction, nothing more. Your African friend has paid for his delivery and I'm facilitating the process. He's a package that posted himself."

"What about that other package, the one you slit open?"

Ben didn't answer for a second, sighed, then said, "He was already dead."

"You found his diamond?"

"How do you know about that?"

"Jonah told me. How did *you* know?"

"It's common with the Africans. I found the diamond, then lost it again. Whoever took my knife took the stone as well. I wouldn't be so careless to leave either behind. Your African friend has it, I presume, though I can't find it on him."

"It belongs to Jonah more than you."

Ben gave a short, ironic laugh, then fired up the engine of the lobster boat. Fraser heard the familiar clang of pistons and screws as the old vessel coaxed itself back to life. A drop of sweat trickled from the nape of his neck down his spine as he boiled behind the glass of the wheelhouse.

Slowly the boat began to move, Ben turning the wheel with one hand and brandishing the knife with the other. Fraser looked through the open door of the wheelhouse to where Hayley and Jonah stood at the side of the boat, hanging on to the rusting rail. Jonah stared at the water with a look of defeat and Fraser felt the heavy weight of failure rest on his shoulders. It mingled with the heat and made him giddy. He stuck his head through the door and words burst from his mouth in a spontaneous, frantic shout.

"Swim for it, Jonah!"

He felt a boot on his backside and went sprawling through the doorway onto the deck.

"Give it a rest, Fraser," Ben shouted angrily. "The man's going nowhere."

Fraser rolled onto his back and felt the sun warm on his face. Ben leaned out of the wheelhouse and waved the knife toward Jonah.

"If you go for a swim, they all go for a swim."

"I will stay here," Jonah said firmly. "Do what you must do."

Fraser felt a tug on his arm and Hayley helped him up. Ben went back to the wheel, slamming the door behind him, shooing Dunny over to the far side of the wheelhouse. Fraser turned to Jonah and said, "Don't worry about us. We'll be fine. Swim for the shore while it's still close."

"I will stay here," Jonah repeated. "I will not put any of you at risk."

"Ben's just bluster."

"He cut open the belly of a dead man and reached inside. Perhaps you underestimate what the man might do."

Fraser looked to the stern and watched the growing speck of the other boat. If it wasn't the police, it was a boat heading in their direction very fast and for no good reason.

"You can't just give in."

"I will never give in," Jonah said. "Sotho men never give in."

"How does this end, then?"

"We are barely at the beginning. It is too soon to think about the end."

"Then swim!" Fraser implored. He looked toward the shore; the gap between the boat and the beach had widened. "It has to be now."

Jonah didn't move. The *Moby Dick* was sailing hard, its propeller churning all the water it was engineered to churn. Ben seemed determined to reach the drop-off point on the island of Skye and pass on his African package before he was stopped and boarded. If Jonah wasn't there, what could they prove?

Fraser saw a flicker of indecision cross Jonah's face. "Go now," he said quietly. "Trust me, Ben will not throw us overboard."

"The boat is moving too fast," Jonah said.

"Then we'll stop it."

Fraser turned and moved with purpose toward the wheelhouse. He heard Hayley say, "Fraser . . . ?" but he ignored her and yanked at the door.

Ben had fastened the latch and it stayed shut.

"Open up, Ben."

"Go away, Fraser." Ben didn't turn his head; his hands

gripped the wooden wheel, his body craned forward as if that would make the boat go faster.

"Stop the boat."

"We'll be stopping soon enough when we reach Skye."

Fraser tugged harder on the door handle. "Stop the boat now."

Ben glanced at him and said angrily, "You're putting your brother's health in jeopardy."

"You're all talk. You wouldn't dare."

"You've no idea what I might do. I've no idea what I might do. It's probably best not to test me."

Fraser punched the door a final time and turned to face the ocean. He banged the rail in frustration and screamed to Ben, Dunny, the whale, and anyone else who could possibly bring it about,

"Stop the boat!"

THIRTY-EIGHT

Hayley watched Fraser ready himself to crash through the wheelhouse window, and then the pitch of the engine changed and the boat swung violently to the side. She was thrown across the rail, held on tight as her side of the deck dipped toward the water. The throttle was pulled back and the boat decelerated sharply, rocking hard in its own wake. It moved forward slowly, carried by momentum, but the engine had been cut to a growly purr and Ben was swinging her around so they now faced the shore on the far side of the sound.

"We've stopped," Hayley said.

Fraser turned to Jonah. "Now's your chance."

Jonah stared at the distant mainland, but before he could do anything, the boat's engine picked up and they began to move again, the propeller once more whisking the flat water into froth.

"Too late," he said, turning to Fraser. He looked agonized.

Ben swung the *Moby Dick* back around to sail up the sound toward Skye. A moment later they were again traveling at full speed. Hayley looked back at the vessel that was following. It was closer but still not close, still impossible to tell whether it was police or a trawler. They would know soon enough.

Again with a violent suddenness, Ben swung the boat hard around and pulled back on the throttle. Once more, Hayley clung to the rail as the boat pitched on the flat ocean as if battered by a sudden storm. Ben hugged the wheel and craned his head forward, searching ahead for something.

"Have we hit a rock?" she asked Fraser.

Fraser moved toward the bow. "We can't have," he said, frowning. "Ben knows every shoal and skerry out here. It's perfect weather, the sun's even shining."

Hayley thought, *If we've collided with the sun, we've sailed too far.*

At the bow she stared ahead at the ocean. There *was* a rock in the water: a small island, a dark reef, except this island moved.

"It is the whale," Jonah said.

"*Leruarua*," Fraser said.

"You remember."

"*Muc vara*," Hayley said.

"Something like that," said Fraser.

As they watched, the whale sank slowly beneath the water and a moment later the ocean was again a flat shimmer of sparkles from the high, hot sun. Ben pushed forward once more on the throttle and the boat began to move.

The tail flukes and then the broad back of the whale reemerged just ahead of the boat. Again the engine died.

"It's almost like . . ." Hayley hesitated. "Like it's doing it on purpose."

She glanced at Fraser and a look passed between them, the unspoken acknowledgment that *of course* the beast was doing it on purpose, that Dunny could command a whale to slow a boat.

The wheelhouse door flew open and Ben strode toward them. He no longer carried his knife, seemed to have forgotten about Dunny, who inched out onto the deck behind him.

The whale rested in front of the boat, gentle ripples emanating from its giant hulk. It blew—a sharp whoosh that Ben seemed to take as a mocking jibe.

"What's it doing?" he spat in fright and anger. "Why won't it let me past?"

"You're the whale scientist," Fraser said. "You tell us."

Ben moved to the starboard side and leaned out across the rail. Behind them the other vessel had closed the gap. Its identity was clear now: a dark blue hull with light blue and yellow squares on the wheelhouse. If Ben still had doubts, there was a word written large across the side of the boat: POLICE.

"Aw, crap," Ben said.

"I was right, then," said Fraser.

"Don't be a clever ass, Fraze. When that police boat reaches us, we're all done for." He jabbed a finger toward Jonah. "Especially him."

"The whale has decided," Jonah said quietly. "I am returning to Lesotho."

"No," Fraser said. He turned to Ben. "Take him to shore. Give him a chance at least."

"Don't be ridiculous. He has to be delivered."

"That's not going to happen. And this way you won't be caught *people trafficking*."

"And what would I tell my . . . friends?"

"Tell them you threw him overboard and he was swallowed by a whale."

There wasn't even a hint of a smile on Ben's face. He looked at the whale floating serenely in front of the bow. "Even if I wanted to, I can't go anywhere."

"It will let you past."

"Oh, will it? You're going to ask it nicely for me?"

"Not me. Dunny."

Ben looked incredulous and Hayley knew that whatever Fraser said next would sound far-fetched and odd. She hoped he would tell the truth, or the little he understood of it.

"Dunny's a *gairmie*."

Ben said nothing for a few moments. "A whale summoner? They're just a myth, there's no such thing." He glared at Dunny. "Your brother is not a *gairmie*."

"I wouldn't be too sure," Hayley said.

"Think about it, Ben. Whenever Dunny was out in the boat with us, we saw whales. And when we saw those orcas offshore, Dunny was on the beach."

"It's nonsense," said Ben. "You can't just summon a whale. And you can't make one disappear."

"Dunny can."

They all turned to look at Dunny. Throughout his young life, actions had always spoken louder than words; now he raised his arms and gave a musical whoop that, Hayley thought suddenly, had a hint of whale song about it. The humpback sank slowly beneath the surface with barely a splash.

"No way," Ben said quietly.

The small lobster boat sat on a sheet of glittering glass and even the usually raucous seagulls had the good grace to be silent. All that spoiled the picture-perfect seascape was a rapidly closing police boat.

THIRTY-NINE

"I told you," Fraser said, a note of troubled triumph in his voice. "Sail for the mainland, Ben. We can still make it."

Ben gave each of them a withering, weary look and said, "This is just madness." He moved past them back to the wheelhouse, flung open the door, and resumed his position behind the old circle of wood.

Hayley faced Fraser and said, "*You* can sail the boat to shore. Jonah can take care of Ben."

Fraser shook his head. "Ben will do it. He knows now that we're telling the truth. He'll do what's right."

The engine roared as Ben worked the throttle and fired it back up. Jonah wasn't quite home and dry, but at least he had a fighting chance now, and Ben could worry about the police. They were just local teenagers on an innocent boat ride: What did they know about illegal immigrants and people traffickers and smuggling rings? Not even Mr. Wallace could prove anything, not before Jonah was on the London train.

The boat began to move again and Fraser waited for the rudder to start a slow turn toward the mainland. It didn't happen. He looked back at the wheelhouse and saw Ben's face at the window, his eyes narrowed, his face twisted as if he had a bad taste in his mouth, his hands gripping the wheel as if someone was trying to prise his fingers from the wood. He was not heading for the far shore; he was sailing up the sound to make his rendezvous.

Fraser spun around, looked in anguish at Hayley and Jonah. "He hasn't listened. He doesn't care."

He knew what he had to do. He was going to wrench the wheelhouse door off its hinges, drag the self-destructive fool onto the deck, pummel his head, then toss him overboard as chum for sharks and orcas.

Jonah grabbed his shoulder.

"Leave it be, Fraser," he said in a quiet voice. "I will try again some other day."

"No, it can't end like this!"

Fraser looked at his brother. Dunny stood in the bow like the figurehead on a pirate ship, his face to the ocean, with an imperious air as if here was his dominion, his subjects scattered beneath the waves. And then he stretched out his arms, his fingers uncurled, and he lifted his chin to the sky. His eyes closed for a moment and then he opened them wide and he repeated the musical phrase, the wavering note—rising from low to high—that coaxed or cajoled or commanded the whale.

"That's it, Dunny," Fraser whispered. "Do something."

For a few seconds the boat plowed on, the engine thumping away, the distant shore a line of black, unreachable hills. The water was calm, stirred only by the arriving pressure wave of the oncoming boat, but then, a hundred feet or so ahead, ripples began to form, then a froth of foam, and then the black, pitted back of the humpback whale emerged once more above the surface. Its giant tail flukes flicked into the air, then slapped hard against the sea, sending up a spume of ocean with a loud crack.

"Way to go, Dunny," Fraser said.

Ben would surrender now, he had to. There was no other choice when a whale was in the way.

But the thump of the engine didn't change; in fact, the pitch rose slightly, as if the throttle had been pushed beyond the mark that said maximum. The boat didn't turn; instead it seemed to straighten so it was dead-on to the whale.

"No!" Fraser cried, spinning round to face the wheelhouse, realizing now how events were about to play out.

Ben's face was pressed to the glass, his eyes wild, his mouth between a smile and a sneer, his small boat at ramming speed, the only course, collision course. The boat was a whale-seeking missile; the whale was an iceberg, a skerry, a reef of vulnerable flesh and blubber. There would be no winner here. The boat's hull would splinter against fin and fluke. The whale's back would gash against propeller and keel.

Fraser clutched the rail and watched, paralyzed with horror, as the boat steamed at full speed toward the floating whale. Ben was not for turning, was no longer for stopping. This was how it was to end, as it had ended throughout history, with sinking boats and dying whales and bodies floundering in the water far from shore.

The ocean sliced apart as boat and whale converged. The whale's head was above the water. Fraser saw the big, black eye staring straight at them and for a moment he imagined a flicker of fear. He braced himself against the rail, looked over at Jonah and Hayley. Both could also see clearly what was coming. Jonah raised his eyes to the sky, thinking perhaps of his absent brother. Hayley looked at Fraser in anguish. He turned back to the whale, dead ahead and close. It gave a great blow, as if steeling itself for the impact, and Fraser felt its breath break over him. He tried to say something, felt himself mouth *I'm sorry*, but he was all out of words.

Then came the cry.

"Stop!"

It was loud and desperate and wretched. And it came from Dunny.

As the cry echoed across the water, the lobster boat pulled hard to port. At the same moment the humpback ducked beneath the surface, its tail flukes lifting from the water. Fraser felt the boat tip, thought it was going over, waited for the collision, clung to the rail, heard a smack like a cannon. He was engulfed by a wave of water, felt the boat tip back, was swirled around as the ocean drained from the deck.

And then all was still and quiet.

He lay on his back, breathing hard, and realized slowly that the boat was afloat and he was alive. There had been no shipwreck, no dying whale. A cry had averted disaster. As he blinked in the sunlight, he remembered whose cry it had been. Fraser grabbed the rail and hauled himself to his feet. The boat pitched slightly in the swell it had created, its engine dead. Hayley, Jonah, and his brother stood on the deck, dripping with water. The wheelhouse door banged and Ben emerged. He looked broken.

"I couldn't hit a whale." He slumped against the gunwale. "I love whales, that's why I'm here. I couldn't hit one."

Dunny was breathing hard and his whole body was shaking. Fraser reached over and wrapped a hand around his arm. He wanted to say something, couldn't muster anything, recognized the irony that words wouldn't come.

"The whale is saved," Jonah said. "As are we."

Dunny leaned over the rail to check, but the whale was gone. His breathing slowed and he looked at the ocean, nodded and smiled, turned to Fraser, nodded and smiled again.

"That was . . . brilliant, Dunny," Fraser said.

He waited for his brother to reply, as if that first word would open the floodgates to many more, but Dunny simply turned back to the ocean. Perhaps he had only one word in him.

And now Fraser remembered the police boat. He looked behind him and the vessel was almost upon them. Figures could be seen on the deck and he wondered if somehow Mr. Wallace had managed to get on board.

"Your friend is finished," Ben said flatly. "We all are."

"I'm sorry, Jonah," Fraser said. "I thought I could get you away."

Jonah shook his head. "No, I am the one who is sorry. You did more than I could have asked, more than I should have asked. If all I achieved in landing on this shore was finding a friend . . ." Jonah looked around him. ". . . finding three good friends, then it is a trip I am glad I made."

For a moment, four of the five souls upon the small boat stood thinking of dreams dashed and hopes ended. Only Dunny looked the other way, up the sound, across the water toward the far horizon, his dream perhaps only beginning.

"I cannot stay here," Jonah said. "I put you all in danger. I bring trouble."

"No, not for us," Fraser said.

Ben gave a scornful laugh. "Oh, I think the African is right. There is trouble coming to us all, even your brother, when word gets out about his special gift."

Ben said *special* as if the word was distasteful, and Fraser saw the harsh truth in the statement. If the world discovered that Dunny was a *gairmie*, then the world would descend on Skulavaig. He pictured the newspaper headline above his brother's photograph: LAST OF THE *GAIRMIES*. Dunny would be a freak show, a circus act—as if he wasn't sometimes those things already.

And yet . . . Dunny's gift could bring jobs and money to the island along with the whales. Tourists would flock to see the spectacle of orca pods and breaching humpbacks. The island economy could be revived and young people would no longer have to leave to find a life.

Fraser thought, *I won't have to leave.*

And it dawned on him that maybe this was why Dunny had summoned the whales in the first place. To save the island. To keep his brother at home.

"No one need know about me, Dr. McCaig," Jonah was saying. "And no one need know about the boy. And if I am gone, no one need know about you."

"Oh, I think I'm going to jail," Ben said, bitterly scoffing. "Someone will snitch." He looked at Fraser and Hayley.

"Give it all up," Fraser said. "Go back to Aberdeen and do your whale research. And never come back." He looked at the man he had so admired and there was anger, but there was also pity. "Do that and I won't tell."

He looked at Hayley and an unspoken agreement passed between them.

"No one will hear anything from me," she said. "This time, I truly promise. Not even my mom."

Fraser believed her. Gone from her face was that superior look; her hair was bedraggled from the wave that had crashed over the boat, her face was smeared with dirt from crawling across the deck. She looked like an island girl just come in from a storm. She had never looked more lovely.

"I deserve to be whale food," Ben muttered, looking at the deck. "Why would you stay quiet?"

"It's a simple deal," Fraser said. "Don't mention Jonah, don't mention Dunny, and give up the smuggling. Then we won't tell."

"But I owe these people money. I haven't delivered my package."

"That's your problem, not ours. Go back to being a whale scientist, you're good at that. This, not so much."

Ben sighed and nodded, said quietly, "I never stopped being a whale scientist."

"I must go," said Jonah, looking at the approaching police boat.

They were adrift in the middle of the sound, the coastline of mainland Scotland far in the distance, a black line beneath the endless blue sky. The sun was warm and the sea was calm, but the water would be cold and they were a long way from land.

"You'll never make it," Fraser said.

"I have made it before."

"Not from this far out. You were much closer to shore that first night. We all were."

"Today there is no wind, there are no waves."

"It doesn't make the water any warmer."

Dunny moved across to where Jonah stood. He fished in his pocket and Fraser expected a shell, but instead, Dunny pulled out a small glasslike object. He held it out in the palm of his hand.

"You!" exclaimed Ben. "I might have known."

Fraser was hit by a sudden memory. He remembered a shell, sitting on his bed, that Dunny had left. And inside the shell was a small piece of glass. Except it wasn't glass, it was the diamond from the belly of a dead man. Ben didn't have the diamond, Jonah didn't have the diamond, Dunny did. And if Dunny had taken the diamond, then he had taken the knife and planted it by the body, maybe even dipped it in blood first to implicate Ben.

His brother had always seemed on the periphery of life, on the edge of things, sometimes quite literally in the way he stood on a high cliff with the drop below. Now Fraser was certain that Dunny was actually at the center of every incident, at the heart of every event. Dunny had known everything, had seen everything; observing, directing, controlling.

"Thank you, my young friend," Jonah said. He took both of Dunny's hands in his and bowed, tears in his eyes. He held himself there for a moment, then put the diamond in his pocket. "With this I can find my brother."

He moved toward the edge of the deck and wrapped his fingers around the rail. "It is time to end this. End it the way it began."

Hayley cried, "No, Jonah!"

She looked to Fraser for support. The voice of reason whispered in his ear, urging him to convince Jonah to let him take his chance with the authorities. In the other ear was a stronger voice, more compelling, which willed Jonah to give it a try, to swim across the sound to freedom.

"Jonah is right," Fraser said. "We should end this how we began it."

He remembered that first night, the night of the storm. They were all there. He and Ben were on the water, Jonah was *in* the water, Dunny and Hayley were on the clifftop. They all saw the same breaking waves, they all felt the same wind; the same rain whipped their faces. That night a man had drowned. It couldn't end like that.

Fraser gave a long sigh, like a whale blowing.

"Thank you, my friend," Jonah said, then turned to face the sea.

It seemed for a second that he had other words to say but then he placed one foot on the rail, pulled himself up, and with the same movement jumped over the side of the boat. There was a splash, he disappeared under, then reemerged a short distance away. Without looking back, he began to swim toward the faraway shore.

Fraser, Hayley, Dunny, and Ben leaned over the side of the boat and watched him stroke powerfully away. A blast on a boat's horn made them turn as one and they saw the police vessel maneuvering to come alongside the little lobster boat.

"They're too late," Fraser said.

"He won't make it," said Ben.

"I think he might."

"I think he will," said Hayley.

Jonah had swum a distance from the boat now, his head a dark circle against the bright water, but Fraser realized that it would take him an hour, maybe longer, to swim that expanse of open water, water that was frigid even with the summer sun beating down. If the cold didn't take him under, then the police boat would spot him and haul him out. All Fraser could do was stall the police for as long as possible. Jonah was on his own . . .

Or was he? He turned to his brother, but Dunny's arms were already raised. He was already humming, that low, rising note that came from deep inside him. Fraser felt it tingle his whole body. It was a strange, magical tune, not so much a song as a chant. Not so much a chant as a sound. The sound of whales.

For a minute more, the sun continued to shine, the sea continued to sparkle, and Jonah grew more distant. Then something broke the water behind the swimming man, something dark and sleek and sharp. Then another, and another and another. Fins. The black fins of a pod of orcas. They were moving fast toward the spot where Jonah stroked for shore.

"Do you see them?" Hayley asked quietly.

"Aye, I do," Fraser said.

"Unbelievable," whispered Ben.

Fraser laughed. "I knew they'd come." And he knew at last it was going to be all right.

They watched the orcas catch up with Jonah and surround him and then they couldn't see him anymore. Perhaps he was too far away now; perhaps it was the glare of the sun upon the water. Or perhaps, as Fraser imagined he saw in his final glimpse of his castaway friend, Jonah was being carried to shore by whales that were answering the call of a boy who was not so silent after all.

CHAPTER
FORTY

Fraser sat with his back to the wheelhouse of the *Moby Dick*, his face in the sun, but it was no longer summer warm. The water in the harbor had a swell to it, the first hint of an autumn breeze.

"Are you ready for school tomorrow?" he asked the girl who sat beside him on the deck.

"No!" Hayley said emphatically. "Don't make me go."

Fraser laughed. "I'm afraid it's all arranged."

"Well, I'm not wearing the stupid tie," she huffed.

"But that would contravene our strict uniform policy."

"Well, you can stick your policy in the same place I stuffed that book you gave me."

"Which book was that?"

"*An Introduction to the Sport of Shinty.*"

Fraser laughed again. "It's a great game."

"If you like hockey without ice, played by morons."

"It just needs a cheerleading squad."

"Go for it, then. I'll lend you my pom-poms."

"Can't do it—I play for the team."

"As I said, morons."

They laughed and Fraser thought how interesting this new term was going to be with both his American girl-friend and Dunny starting school. They were both going to create quite a stir. If he could have told his friends about their summer, it would have been even better, but it was a story that would remain a secret among the three of them. There was a bond between them, one he was sure would survive the separation of the Atlantic Ocean when the time came.

"So when do you get your learner's permit for driving this thing?" Hayley asked.

"You mean my boatmaster's license? The training course starts next week."

The girl shook her head and smiled. "I can't believe you own this boat now."

"Ben McCaig needed some quick cash and my dad thought Dunny and I should have a proper boat instead of a rubber dinghy. It's Dunny's boat as much as mine."

They both looked at the bow, where Dunny stood, his legs spread, his arms outstretched, face raised to the sky, a smile on his face.

"Who's he talking to now?" Hayley asked.

"I believe it's a blue whale called Bob."

"Really?"

Fraser laughed and scoffed. "No. I've no idea what he's doing. Maybe he is talking with the whales, maybe he's just working on his tan."

"I used to have one of those," Hayley said sadly.

They sat for a moment with only the slap of waves against the hull to break the silence.

"Still no voice from him?" Hayley asked.

"No. I think he's thinking about it but he hasn't felt the need yet. But we know he can do it now. It can only be a matter of time. Or it may be another eleven years before his next word."

"So when does the whale watching start?"

Fraser gave a satisfied grin. "Next summer. Once we have all the permits. You'll need to come back so I can take you for the first sail up the sound. Whales guaranteed."

"The way things are going, we may still be here next summer." She gave another huff but it was a halfhearted effort.

The sound of footsteps above made them look up. Jessie Dunbar stood on the stone jetty, looking down.

"I thought I might find you here," she said. "You'll be moving in next."

"Can I?" asked Fraser.

"No, you can't. And that engine doesn't start until you've done your certificates."

"Aye, Mum. I know."

"Here," Jessie said, reaching down with something in her hand. "This came in the post today."

Fraser got to his feet. "What is it?" he asked.

"It's a postcard. Peculiar thing. Who do you know in London?"

Fraser stifled a gasp. "No one I can think of."

"Aye, well, someone knows you." She started back up the jetty. "Be home for dinner, the pair of you." She said over her shoulder, "Keep an eye on them, Hayley."

"Always," Hayley said.

Fraser stared at the postcard as he sat back down. It was a montage of various London landmarks: Big Ben, the Tower of London, Tower Bridge, the London Eye, with the River Thames winding across the picture. He flipped it over. There was no message and the address read simply, "Fraser Dunbar, the Island of Nin, Scotland." He handed it to Hayley.

"Is it?" she asked.

"There's no message; it's hard to tell."

"So it could be from anyone?"

"I suppose, but it must be from him."

Dunny had joined them and Hayley handed him the postcard.

"It might be from Jonah," she said. "Or it might not."

Dunny stared at the postcard for a few moments and then his face broke into an enormous smile.

"What is it?" Fraser asked.

Dunny pointed at the postcard where the River Thames flowed past the Houses of Parliament.

"What?" Fraser said, and then he saw. On the river, in black pen, someone had drawn four triangles. They were crude but unmistakable. Fins. And not just any fins; they were the high pointed fins of a pod of orcas.

Hayley looked at the postcard and said, "He made it."

"I think he did," said Fraser.

And then Dunny stood there with a scallop shell in his hand. He offered it to Fraser and Fraser took it because he never threw them away anymore.

He read the shell and said, "Seriously?"

Dunny nodded.

"Coming here? To the sound?"

Dunny nodded again.

Hayley saw the frown on his face and asked, "What is it?"

Fraser laughed. "You don't want to know."

He looked out upon the sound and the water that had been the witness and the whereabouts of so much adventure. And so much to come.

"You don't want to know."

ABOUT THE AUTHOR

Kerr Thomson is a teacher of geography at Cathkin High School in Glasgow, and is the father of two young children. After studying geography at universities in Glasgow and Arkansas, he worked at various jobs in various places, including hospitals, sports centers, and country parks. Eventually, he could resist no longer and entered the teaching profession, which is something of a family business.

In every place and at every time, Kerr has always written stories. *Washed Ashore*, which won the Times/Chicken House Children's Fiction Competition as *The Sound of Whales*, is his debut novel. You can find him online at @kerr_thomson.